"I'd hoped my first sexual experience would be...different," Dustin admitted

"I loved every minute of being in that back seat with you," he added quickly, then shook his head. "Or should I say, every second. But once I was inside you, the sensation was better than I ever dreamed it could be.... I'm afraid I went a little crazy."

Erica's tension became more centered, setting up a deep throbbing between her thighs. Outside the truck, a cricket began to chirp. If she closed her eyes, she could imagine they were back on that country road.

"Turns out I have the same reaction now that I had ten years ago," Dustin said softly. "Get me alone with you in the dark, and all I can think about is being inside you." He paused and cleared his throat. "I know we've had good sex, and you said we've wiped out the old memories. But I really can't agree."

Erica opened her eyes and looked at him. In the shadows, he could still be that eighteen-year-old boy she'd had such a crush on.

"I'm not asking you to go back to my hotel," he said. "I realize now that what I've wanted all along is for you to climb into the back seat of this king cab with me and re-create one of the most important moments in my life. Only, this time I want us to do it right...."

Dear Reader,

What a thrill to be linked to that terrific continuity series, TRUEBLOOD, TEXAS! So many lives have been touched by the Finders Keepers Detective Agency, founded by Lily and Dylan Garrett, descendants of Isabella Trueblood. And like the Rio Grande surging toward the Gulf of Mexico, the saga grows wider and richer with every story. And wilder, too! Somehow, I doubt good old Isabella ever imagined a pursuit quite like this one....

Because now TRUEBLOOD, TEXAS is heading into Blaze territory! It doesn't get much hotter than Texas in August. And the torrid encounters between Erica Mann and Dustin Ramsey sure resemble spontaneous combustion....

And the heat wave is going to continue into the fall. Next month Tori Carrington sets Houston on fire in *Every Move You Make*. And then in October, Debbi Rawlins fans the flames in *Hands On*. So don't miss out. Join us for a Blazing good time, TRUEBLOOD, TEXAS style!

Enjoy,

Vicki Lewis Thompson

P.S. To drop me a line, or find out about upcoming releases, visit my Web site at www.vickilewisthompson.com. And please check out tryblaze.com!

Books by Vicki Lewis Thompson

HARLEQUIN BLAZE
1—NOTORIOUS
21—ACTING ON IMPULSE

HARLEQUIN TEMPTATION
744—PURE TEMPTATION
780—THE COLORADO KID
784—TWO IN THE SADDLE
788—BOONE'S BOUNTY
826—EVERY WOMAN'S FANTASY
853—THE NIGHTS BEFORE CHRISTMAS

TRULY, MADLY, DEEPLY

Vicki Lewis Thompson

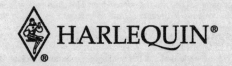

TORONTO • NEW YORK • LONDON
AMSTERDAM • PARIS • SYDNEY • HAMBURG
STOCKHOLM • ATHENS • TOKYO • MILAN • MADRID
PRAGUE • WARSAW • BUDAPEST • AUCKLAND

To Sebastian, my most excellent writing partner.
You're a great cat.

ISBN 0-373-79056-2

TRULY, MADLY, DEEPLY

Copyright © 2002 by Vicki Lewis Thompson.

This edition published by arrangement with Harlequin Books S.A.

Visit us at www.eHarlequin.com

Printed in U.S.A.

Prologue

PEERING AT THE COMPUTER screen, P.I. Jennifer Madison muttered a few swear words in her native Spanish. The investigative software she'd installed was malfunctioning yet again. Finding Erica Deutchmann should have been a snap, but computer glitches were turning it into a two-day nightmare.

Then, miraculously, the program coughed up the information she'd been struggling to find.

"*Ayiyi!* There she is, living in Dallas!" The minute the triumphant words left her mouth, she cringed. Sure enough, the baby in the crib next to her desk woke and started to cry.

"Ah, baby Annie, your mama didn't mean to shout." Quickly activating the print icon on her computer screen, Jennifer rolled her chair to the crib and reached for the wailing baby as the printer began to hum.

"What happened?" Still holding a whirling automatic toothbrush, her husband Ryan charged into the home office. "Is Annie okay?"

"She's fine." Jennifer held Annie against her shoulder and rolled the desk chair back and forth. "But you're getting toothpaste all over."

Ryan glanced down at the toothbrush and shut it off. "Whoops." He swiped at the droplets on the door. "But I heard you shout and then Annie started to cry...."

"That's my fault." Jennifer stood and carried the baby over to Ryan. "I got excited when I finally found Erica Deutchmann, and I scared Annie. She's okay, now, see?" She turned so that Ryan had a view of the baby as she settled back to sleep on Jennifer's shoulder.

And the agency was all hers now that Morales and Budnicki had both retired. She loved being in charge. She'd closed the downtown office and moved home temporarily, but now that Annie was two months old, Jennifer was looking for a new office close to home, a place where she could meet with clients a couple of days a week. With her recent software problems and the time spent office-hunting, she was way behind. No, she really couldn't have Ryan staying at home. He needed to be out inspecting his drilling sites so she could do her job.

"I see." Ryan's voice softened with love. "She's so sweet, Jen. I hate going to work. I'd rather stay home with you guys."

"I wish you could, too." Although to be truthful, she wondered if she'd get any work done if Ryan stayed home. They'd both waited impatiently for the doctor's permission to have sex again, and abstinence had made them ravenous for each other. It seemed as if whenever Annie slept, they got it on.

Ryan placed a soft kiss on the baby's head. "At least one of us can stay with Annie."

Jennifer laughed softly. "Too bad it's the one with the big mouth. I get involved in what I'm doing and forget she's right there next to me. Well, I guess I'd better put her down and let you scrub the toothpaste off your shirt so you can get on with your day." She walked slowly to the crib and eased Annie back into it.

"I could call in and say I'll be a little later than I thought."

Jennifer turned to discover that tenderness for the baby had been replaced by good old-fashioned lust directed at her. If she looked into his eyes for very long she'd give in to that sexual pull. Making love to Ryan Madison was one of the best things life had to offer.

Slowly she shook her head. "Now that I've found Erica, I need to call Dustin Ramsey right away."

Disappointment clouded his expression. "He couldn't wait a few hours?"

"I projected I'd have this information two days ago. Considering how influential the Ramseys are in Midland, I want to make the best impression I can."

Ryan sighed dramatically. "Everyone told me it would happen sooner or later."

"What?"

"My wife would get bored with the same old routine. Maybe it's time for me to buy some sex manuals and—" The rest of his sentence was obliterated as Jennifer threw herself into his arms.

"Take me, you wild man. Take me, now."

He grinned down at her. "What about Dustin Ramsey?"

"He can wait a few more hours." She grabbed a fistful of Ryan's shirt. "Did I ever tell you that the smell of tooth-paste gets me hot?"

1

Dear Erica,
My boyfriend loves it when I give him oral sex, but
he's stingy about returning the favor. Should I keep
him or dump him?
Sincerely, Sugarlips

ERICA DRUMMED her fingers on the edge of the keyboard while she contemplated her answer. Then her clock chimed the half hour, reminding her that Dustin Ramsey would show up in thirty minutes, and her stomach began to churn.

She needed to make use of this time before he arrived. Her newsletter was due at the printers by noon tomorrow. If she'd had any backbone whatsoever, she'd have told Dustin this wasn't a good time for him to make the trip from Midland. The first of next week would have been better.

But no, she'd been too dumbstruck by the call, too eager to see him after all this time. *Too awed by the great Dustin Ramsey, just as she had been at eighteen.* Now she was so nervous about the meeting that she couldn't concentrate on her work. Her New Age mother would tell her to "live in the moment" and stop obsessing, but Erica hadn't perfected that yet.

With a sigh, she rolled her chair away from the battered desk. Then she stood and wandered around her small living room, adjusting the cushions on her flea-market rattan furniture. She also should have suggested meeting him at some neutral location instead of going along with his too-intimate suggestion of coming to her apartment. She couldn't imagine that soon he'd be standing on her sisal rug. Once she'd left Midland ten years ago, she'd never expected to see him again.

Never wanted to see him again, either. In her view, if you had embarrassingly bad sex with a guy there were only two options—hang in there and try to get it right, or avoid each other forever. She would have voted for Option A if she'd had an ounce of sexual confidence. Instead she'd allowed Dustin to dictate what happened next, and he'd chosen Option B. She could hardly blame him. Virginal and fumbling, she'd been more of a liability than an asset in the back seat of his Mustang on that warm April night.

Years later she'd realized that a more experienced woman could have changed the wham-bam-thank-you-ma'am into a night of ecstasy for both of them. She could have taken charge of the situation by teasing him, petting him, suggesting varied positions, moving the action outside, even performing a striptease. Instead she'd simply spread her thighs. No doubt a savvy guy like Dustin had been bored, so bored that by now he'd forgotten the whole incident. Unfortunately, she believed him when he said he'd looked her up to discuss a business proposition, something to do with her newsletter for singles.

She could have told him that she'd started *Dateline: Dallas* on a dare and that she planned to abandon it the minute she landed a juicy hard-news slot on a major daily. But then he might have changed his mind about discussing this business proposition, and she couldn't resist the possibility of spending a little time with Dustin. She'd never been able to resist that prospect.

Ten years, and she hadn't progressed an inch when it came to that guy. Damn it. She forced herself to return to the computer. Sugarlips was the only one who could save her.

When she eventually gave up the newsletter, she'd miss writing replies to the letters column. She'd miss the free food from the restaurants she reviewed, the complimentary movie tickets, and the free drinks handed out by West End nightclubs hoping for a mention. She'd had fun this year making lemonade out of her inability to land the job she really wanted, but she had to agree with her parents that *Dateline: Dallas* was on the superficial side and a waste of trees.

As she typed, she smiled at the writer's self-description.

Dear Sugarlips,
Your guy is loafing on the lead, girlfriend! You might try enticing him with flavored oils, but my gut feeling is that you're dealing with a sexually selfish dude. I'd give him one more chance, but only one. If he fails that test, it's Dumpsville, baby. Good luck.
Erica

Saving both letter and reply to a new file, she moved on to the next letter.

Dear Erica,
My boyfriend has no staying power, and I'm left un-satisfied. He says I should be able to come sooner, and I say he should be able to last longer. Who's right?
Sincerely, Frustrated Franny

Erica began typing with more enthusiasm. On this particular subject, she was a certified expert.

DUSTIN RAMSEY STOOD outside a three-story brick apartment complex on McKinney Avenue, the results of Jennifer

Madison's investigation tucked into his briefcase. The sweat trickling down his backbone had little to do with the August heat and a lot to do with anxiety. Because of the ninety-five-degree temperature he'd left off the tie, but a business deal required a jacket as a bare minimum, and he'd also worn his best snakeskin boots.

He might feel like a fraud on the inside, but on the outside he would look like the professional businessman he should be, given his heritage. People in Dallas paid attention to clothes. He'd left Midland at dawn, and the knot of tension in his gut had tightened with every mile.

No doubt about it, he was in deep shit. If he'd asked to be involved in the family business instead of screwing around on the amateur auto racing circuit, he'd have known that his dad was flushing the family fortune down the toilet. It was a common story in West Texas—oil barons unable to compete with the cheap crude coming out of the Middle East.

As if that wasn't disaster enough, Clayton Ramsey had used precious money to buy two weekly newspapers, one in San Antonio and one in Houston. Apparently Dustin's father had always longed to be a newspaperman. Dustin had been oblivious to everything until eight months ago, when a stroke had left his father unable to talk.

Thrust into power, Dustin had considered auctioning the land to developers, selling both newspapers, setting his parents up in a town home and calling it good. But the tears in his mother's eyes and the hopeless droop of his father's shoulders changed his mind. He'd use the land as collateral to rebuild Ramsey Enterprises and hang on to his father's newspapers. Somehow.

The notice for his ten-year high-school reunion had come about that time, which had started him thinking about Erica. He'd goofed off in every class, barely passing, until the semester he took chemistry and ended up as Erica's lab partner. She'd challenged him to do better, and by God, he had. It was his lone A in a crowd of C's.

He must have had some dumb idea that his performance in that chemistry class would transfer to his seduction of Erica in the back of the Mustang. She'd been blond, leggy, slightly drunk and unbelievable sensuous. He'd been…a virgin. A bumbling, eager, too-quick-to-come virgin. While all his jock buddies had managed to get laid in some form or fashion by the time they were juniors, Dustin hadn't.

Naturally he'd let everyone assume otherwise, shy about revealing the romantic streak that had made him want to wait until the moment felt exactly right. That moment hadn't arrived until April of his senior year during a keg party at Jeremy's house. Jeremy threw a party every time his parents left town, and usually the guests were limited to football players and cheerleaders.

But in honor of his senior year, Jeremy had invited the whole damn school, including brainiacs like Erica. A couple hours into the party, Dustin had come up with the brilliant idea of asking her to take a drive into the country, and they'd ended up in the back seat together.

He still winced every time he thought about his abysmal performance that night. What a total disappointment he must have been for a knowledgeable girl like Erica. What a deep disappointment he'd been to himself. To think that the homecoming king, star running back and most eligible bachelor in school was a lousy lover. He hadn't been able to face Erica after that.

Ten years later he could forgive himself a little bit. He'd been naive to think that he could be instantly good at sex the way he'd been instantly good at every sport he'd ever tried. Hand-eye coordination was all well and good, but sex involved coordinating a trickier part of his anatomy. Besides that, he'd been intimidated by Erica. He'd tried too hard.

Okay, now he was better at sex. Without bragging, he could say that he was damn good at it. Several women had told him so. He should be able to forget that he hadn't given Erica Deutchmann, his first lover, an orgasm. But he couldn't forget, and he wanted a rematch. That was a big part of why he was here.

It wasn't, however, the main reason. His reputation as a party animal had attracted other party animals. Now when he had to get serious, he had no friends to rely on. But during that chemistry class, he'd learned that he could rely on Erica. She was intelligent and ambitious, just the sort of person he needed on his side during this business crisis.

He wasn't at all surprised to find her publishing a wildly successful newsletter for singles all by herself. Once Jennifer had uncovered the information about *Dateline: Dallas,* Dustin had contacted a couple of his racing buddies who lived here, and they'd said everybody over eighteen and under forty knew about the newsletter. It was savvy, sexy and just plain fun.

Erica had tapped into a gold mine, and that was exactly the kind of drive and initiative he needed as part of his campaign to reorganize Ramsey Enterprises. He already had printing capability in San Antonio and Houston. Revenue from a hot newsletter could shore up the bottom line for the weeklies his father was so attached to.

Plus, if everything worked out, Dustin would have many opportunities to erase old memories and create new ones with Erica. It was a good plan, and it had to work. Yeah, the strategy might look like a Hail Mary pass in the last minutes of the game, but it was all he had going for him.

He took a deep breath and headed for the set of glass double doors leading into the building. Before he left Dallas, he would prove to Erica that he was capable of excellence in business *and* pleasure.

Inside the building he discovered stairs and no elevator. Damn. He liked the idea of whisking up to the third floor in an elevator before he could lose his nerve. Taking off his jacket, he started up.

By the second flight he'd convinced himself that this was the most insane idea he'd ever had. Erica wouldn't be interested in sharing either business or pleasure with him. She'd sounded sort of distant on the phone. He'd been obsessing about her for years and it was possible she barely remembered him.

Still, he'd see this through. He might have screwed around most of his life, but he wasn't a quitter. That's why he'd scored so many touchdowns in high school—point him toward a goal and he was unstoppable. He'd just never seen any other goals worth the effort. Until now.

On the third floor he paused and put on his coat. Hefting his briefcase again, he started down the carpeted hallway toward number 310. His heart pounded like a sonofabitch, and not from the climb, either. He hadn't been this nervous since...since driving out into the country with Erica.

He stood in front of her door for a good thirty seconds, working up to pushing her doorbell. Finally he squared his shoulders and did the deed. Footsteps sounded on the other side of the door.

When she opened it, he managed an automatic smile. He was a Ramsey, and Ramseys always led with a big, Texas-style grin. But he was afraid his eyes popped.

At the high school reunion a month ago, he'd had a chance to see how ten years had treated his classmates, and not a one of them had blossomed like this. Erica had been pretty back in high school, but not especially stylish, wearing both her blond hair and her denim skirts long. Now both were short. Very short.

Her hair was cut in the jaunty style so popular now, and her jungle-print skirt and black tank were the kind of seductive clothes that women wore these days. Not many wore them with this kind of flair though, because not many had been blessed with a long-legged, full-breasted figure that would never go out of style. She wore large wooden earrings and open-toed mules. Urban chick all the way.

He quickly checked her left hand and found bright red nails but no engagement ring. That was a relief.

"Hey, Dustin. It's been a long time, huh?"

Way too long. "Sure has. You're looking terrific." It was lame, but the best he could do considering his jangled brain and dry throat.

"You, too." Her tone was cautious. "Come on in." She stepped back and gestured for him to enter.

"Thanks." He could understand her caution. She wouldn't want him to get the wrong idea, like maybe she was interested in a date. Assuming she remembered their history, he'd be the last person on earth she'd want to date, old Instant-o-matic Ramsey. Although he was mesmerized by the curve of her breasts and intoxicated by the exotic fragrance she wore, he managed to walk past her and into the room with what he hoped was confident ease.

He kept his voice casual. "So why didn't you come to the reunion?" She'd cost him precious money by staying away. He'd expected to hook up with her there. When she hadn't showed up and nobody had known her whereabouts, he'd tried the phone listings in various Texas cities, never suspecting she'd shortened her last name to Mann. He'd had to hire Jennifer to dig up that information.

"Reunion? Oh, yeah, I guess it is ten years, isn't it? I didn't get the notice, probably because of my name change."

"I wondered why you decided to change it." He inhaled her perfume with relish. It was much more blatant and sexy

than what she'd used in high school. Her makeup was more
out there, too—pouting red lips and dramatic black lashes,
even though he knew for a fact she was a natural blond.
While taking off his Jockeys in his room after that fateful
night with her, he'd found a blond hair tangled in with his
darker ones.

"When I was in journalism at U.T. I decided I wanted
a more dramatic byline."

He nodded. "That sounds like you." Dazed as he was
by Erica, he had trouble focusing on his surroundings.
Vaguely he registered a bright, sunny living room with lots
of bookshelves, rattan furniture that gave the apartment a
tropical look, a counter defining a small kitchen to his left
and a hallway leading to the bedroom and bath to his right.
Over her sofa hung a huge picture of some kind of flower.
The rosy colors inside the flower made him think of sex,
but anything would make him think of sex right now.

On an old wooden desk sat her computer, still turned on.
The desk was cluttered with paper and advertising flyers.
"I see you've been working on the newsletter."

"Yeah, deadline coming up."

He set down his briefcase and wandered over to the desk.
He'd already seen a couple of issues, and he knew the
advice column was the juiciest part, with the letters usually
focused on sex. He glanced at the screen.

Dear Frustrated Franny,
You deserve long and delicious bouts of sex with many
orgasms. Teach your guy to go the distance. Here's
one technique:

"Would you like some iced tea?"

He glanced up into those gray eyes of hers and swallowed. He'd give his cherished Harley jacket to know what
she was thinking, now that they were face-to-face again.

He'd become more experienced, but so had she. For example, she knew techniques for prolonging an erection. He might not have the edge, after all.

Wired as he felt, he could use two fingers of Jack Daniel's to settle him down. "Tea would be great."

She broke eye contact, as if she wanted to preserve her secrets. "Have a seat anywhere you like."

"Okay." He walked over to the sofa and sank down on the soft cushions. It would be an excellent make-out sofa, but he had a long way to go to overcome his previous reputation and be allowed to test-drive it.

"Are you hungry?" she called out again. "I have cookies."

Sharing food with a business associate was always a good thing. He should keep his wits about him and remember tactics like that. "What kind?" he asked, remembering one of the other tricks of the food maneuver.

"Fig Newmans."

He must have misunderstood her. "Fig *Newtons?*"

"Better. These are the organic version put out by Paul Newman and his daughter Nell."

"Oh. Sounds good." The cookies might be made from seaweed and tofu, but he'd eat the damned things. Urban chick or not, Erica obviously was still into the environmental stuff. He glanced at the magazines on the coffee table and noticed they were back issues of *Mother Earth News*.

He wondered if he had time to sneak back to the computer and read about her techniques for prolonging an erection. Not that he needed to read them, of course. He didn't have that problem anymore. For another thing, focusing on the problem might even make it happen when he finally got his second chance. Now that would be a pisser.

"Here we are." She walked into the room carrying a wooden tray with a pitcher of iced tea, two frosted glasses and a plate mounded with what looked like fig bars. "If you'll pick up those magazines, I'll set the tray there."

He leaned over and scooped up the magazines. From this angle, if he made any kind of effort, he could look right up her skirt. He made no effort. Just watching the way her thighs brushed lightly together as she walked was causing enough damage. He couldn't seem to concentrate on anything but sex where Erica was concerned.

First things first. He needed to sell her on the idea of expanding her newsletter. Once they'd agreed on that he could turn his attention to other things, and not before.

She poured the tea and sat in the chair on the other side of the coffee table. "So. You have a proposition for me?"

He wondered if she'd deliberately made that sound like a sexual challenge, as if she found it difficult to believe a three-minute wonder could manage a decent business proposal. Maybe his performance ten years ago was coloring everything for her, too. God, he hoped not.

Wrapping his hand around the cold glass of iced tea, he picked it up and took a swallow. Good, strong tea. He looked her straight in the eye. "I'd love to take you and your newsletter to the next level."

Her gaze flickered. "My newsletter?"

At least she hadn't laughed. If she'd laughed, he would have been toast. "I think you should consider widening your scope. Ramsey Enterprises could provide a support structure that would allow you to really try your wings and achieve greater satisfaction from your efforts."

Hey, that sounded pretty good. Maybe he was better at business negotiations than he thought. He'd decided not to mention the weeklies until later on, after she was hooked on the idea. According to Jennifer's info, Erica used to work for the *Dallas Morning News*. After being involved with a major daily, she might think a weekly wasn't impressive enough.

She frowned in obvious confusion. "I have no idea what you're talking about."

Then again, maybe he sucked at business negotiations. He sighed. "You have a great product. I think you could franchise it."

"*Oh.*" She shook her head. "I'm not really into the newsletter. It's just something I'm doing while I wait for the right opening on a big daily."

He stared at her, unable to believe that this brilliant newsletter idea was a throwaway job. "But everybody's talking about *Dateline: Dallas*. You have a hot commodity there with all kinds of potential."

She shrugged and picked up a cookie. "Sure, it's fun, but—"

"If you expanded into other cities, the sky's the limit. Compare that to slaving away on a reporter's salary."

Her eyes flashed. "As if I cared about money. I want to make a difference, and I quit my job at the *Morning News* when I wasn't getting the stories I wanted. The newsletter is tiding me over until a good job opens up somewhere else, but I don't kid myself that it has any socially redeeming value. At least I print it on seventy percent postconsumer recycled paper, so that salves my conscience."

Dustin was astounded. He'd never imagined that she wasn't going to continue with this fantastic project. "It has lots of redeeming value," he said without thinking.

"Like what?" She bit into her cookie with even white teeth.

"Like…being single is tough these days. Sexual marathoners, born-again virgins, cross-dressers. It's a jungle out there. People need a guide."

She chewed and swallowed her bite of cookie. "I want to deal with bigger issues."

He had a feeling that saving Ramsey Enterprises

wouldn't count as a big issue with her. "So you're not interested in what I'm suggesting."

"I have to admit I'm intrigued, but I can't see any point in talking about it when I'll abandon the whole thing the minute I get the right job offer."

Intrigued. He could work with that. Maybe he hadn't bobbled the Hail Mary pass, after all. Maybe it was still hanging suspended in the air. "Any good leads on that job?"

She sighed. "No. With the economy still uncertain, people are keeping the jobs they have. Openings are scarce."

"Then why not think about the franchise idea?"

"Because if I expanded, then I wouldn't be able to drop it and run so easily."

"We could anticipate that you'd be leaving, put people in place who could take over." That would be easier said than done. Judging from the editions he'd seen, her personality was stamped all over it.

"Why are you so hot to do this?"

Now there was a loaded question. "What you're doing is unique because it's city-specific." He had no idea where that term had come from, but it sounded professional. Thank God for his natural ability to BS his way through anything. The talent had served him well in college, and it might work here.

But talk about hot—all he had to do was glance over at her sitting in the chair with her long legs crossed, and he began to salivate. Desperate for some sort of oral satisfaction, he picked up a cookie and bit into it. Not bad. Tasty, even. But figs made him think of fig leaves. And fig leaves made him think of nearly naked bodies. And sex.

"What sort of expansion are we talking about?"

Surely she hadn't just glanced at his crotch. He was imagining things. "Whatever you think you could handle."

She nibbled at her cookie. "Fort Worth would be the logical first step. Then maybe Houston."

"Houston's good. San Antonio, too, maybe." He watched her eat the cookie, watched as she licked a crumb from her lower lip, leaving it red and glistening.

"I'm not saying I want to do this," she said, "but I wouldn't mind having a little time to think about it."

"Take as long as you want." Yes, the Hail Mary pass was still in the air.

"Are you heading back to Midland today?"

"Not necessarily." He didn't plan to let her know how critical her little newsletter was to the fate of Ramsey Enterprises. That could spook her completely.

"Do you have other business in Dallas?"

Only you. "Not really. In fact, I'm due for a couple of days off." He picked up his briefcase, opened it and pulled out a nine-by-eleven envelope. "I've laid out the details of the proposal for you to look over at your leisure. No pressure. I haven't been to Dallas in a couple of years. I can give you a day or so to decide while I take in the sights."

"Alone?"

"If you mean do I have a girlfriend stashed in a hotel room, the answer is no." Good. She'd led the way to a topic he wanted to cover. He finished off his cookie. "And while we're on the subject, is there anyone you need to consult about this? Some silent partner I don't know about?"

She spread her arms. "Nope. I'm it."

You sure are. "If you should change your mind and agree to this, there will be some intense working situations until we get all the machinery in place for the various markets we plan to penetrate." *Penetrate.* God, he couldn't seem to avoid sexual language. "If you have a boyfriend who likes plenty of attention, he should be forewarned."

Her gaze turned frosty. "I wouldn't tolerate a boyfriend who required *plenty of attention,* as you so quaintly put it."

Whoops. "Sorry. I didn't mean to imply that. Whether you have a boyfriend is of no consequence to our business discussion, and I was out of line to bring up the subject."

"Agreed."

Well, he'd outsmarted himself, zigged when he should have zagged, and been thrown for a loss. He needed time out so he could regroup. He handed her the envelope. "Then maybe I should leave you with this and go play tourist. I can check back tomor—"

"Or we can take the envelope with us while we go grab some lunch. I have a restaurant to review for the current issue, and I need to do it today."

"Sounds good." The idea of spending more time with her was the best news he'd had yet, but he didn't want to seem too eager.

"Then we can have more time to talk." She rattled the envelope. "And I doubt if all the questions I have are answered in here. On the very slight chance I might change my mind and consider franchising, I need to get a feel for the company. All my information is ten years old."

"What information?" He was truly bewildered. Ten years ago even he, the only son of Joan and Clayton Ramsey, hadn't known diddly about how the company operated. Hell, ten months ago he hadn't known anything. He had trouble believing Erica had possessed any knowledge whatsoever ten years ago.

She focused those mysterious gray eyes on him. "On your performance," she said quietly. "It wasn't very good."

He could feel the heat working up from his collar. "You mean the performance of Ramsey Enterprises?"

"Of course. What did you think I meant?"

"That's what I thought you meant." He cleared his throat. "Well, that shouldn't be a problem for you now."

"That's good to hear." She smiled. "But I'd like specifics. If we spend some time together, I'll be certain to get all I need from you."

They couldn't be talking about sex. Surely she wouldn't do that. But even if they weren't talking about sex, she was proposing that they hang out together. Good things had to happen eventually.

"Okay," he said. "I haven't rented a hotel room yet. Do you have time to come along while I take care of that?"

"I can do that." She stood and picked up the tray of tea and cookies. "Let me put this stuff away and get my purse."

"Great." Things were looking up. He closed his briefcase and stood as she quickly put the cookies back in the package and dumped out the remains of their iced tea.

"Be back in a sec," she said, breezing past him and heading down the hallway.

While she was gone, he couldn't resist going over to the computer and checking out the rest of her answer to Frustrated Franny.

Practice first with fellatio, keeping your thumb and forefinger around the base of his penis. When he's about to come, squeeze there until he's under control again. Once he realizes that holding off will increase his pleasure, he may be more motivated. You can also consider which positions—

Dustin heard her coming back down the hall and quickly returned to the sofa where he pretended to study the gigantic flower print hanging over it. Theoretically, looking at a flower should quiet his erection, but damned if the soft, plump interior of that flower didn't look like a woman's—

"Georgia O'Keefe," Erica said, coming back into the room. "On loan from the library."

He must have looked confused.

"You can check out prints just like you can check out books," she explained. "That cuts down on the materialistic acquisition of things."

"Oh." He thought of the Western art, all originals, hanging in his mother and dad's house. He hadn't been able to bring himself to suggest selling those, either. He studied the print more closely and found the signature. "I thought Georgia O'Keefe painted cow skulls."

"She did that, too. But her work with flowers is quite sexual, don't you think?"

He turned to look at her. "So it wasn't my imagination."

"No." Her color was high, but she met his gaze without hesitation. "Do you like it?"

"Yeah," he said softly, thinking about the hours that lay ahead of them, hours that just might unfold with promise like this exotic flower. "I definitely like it."

2

AS ERICA LOCKED UP her apartment and walked to the stairway with Dustin, she wondered what in hell she was doing, inviting him to have lunch with her. Testing her courage, most likely. Venturing into the scary old haunted house to see if the boogeyman really lived there.

She wanted Dustin to think of her as a sophisticated, sexual creature, and so far she believed she'd pulled it off. The smart thing would have been to take his envelope and send him out the door with his new vision of her intact. She had a deadline to think about. Instead she was accompanying him out the door, as if she had to continue proving her point.

Apparently she did. He'd showed signs of being very turned on by her. She'd detected a bulge behind his fly as they'd been talking. The possibility that he still wanted her was so fascinating she had to follow up on it.

Besides, he looked damned good—more of a hottie than she'd remembered, and that was saying something. Although she'd been taught by her parents to be suspicious of men wearing expensive sport coats, she had to admit Dustin looked excellent in one and even better out of it.

For the trip down the stairs, he'd taken off his jacket and slung it over one shoulder. The western cut of his shirt emphasized those shoulders, which had broadened since high school. His voice was a shade deeper, too, and listening to him gave her goose bumps. She liked the tiny character lines fanning out from the corners of his blue eyes and the leanness in his face that had turned a handsome boy into an awesome man.

Maybe she'd decided to spend more time with him so she could figure out why he turned her on. Because he definitely did. All she had to do was look at him and she got all warm and pliable. But that reaction was very inconvenient, because he was not her type. Her type wore loose cotton pants and sandals, not snug western-cut slacks and snakeskin boots.

"Have you been working for your parents since college?" she asked.

"Uh, no, not exactly. I got back into the family business a few months ago."

"Really?" She would have thought he'd slide right into a job with Ramsey Enterprises. "Then what have you been up to?"

He hesitated, as if he didn't want to discuss it. "Amateur auto racing," he said at last.

"Oh." In other words, he'd extended his childhood so he could race around a track burning up precious fossil fuels while he helped destroy the ozone layer. He was so not her kind of guy. She dated men who held environmentally responsible jobs and spent their weekends browsing used bookstores or seeking out interesting foreign films. Any day now she was going to find a man like that who also excited her sexually.

He glanced at her. "You don't approve of the racing thing."

"I didn't say that."

"You didn't have to. I could hear it in your voice." He sighed. "I knew you wouldn't."

He sounded much like a remorseful little kid and she smiled.

"Well, if it makes you feel any better, I'm a little embarrassed that I stayed with it so long," he continued. "I realize it was a purely selfish deal—I barely made enough money to support myself, and although I had a hell of a good time, I probably should have been doing something more constructive.''

She tried to banish a picture of him emerging from a fast car with a triumphant grin, because the image was so damned sexy. ''Then you can understand why I don't want to devote my life to putting out a newsletter for singles, when I could be investigating important stuff like the disposal of toxic waste.'' She hoped she wasn't attracted to his flash and dash. As they continued down the stairs, she studied him with covert glances, trying to decide if that was the appeal.

''There's a huge difference between my racing days and this newsletter,'' he said. ''I loved the racing, but nobody benefited from it but me. By putting out the newsletter, you're bringing people together, making things better.''

''In a small way, maybe, but—''

''I know, I know. You want to change the world. I always admired that about you.''

''You did?'' She'd never imagined herself the focus of his admiration. The focus of his temporary lust, maybe, but not admiration.

''Sure. Most of the girls were concentrating on makeup and clothes, but you picketed the administration for recycled TP in the bathrooms.''

''Which we didn't get.''

''You were ahead of your time.''

''Thanks. I think so, too.'' She also thought it was pretty cool that he'd paid attention to her antics. She'd paid attention to him, too, but not for such noble reasons.

He'd worn those sleek satin football pants to good advantage. No doubt about it, he had great buns then and still had them now. The baggy look so many of her dates liked didn't give her a chance to find out if she liked their buns or not.

"I'm really sorry I didn't get to the reunion," she said, meaning it. She could ask him to give her the name of the coordinators so she could attend the next one. "How many people showed up?"

"About two hundred graduates, so the kids and spouses made it closer to four hundred at the picnic."

"I can't believe the kids in our class have kids of their own."

"Some have two or three. Jeremy and Lucinda have four. Some people are on their second marriages already."

"Unbelievable." Speaking of Jeremy and Lucinda took her right back to that party where she and Dustin had become involved. They'd shared their first kiss out on the patio beside the swimming pool. She'd loved the shape of Dustin's mouth. His lips were full enough to qualify him as a great kisser, yet not so full that he looked feminine.

As they reached the bottom of the stairs, she had a sudden thought. "Do you have kids?" No wedding ring didn't necessarily mean no kids.

He shook his head. "Nope. No ex-wife, either. Not even an ex-fiancée." He gave her that winning smile of his. "I've been having too much fun to think of tying myself down."

Fortunately she remembered her savvy chick line as they walked out into the midday heat. "Me, too. Way too much fun." His smile was another thing that made her tummy quiver with anticipation. Not every guy could smile with that level of confidence, as if he could spin the world on the tip of his finger if he chose to try.

"Footloose and fancy-free, huh?"

"So many men, so little time."

He took sunglasses from an inside pocket of his jacket

and put them on. ''I guess I should be honored that you're spending your lunch hour with me, then.''

She put on her own shades. ''So, are you honored?''

''Yeah. Yeah, I am.''

She smiled, liking that a lot. Ten years ago he'd held the upper hand, but today she'd felt a shift in the balance of power. She couldn't be blamed for wanting to savor that a little.

He was definitely flirting with her, and for the time being, she'd flirt back. But if he wanted to take it further, she'd back off. No point in pushing her luck and risk getting dumped a second time. Besides, she had a deadline. That should keep her from making a fool of herself today.

When they reached the apartment complex parking lot, she noticed a shiny new red Mustang and started toward it, thinking he must have traded in his vintage ride for a new model.

''I'm over here.'' He headed in the direction of a silver king-cab with Ramsey Enterprises stenciled on the driver's door.

''Oh.'' She hated giving herself away by letting him know that she remembered the Mustang. ''Somehow that red car looked more like you.''

''As a matter of fact, I do have a soft spot in my heart for Mustangs.''

So did she. ''Is that red car a Mustang? I can never tell one model from the other.''

He rounded the truck and unlocked the passenger side. ''I had a Mustang in high school.''

''Did you?''

He held out a hand to help her up into the cab. ''You don't remember it? The convertible?''

She put her hand in his and a quiver of recognition rippled through her. Thank God for sunglasses, so he couldn't see the aftershock registered in her eyes. ''Ah.'' She managed a little laugh. "The convertible. Now I remember." Then she stepped up into the saunalike interior of the truck and released his hand. At least he'd used a sunshade to shield the interior, or the heat would have been unbearable. "Those were the days, huh?"

"Those were the days." His voice sounded a little strained. "Listen, I'll leave the door open until I get in and get the air going."

Thoughtful. The truck had automatic windows she wouldn't be able to open if he closed her inside the hot cab. But she was more concerned about the topic of conversation than the temperature. She didn't want to talk about that night and risk letting him know how much she still thought about it, or worse, remind him of what a little bumpkin she'd been.

"Do you have a favorite hotel in town?" she asked the minute he swung into his seat and started the engine. An easy-listening station came on along with the air. "Because I'd like to make a suggestion."

"Go ahead." He turned up the air-conditioning and removed the sunshade, lightly bumping her shoulder in the process.

She noticed the contact and pretended not to. "The Fairmont."

"The Fairmont it is." He turned the air conditioner to full blast, but he made no move to back out of the parking spot. Instead he rested an arm on the steering wheel and turned to her. "You've probably forgotten about the night of Jeremy's party, but—"

"Wasn't there a lot of beer involved?" Damn, he wasn't going to let it go. "You're right, I'm pretty foggy about what happened. I remember I'd had too much beer."

"Maybe. But foggy memory or not, I'd like you to consider the franchise proposal. I don't want lingering thoughts about that night to interfere with your decision."

Swallowing, she glanced over at him and hoped he couldn't hear her heart thumping. The radio switched to an oldie, *Save The Best For Last.* She'd always associated that song with Dustin. With both of them wearing sunglasses, she couldn't read his expression. Fortunately he couldn't read hers, either. "Wouldn't it be best if we agreed to put that night behind us?"

"And start fresh?"

"Meaning what?" She wasn't planning to have sex with him again, that was for sure. Never mind that she was feeling warm and tingly with both of them settled cozily in the cab and the radio playing a song from their high school days.

"A clean slate. Two friends from high school meeting again after ten years."

"Were we friends?" God, but he looked sexy. The shirt fit beautifully, showing off his solid chest and firm stomach. She'd unbuttoned his shirt that night and run her hands over his chest. She still remembered the texture of his skin and the tickle of his hair beneath her exploring fingers. Then she'd unbuckled his belt...

"I like to think so. You pulled me through chemistry."

She'd developed a huge crush on him in chemistry class. Her crush had been mostly about his gorgeous body, but to her surprise, she'd discovered his mind wasn't too bad, either. Apparently he hadn't been accustomed to using it. He'd scored higher on the final than she had, which had annoyed her, but she'd been secretly thrilled to find out he could match her intellectually.

"You didn't need me to get through chemistry, and you know it," she said.

"But I did. I discovered you're a good influence on me." His slow smile took her breath away.

If his goal was to charm her, he was doing a hell of a

job. "I thought boys liked girls who were a bad influence on them."

"Boys do. Men know better."

Oh, baby. Keeping him at arm's length would take some doing. They had serious automobile history, and the combined scent of aftershave and leather upholstery was stirring up memories in color with surround sound.

If anything, this experience was even more erotic, because the deep timbre of his voice reminded her that he was older and more experienced now. So was she. If they started something in the back seat of this truck, it wouldn't be over in a few minutes.

At eighteen she'd had no yardstick, so to speak, for measuring Dustin's attributes. Now, combining her own experiences with her girlfriends' tales, she realized that he was *really* well-endowed. Fortunately she'd been very excited that night, or he could have done serious damage. Instead she'd felt a moment of slight discomfort and then some wonderful sensations that had been over way too soon.

"I've missed you," he said simply.

She wasn't sure how to respond. You missed someone you felt emotionally close to. Dustin had rocketed through her life and changed her forever, but she'd always recognized the distance between them. He'd been a fantasy then, and he was a fantasy now.

"But obviously you haven't missed me." His voice registered disappointment.

She turned more fully toward him. "I'm not sure what you want from me, Dustin."

He gazed at her for a long moment. "Just what we said. A fresh start."

"Okay. A fresh start, then." She had a feeling the situation was more complicated than that, but she decided not to press the matter.

"We'll talk more about it during lunch." He reached

across her to adjust the air-conditioning vents and brushed her breast with his elbow. "Sorry."

"No problem." Ha. No problem, indeed. Her nipples had gone on instant alert.

Apparently satisfied with the outcome of the conversation, Dustin eased the truck out of the parking space. She was aware of his every move. He wanted a fresh start, and she couldn't help wondering if he meant a fresh sexual start. If so, she'd be a much better lover now. But that was adolescent, to think she had to prove something sexually to this guy.

Even if she wanted to do that, she didn't have the time. As it was she'd have to burn the midnight oil putting together the newsletter. Over lunch she'd find out what kind of company Ramsey Enterprises was these days and get a better handle on why Dustin intrigued her so much.

Maybe his choice of vehicle figured into it. The Mustang had been a souped-up muscle car, and this truck oozed testosterone, too. She preferred fuel-efficient cars, but she couldn't pretend they were as sexy.

She hadn't ridden in a truck for a long time, not since her days in Midland. The deep rumble of the engine exuded macho power. Watching Dustin at the wheel of this truck was a completely different experience from riding with her other male friends in their import sedans.

She'd thought she was beyond this sort of obvious symbolism. Then again, maybe not. She'd put herself on the library waiting list so she could borrow the Georgia O'Keefe flower print. Dustin had placed himself in a powerful truck that thrust into traffic with masculine authority.

Maybe her Midland roots were showing. During puberty she'd been exposed to truck-driving cowboy types, so perhaps they'd imprinted on her budding womanhood. What a shame if she couldn't get excited without throbbing engines, considering how much she disapproved of eight-cylinder gas-guzzlers like this monster.

But facts were facts, and she was turned on by watching Dustin at the wheel of his truck. She sincerely hoped he couldn't tell that the longer they were together, the more she wanted to strip him naked and jump his bones. While giving him directions to the Fairmont, she kept her voice steady and her eyes on the road. She'd never known men to be good mind readers, so her desperate longing for his virile body could be her little secret.

He navigated the heavy city traffic with ease, handling the truck almost like a sports car as he gunned the engine to switch lanes. She was thrilled down to her painted toenails with every aggressive tactic.

The radio station started broadcasting the headlines and he switched it off. "How did you happen to get the idea for the newsletter?"

"From my girlfriends at the *Dallas Morning News*." Talking about her work might take her mind off sex. "We were sitting around the break room one day wishing out loud that there could be a singles magazine along the lines of *Cosmo* that was specifically geared to the Dallas area. I claimed that I could desktop-publish a singles newsletter, and my friends dared me to try."

"Can't resist a dare, huh?"

"Depends upon the dare."

"See, that's what I'm talking about. You're not the type to lose your head and do dumb things."

I wouldn't say that. I had my first sexual experience with you. "You make me sound dull and uninteresting."

"Are you kidding? You were about the most interesting girl in the senior class. Granted, your ideas were sort of strange, but—"

"Not so strange! Time is proving me right, you know. If we don't wake up, this planet will be ruined." She was glad he'd slipped and called her ideas strange. Maybe she'd get over her sexual attraction to him, after all.

"Hey, I care about the environment."

Now she was in familiar territory. "Excuse me if I don't believe that. You've spent years polluting the air with exhaust fumes, just for the fun of it. Of course, with your parents in the oil business, why not? Who cares about air quality when more oil consumption lines your pockets?"

"Do you know what would happen to the economy of this country if everybody thought like you?"

"Dustin, that argument is full of holes. We could switch this economy to alternate fuel and keep it humming along nicely. But that would mean shaking up your comfortable little world, giving up your favorite toys."

He was silent for so long she was sure she'd offended him. Well, so be it. They were completely different, and they might as well acknowledge that up front.

"Maybe I'm ready to shake up my world," he said at last.

She glanced at him in surprise.

He shrugged. "As I said, you're a good influence on me."

Well, now. This cast a new light on things. He was hinting that she might make a convert of him. To take the son of an oil baron and turn him into a liberal conservationist might be a job worth tackling.

"What's your position with Ramsey Enterprises, now?" she asked.

"Looks like I'm running the show. My dad had a stroke right after the first of the year and can't handle the job anymore."

"Oh, Dustin." Remorse washed over her. Now wasn't the time to chide him about his *comfortable* situation. It was anything but comfortable. She laid a hand on his arm. "I'm so sorry. That must be very rough."

He nodded. "Yeah, but maybe it was time I grew up."

"Forget what I said. I had no idea what you were dealing with."

"No offense taken."

She drew her hand away when she realized she'd begun lightly stroking his sleeve. "How is your father?"

"He's in rehab, and gradually learning to walk again. But his problems with communication are the biggest reason he can't run the company. He can't read or write, and he has trouble finding the words he needs when he talks."

"Thank goodness you have the resources to give him good care." She worried about her own parents, who were living on a little farm in Ohio and had no health insurance. They claimed healthy living would keep them out of hospitals, but she thought they were skating on thin ice.

"Right," Dustin said.

Her impression of him was changing by the minute. Ten years ago she'd tried to soothe her broken heart by thinking of Dustin as the dark prince from an evil empire. But rich or poor, when you were the only child of an ailing parent, the worry was still the same.

"They're doing wonderful things with stroke patients these days," she said. "With the right therapy, he could have a full recovery."

"I hope so. But the doctors warned me not to expect it. I have to operate as if he'll never be in charge of Ramsey Enterprises again."

"I'll bet you know more about running the company than you think you do."

"We'll see." He pulled the truck under the portico in front of the Fairmont and handed the keys to the valet with the air of someone who'd done it a million times. No doubt he had. With the same ease he tipped the bellman who helped Erica out of the truck and took Dustin's overnight bag from the back.

Then Dustin grabbed the dove-gray Stetson that had been lying brim up on the seat and settled it on his head. With that gesture, he suddenly became Dustin Ramsey, heir to the throne of Ramsey Enterprises. She'd do well to remember that, dutiful son or not, he was still aligned with corporate America.

And she was not. Therefore she couldn't allow herself to be thrilled by a man who knew exactly how to check into a luxury hotel. Maybe for a brief moment, as she walked with him into the flower-decorated lobby, she fantasized spending the night with him here. Even without her deadline looming, that would be a gigantic mistake.

He reserved a room for two nights. Interesting. By tomorrow night she'd have met her deadline. Not that it mattered that she'd have free time then. Of course not.

"You'll come up with me, won't you?" He pocketed the folder containing the card key and walked away from the check-in desk. "I'd like to drop off my jacket and briefcase, and there's no point in having you hang around the lobby waiting for me."

"Okay." She walked with him toward the bank of elevators and tried to convince herself there was nothing forbidden or exciting about going up to his room. Hanging around in the lobby like some scared little rabbit would be stupid.

They rode up with a couple of men wearing suits and toting briefcases. Erica stood well apart from Dustin and watched the floors blink by above the elevator doors. No matter how she tried to diffuse the feeling, the little trip upstairs seemed to have sexual liaison written all over it.

She wondered if agreeing to go up to his room had meant more than she'd intended. Ten years ago he'd invited her for a ride in the country, and he'd assumed she'd wanted more than fresh air out of the deal.

Well, if he thought something would happen once they

reached the room, he'd better think again. Offering sympathy for his situation with his father was one thing. Losing her head and jumping into bed with him was quite another. She wasn't the same person he'd dazzled back in high school.

His silence as they walked toward the room was extremely suspicious. Maybe he was busy planning his seduction. She'd bet the great Dustin Ramsey had never been turned down, and he took it for granted that once a woman stepped inside his hotel room, she would go along with his every desire.

By the time he opened the door and ushered her inside, her heart was pounding wildly and her imagination was in overdrive.

The room was hushed and seductive, light filtering through sheer curtains. The bulk of the room was taken up with a king-size bed, a piece of furniture that was impossible to ignore and difficult to take casually. She should have waited in the lobby. Looking like a scared rabbit was preferable to an awkward scene when she refused him.

And she absolutely would refuse him. Her self-esteem required it.

Dustin tossed his jacket across the burgundy-and-green quilted bedspread and put his briefcase on the lacquered desk. "Do you want anything to drink before we go back down?" He opened an armoire. "There's a courtesy bar in here."

She could imagine only one reason he'd offer her a drink in the middle of the day in his hotel room. "No, thanks. Dustin, I think we should—"

A knock on the door interrupted her. She waited, fidgeting with her purse strap, while he let the bellman in and tipped him for bringing up the overnight bag.

Once the door closed, she tried again. "I need to ask you something."

He stowed his bag in the closet. "What's that?"

"Why did you come to Dallas?"

"I found out about your newsletter and thought franchising would be a great opportunity for both of us." He closed the closet door.

"That's it?"

He studied her from across the room. "Why?"

Her heart thudded faster. People didn't ask *why* unless they had something they weren't telling you. "Because I have the feeling that there's a whole other thing going on. I want to know what it is."

3

DUSTIN HAD HOPED his dealings with Erica would run a little smoother than this. First of all she hadn't jumped at the franchise offer. Now she was demanding to know if he had ulterior motives for making the offer. He hadn't asked Erica up to the room to seduce her. He wasn't sure why he'd asked her to ride along, other than a desire to keep her close by.

Sure enough, he was drawing strength from her, as he'd thought he would. For the first time since his father's stroke, he was beginning to feel optimistic about his ability to run the company. That didn't make sense considering that Erica seemed ready to reject the franchise deal.

But she'd offered him comfort when he'd told her about his dad, the kind of comfort he couldn't expect from his good-time pals on the racing circuit. She'd also implied that she thought he could handle all these new challenges. He didn't remember anyone else saying that, not even his mother. Yep, he definitely liked having Erica nearby.

He wouldn't mind having her even nearer, and she'd picked up on that. But he wasn't so crude that he'd try to lure her into bed during their first couple of hours together. She didn't know that, though, and obviously riding up in the elevator had given her time to concoct all kinds of scenarios. He should have made small talk, whether there were other people in the elevator or not. Giving a woman like Erica extra time to think wasn't a good idea.

Now she was demanding explanations he wasn't willing

to give. He hadn't decided how honest to be with her about the sex thing. Considering how soon it was into the encounter, he didn't want to bare his soul and all his insecurities. That time might never come.

She stood silhouetted by the light coming through the sheer draperies. He couldn't see her face very well, but her rigid posture suggested she was feeling under attack. He would have liked to move closer, but she might interpret that as being too aggressive.

He decided to give her part of the truth and hope that worked out. "You're right, there's more to my visit than working out a franchise deal for *Dateline: Dallas*. That's a bonus, but it could be a very promising bonus for both of us. I'm dead serious about wanting to expand the newsletter to other cities."

"You're not offering me a business deal out of guilt for what happened ten years ago, are you? Because if that's the reason, I—"

"Not a chance." He held back a smile. Guilt, hell. She'd jumped to the wrong conclusion, which temporarily saved him. "There's no place in business for guilt." He'd heard that line from his father, although personally he thought his father had many things to feel guilty about. "The offer is legitimate, and I hope you take me up on it."

Her breasts lifted and quivered as she took a deep breath. "So what else is going on?"

Damned if his mouth didn't literally water as he imagined uncovering those full breasts and rolling her taut nipples against his tongue. "Ten years ago we obviously were attracted to each other. I was too...well, too young to recognize the potential, but I haven't been able to forget you."

That was way more than he'd wanted to say and it left him vulnerable. He didn't like to appear needy, but that was better than saying he wanted another chance because he'd been a stupid virgin the first time they'd had sex.

She regarded him silently for a long time. Too long.

He finally broke the silence. "Obviously you've been able to put me right out of your mind, though," he said at last. A guy had to salvage a little pride. "Don't worry about it. I'm a grown-up, and I can put the whole thing aside and focus on business. We can go get some lunch and talk about—"

"I haven't put you entirely out of my mind, either."

Thank God. Maybe he wouldn't end up roadkill, after all. "That's how you've made it seem."

"I…okay, maybe I have."

"Playing it cool?"

"Sort of." A smile flitted across her mouth and was gone. "But I do remember that night, Dustin."

And it was entirely possible that, whenever she remembered it, she focused on his miserable performance. He hated that. "Look, we really don't have to get into the subject now. The franchise deal is what we should concentrate on." He'd been trying to tell himself that, but repairing his sexual record seemed equally important. That only showed that he wasn't a true businessman like his father.

"You know what? I want to get into this right now." She sat down on a chair positioned by the window and crossed those beautiful long legs. "I doubt I'll go for the franchise, but if I thought you were only using it as a way to—"

"I'm not. Swear to God."

She studied him. "I guess I've never fully trusted someone who has a lot of money. They can use it to manipulate situations."

What a joke. Little did she know that he couldn't do that even if he wanted to. But admitting his shaky financial status might make her shy away from throwing in with him. Accepting her sympathy regarding his dad was okay, but he didn't want her sympathy when it came to the money crunch.

He cleared his throat. "So you're afraid I would franchise your newsletter in order to get you into bed?"

"Would you?"

"No. That's sleazy. I'm sorry you think I would stoop to that kind of thing."

"I don't think it's so hard to imagine." She used her captain-of-the-debate-team voice. "Which came first, finding me or discovering the newsletter?"

This conversation wasn't going to end for a while. He decided to walk over and sit on the side of the bed so he could face her. By moving closer, he could judge her expression better. Maybe he'd lose the feeling that he was on a runaway train. "Finding you."

"And why were you looking for me?"

He sighed. "This will sound lame, but it all goes back to chemistry."

"Aha! That's what I—"

"Chemistry *class*."

She stared at him.

"In the months since my dad's stroke, I've felt this growing sense of panic that I was in over my head, that I couldn't manage the company. And I—"

"Doesn't your dad have assistants, secretaries, people who can help you catch up?"

He shook his head. "Clayton Ramsey didn't delegate. He was also a hard guy to work for, and no secretary stayed for long. The last one quit and moved to Alaska right before he had his stroke." Dustin decided not to add that his father hadn't paid those secretaries enough to get decent ones or make them feel any sense of loyalty. The office was still a mess from the last secretary's slipshod work.

"Anyway," he continued, "to say that I don't feel confident is an understatement. My successes have come on the football field and the racetrack. The only time I've accepted an intellectual challenge was in that chemistry class with you. When I said you were a good influence on me, I wasn't kidding.''

"You want me to help you run the company?'' Her eyes widened. ''Dustin, I'm not remotely qualified.''

"No, I'm not asking for that. I want…'' He paused and rubbed the back of his neck. ''I'm going to run the company. Come hell or high water, I'm going to accomplish that. But Ramsey Enterprises needs to diversify so that it's not so dependent on oil.''

"Ah. Middle Eastern oil is cutting into your profits.''

"Yes.'' Wiping out his profits was more like it. He shouldn't be surprised that she'd have information on that. She was a journalist. ''I thought you might have some ideas to offer, and when I found out about the newsletter, I had the brainstorm that it could be the start of Ramsey's diversification program.'' He glanced at her.

"My little newsletter?''

"It's growing, and it could grow bigger.'' Apparently his business degree hadn't been a total waste of time, because he'd recognized a potential gold mine when he saw one. ''Every major city in the country is a potential market. That's not a little concept.''

With a self-deprecating smile, she relaxed back into the chair. ''And here I thought it was all about sex.''

He had a split second to make a decision. ''Actually, it is.''

She sat up with a jolt. ''But—''

"Everything I've told you so far is the absolute truth, but there's more.''

Her throat moved in a slow swallow. ''Then I guess…you'd better tell me.''

"The thing is, ten years ago, when we…well, it wasn't exactly perfect.'' He looked into her eyes. ''Was it?''

Her gaze was wary. "Well, maybe not, but I think we could blame that on the beer."

"Yeah. Sure. But I remember how much we both…how excited we were. That's mostly what's bothered me all these years. It should have been a better experience."

"We were young."

"Exactly." He took a deep breath. "I know this will sound outrageous, but…I can do better. I'd like a chance to prove it."

ERICA USUALLY HAD a comeback for everything. In fact, she could count on one hand the times she'd been stricken speechless. No question, this would rank as the most memorable. Never in a trillion years could she have predicted those words would come out of Dustin Ramsey's mouth.

Finally she found her voice. "You want a do-over?"

"Yes. No. Well, in a way. Damn, I had no idea this would be so—"

"I am incredibly flattered." *And unbelievably aroused.*

"But you're not interested. People always start a rejection speech by saying they're flattered, but they couldn't possibly do whatever it is. Listen, don't worry about it. You wanted to know what the other part to this was, and now you know. We can forget the whole thing and concentrate on the franchise."

"Forget the whole thing? You must be joking."

He groaned. "I've screwed it up. Now you won't consider the franchise because all you'll be able to think about is that I asked you to have sex with me. But I couldn't lie to you, Erica. I respect you too much for that."

She took several deep breaths and tried to calm her racing heart. Dustin wanted to franchise her newsletter, but he also wanted to give her an orgasm. He hadn't said it quite like that, but that's what he meant. She was still trying to process the idea that he'd worried about their less-than-wonderful night for all these years and had taken the responsibility for that failure.

That said so much about him. She'd blamed her inexperience, but he hadn't. And now he wanted to show her that he'd improved. Amazing that he'd even care about her opinion. Even more amazing that his own self-image seemed to depend on getting it right with her. She'd never possessed such power over a man in her life.

She would handle it carefully. "If we…had sex, assuming we'd both be better at it this time, what would that achieve?"

He gazed at her for several seconds. "Every time I think of you, I remember that night and cringe. I want to fix that."

"You make it sound like a loose wheel on one of your race cars."

"You're kidding, but that's not such a bad way to describe the feeling I have."

She still had trouble comprehending that their silly little experience had affected him this much. "You can't simply forget it?"

"Believe me, I've tried. It probably doesn't bother you at all, but it's been driving me nuts for years."

What a concept. She loved it. "Okay, I'll admit that it bothers me a little, too." She wasn't ready to say that it had haunted her for ten years. She hadn't allowed herself to think that way.

"See? It'll always be an obstacle between us unless we do something to change it." He glanced down at the carpet. "I shouldn't have avoided you like I did after that night, but I was only eighteen and…mortally embarrassed about the lousy sex."

"That's why you didn't call me?" She thought of the weeks of misery she'd endured. "Embarrassment?"

He looked up at her again and nodded. "Sorry."

"I thought once you'd scored, you weren't interested anymore!" And she still wasn't convinced that hadn't been a part of it. Maybe he was revising history to suit his current predicament.

"Then you must have a pretty rotten opinion of me. I suppose you classify me with the guys your readers write about, like the one who wouldn't take time to satisfy Frustrated Franny."

Her body grew warm and restless. "I see you noticed what was on my computer screen."

"I couldn't help being curious. Do you see a lot of that? Guys who aren't willing to give as good as they get?"

The topic was making her squirm in her chair as she fought down her body's response. "A fair amount. First women have to realize they're entitled to good sex, and then they have to educate the guy. It's an evolving situation, but I think the word's getting out."

"Thanks to people like you." His blue gaze grew more intent. "Don't you think helping couples find greater sexual satisfaction is important?"

"The column's only a small part of the newsletter." She couldn't seem to stop staring into his eyes, eyes that made her feel sexually alive. She hadn't felt that way in a long time. "Mostly it's about restaurants, nightclubs, date-worthy attractions around the city."

"And why do you suppose the newsletter is so popular? I'll give you a hint. It's not because of the date-worthy attractions, although I'm sure you provide a good service there, too."

"Well, I'm sure people like the column, but—"

"Listen, I have two racing buddies who subscribe to *Dateline: Dallas*. They might tell everybody else it's for the restaurant reviews, but they admitted to me that the first thing they read is your column. Guys don't like to be obvious about picking up sexual information, so this is a way to do it on the sly. You tell one reader how to help her guy last longer, and a hundred guys will make a greater effort to do that.''

And if they kept up this discussion, she was liable to throw herself at him and beg for that do-over. He'd already promised to give her satisfaction.

She cleared her throat. ''I think we're getting off track.''

''Not really. You've spent ten years thinking I'm the kind of coldhearted guy who would take what I wanted and dump you. We can't renew our friendship if that's what you think of me. I need to clear up that impression.''

''I could simply take your word for it.''

He shook his head slowly and smiled. ''What happened between you and me was physical. It'll take a physical act to override our memory of it.''

Oh, boy, she was ready for that physical act. Fortunately her brain was still in gear. ''Dustin, this is insane.''

''Why?''

''With all those expectations, sex between us would be a disaster.''

His smile broadened. ''When it comes to physical challenges, I perform well under pressure.''

Her nerve endings hummed. ''I can't imagine how we could relax and enjoy ourselves, knowing that this was some sort of test, each of us trying to outperform the other.''

''You'd be trying to outperform me?''

Now there was a stupid slip. ''Well, no, of course not.'' Being around a jock must be awakening her competitive urges.

''Tell you what. Let's go have lunch and you can think it over.''

''I have thought it over, and I think it's crazy.''

He stood. "Think some more. In the meantime, I'm starving. All I've had to eat since five this morning is one Fig Newman."

SEATED IN A SECLUDED little West End restaurant booth across from Erica, Dustin ate barbecue and Erica munched on a veggie sandwich. She'd told him that reviewing required her to taste a variety of things, so she'd eaten off his plate, too. She preferred the veggie sandwich.

He and Erica were different. He'd shrivel up and die on a diet of sprouts and tofu, while that was her favorite. She only ate meat because she had to, for the restaurant review. Although he didn't always understand or agree with her preferences, he admired her convictions. He always had. In fact, he enjoyed playing Texas good ol' boy, just to get her on a soapbox.

When she'd ordered a local microbrew made from organic grain, he'd deliberately asked for a Bud. At the moment, she was trying to convince him to invest Ramsey money in the microbrewery. He liked the idea of making a profit on beer, but he had his doubts about the organic part, which jacked up the price considerably.

She was persuasive, though, and he loved the passionate way she argued a point. The more time he spent with her, the more he became convinced that he'd done exactly the right thing by seeking her out. When they'd hooked up in chemistry class, she'd been the first girl to treat him as if he had potential to succeed at something besides football. Up until then, his ambitions hadn't stretched much beyond winning chugalug contests and the state football championship.

But then he'd pushed his luck and taken her for a drive in the country. After that dismal failure he'd avoided Erica, which resulted in a return to his old lazy mental habits. Now his only option was to retrace his steps, get on a better footing with Erica and move forward from there.

She really *was* good for him. He'd like to believe he could be good for her, too. With her initiative, she could reap benefits from the economic system she liked to criticize. They both could reap benefits of a more personal nature if she'd allow it.

"Just try the beer," she said, holding out the bottle she'd been drinking from.

He liked the idea of putting his mouth where hers had recently been. His fingers brushed hers as he took the bottle and awareness flashed in her eyes. Good. She was still thinking about his proposition.

Holding her gaze, he lifted the bottle to his lips and drank.

"Well?" She looked at him expectantly.

"I like it. Rich and good." Exactly the way sex would be with her. He imagined he could taste the flavor of her mouth along with the beer. Handing the bottle back, he watched as she sipped from it again. Drinking from the same bottle was a start.

"So you'll think about that as a potential investment?"

"Sure. I'll look into it. But organic beer doesn't have sex appeal. Your newsletter does. And you know what they say. Sex sells."

She made a face. "I thought you wanted to educate people, not capitalize on the sexual content of the newsletter."

"What's wrong with doing both?"

"Spoken like a true capitalist. I just don't happen to care about making gobs of money." She took another sip of her beer. "And I honestly don't see myself publishing this newsletter for much longer. Some job will open up for me in the next six months, as the economy improves."

"You're passing up a golden opportunity."

She regarded him from across the table, her gray eyes sparkling. "Are we still talking about the franchise?"

He grinned.

"You're such a flirt. I have to admit you're arousing my curiosity."

"And that's all?"

She didn't comment, just smiled back at him.

He was sure his sexual longing showed right on his face. Fortunately she couldn't see under the table, where even more evidence lurked. He took another bite of his barbecue.

"I still wonder exactly how you found me," she said. "I've lost touch with everyone in Midland. If the reunion committee couldn't locate me, how did you?"

He chewed and swallowed the spicy beef, taking his time while he thought of how to answer. If he told her, she'd know how obsessed he'd been with tracking her down. He'd hoped to keep from mentioning the extent of his search, but now that she'd asked, he had to level with her. "I hired a private investigator."

"Get outta here! You hired a *P.I.* to find me? I can't believe that!"

Sometimes he had a hard time believing it, too. "When I get an idea in my head, I can be…stubborn."

Her eyebrows lifted. "Apparently."

"I'd hoped you'd be at the reunion, but when you weren't, I had to figure out something else."

"You really and truly had a private eye tailing me?" She looked intrigued.

Maybe telling her wasn't such a bad thing. "I did."

"This is beginning to sound like a movie."

"Well, if you're thinking of a guy wearing a trench coat and a snap-brim fedora, that wasn't happening. Jennifer Madison operates out of Midland and she found you using the Internet, with her two-month-old baby asleep in the crib next to her."

Erica frowned in concentration. "Jennifer Madison. I know that name." Then she snapped her fingers. "She subscribes to *Dateline: Dallas*. I wondered why she be interested, living in Midland. So Jennifer Madison is a private eye.''

"Yep. And a good one.''

"A private eye with a baby and a computer. That is sort of anticlimactic. I was picturing reruns of *Magnum P.I.* It wouldn't be so bad to be watched by the likes of Tom Selleck in his younger days. Actually, he's still pretty cute.''

"Sorry.'' Actually he wasn't sorry at all. He wouldn't have hired someone who looked like Tom Selleck in the first place. "It's the electronic age.''

"Even so, it's quite a concept, to think that you actually hired a person to dig around until they located me. I've never been tailed before.''

"So…you're not upset?''

Leaning back in the booth, she gazed at him. "I suppose I could look at it as another example of how people with money operate differently from the rest of us. You wanted to find me so you thought nothing of hiring it done.''

"As a last resort.'' And he'd considered the expense more carefully than she'd ever know.

"But the truth is, this is very good for my ego. I thought I was nothing more than a notch in your belt, and here you are hiring a P.I. to track me down ten years later.''

He winced at her interpretation of his behavior ten years ago. "I'm not a belt-notch kind of guy. That's what I'm trying to—''

"You could be a scorekeeper, though.''

"Excuse me?''

"What exactly was wrong with the sex between us?''

"Well, um—'' He took a fortifying swallow of his Bud. "It was over too fast, for one thing.''

Her gray eyes held his relentlessly. "Some people think quickies are great.''

"They are, if both people are satisfied at the end.'' He

was glad they were seated in a back booth and the place was nearly empty.

Still he didn't feel totally secure about having this conversation right now. The restaurant owner, a guy named Henry, had popped back several times to make sure the food was good. He could show up again and catch part of what they were saying.

She continued to challenge him with her eyes. "And your point is?"

He leaned forward and lowered his voice. "You didn't come, Erica. That's what was wrong with it."

She mirrored his posture, leaning toward him and resting her arms on either side of her plate. "And I suppose all the rest of your sexual partners have come?"

"Damn right they have." He was proud of that. In some cases he'd given them the first orgasm of their lives.

She settled back with a victorious smile. "See what I mean?" she said softly. "I'm lousing up your perfect score."

"That's not the point, damn it." Okay, it was a small part of the point. But not the biggest part of the point.

"I say it is. You're a jock, and jocks can't help keeping score."

"That is not true. It's not about the numbers. Every guy probably has one woman he didn't have any success with, sexually. I could live with that. I just don't want that woman to be you."

"Why not?"

"Out of all the people I've had sex with, you're the one I respected the most." Until he said it out loud, he hadn't realized how true it was.

Her gaze flickered. "Sounds like there's been quite a lineup."

"I didn't mean to make it sound like that." There had been quite a lineup, but none of the experiences had meant as much as that night in the back of his Mustang. And he'd botched that. "I just want to show you that I'm capable of doing it right."

She leaned toward him again. "You know what? I think you're turning this into more of a production than you need to. If giving me an orgasm is all you need to feel better about everything, we don't have to stage an elaborate bedroom scene."

"We don't?"

"Nope. I don't have time for that, anyway. I'm on a tight deadline for the newsletter and I have to work straight through until noon tomorrow if I expect to get it put together."

"I understand that." The gleam in her eyes made him nervous. "But I'm here through tomorrow night."

"Why wait?" she murmured. "If this is so important to you, why don't we take care of it right now?"

His mouth went dry. "What are you talking about?"

She moved to the far corner of the booth and patted the vinyl seat next to her. "Scoot on over here, cowboy. Let's even the score."

4

ERICA WAS REASONABLY SURE Dustin would back down before her challenge. He had a whole other strategy mapped out that involved both of them getting naked, and this suggestion wouldn't fit his preconceived idea. So she'd get credit for being a bold, swinging chick without having to follow through.

All her years of debate strategy were paying off, judging by the startled look in his eyes. Do the unexpected and gain the advantage. His phone call had been totally out of the blue, so he'd had the advantage in the beginning. By confessing that he'd been thinking about her for ten years, he'd lost a good part of that advantage, though.

Now his advantage was completely gone. Obviously she'd shocked him down to the toes of his expensive snakeskin boots.

His throat moved in a convulsive swallow. "I…that's not what I—"

"How are you two coming along?" Henry sauntered back to the booth. "Are you saving room for dessert?"

Erica felt a naughty thrill knowing what she and Dustin had been discussing right before the portly restaurant owner showed up. She'd bet that Dustin was dealing with a major erection right now. The thought made her go all squishy inside, but she didn't really want to make out in a restaurant booth. Of course not.

Sliding back to the middle of her seat, she gave Henry

a broad smile as she glanced up at him. "Dessert sounds wonderful."

"Terrific." Henry clasped his hands in front of him. "We have mud pie, an unbelievable hot-fudge sundae, a raspberry cheesecake that's out of this world, and pecan pie to die for. Why don't I bring all of them and let you sample to your heart's content?"

"Sounds like a great idea." Erica looked over at Dustin and somehow managed to keep her face straight. "Are you up for that?"

He coughed. "Um, sure."

"May I clear your plates?" Henry asked.

"You can take mine," Erica said. "And it was delicious, Henry. Even the barbecue, and you know I'm not much of a carnivore."

"I thought I'd tempt you with that sauce," Henry said. "Be sure and mention the sauce in the review. We're known for that."

"I'll be sure and mention the sauce." Erica reached over to Dustin's plate, swiped up a bit with her finger and licked it off, totally on purpose. She'd never been this motivated to sexually taunt a guy. "A taste that yummy should be illegal."

Henry beamed. "My mom's secret recipe." He turned toward Dustin. "Sir, do you want to keep your plate?"

"No, that's okay." Dustin's voice sounded gravelly. "You can take it." He cleared his throat again. "It was very good, though."

"A positive review in *Dateline: Dallas* guarantees increased traffic." He picked up Dustin's plate. "I've been trying to get Erica in here for months." He glanced at her. "And the review will be out Saturday, right?"

"Absolutely. I'll write it this afternoon."

"Cool. I've scheduled everybody to work Saturday night, to handle the crowd. More beer for either of you?"

"One beer's all I can handle if I'm going to make my deadline," Erica said, "but iced tea would be nice."

Henry looked at Dustin. "And what can I get for you?"

"The same, thanks."

"Good deal. Be right back."

After he left, Erica gazed at Dustin in silence, waiting to see if he'd say anything more about her outrageous suggestion.

"You weren't serious about it, were you?" he asked at last.

"What makes you think I wasn't serious?"

"Well, for one thing, Henry keeps wandering back here."

She'd honestly forgotten about Henry, but that didn't matter, because Dustin wouldn't take her up on her offer. "The possibility of discovery increases the excitement," she said, continuing to have fun with him. "I did one issue on restaurants where it would be possible to fool around. I keep getting requests for reprints of that issue."

"Did you test out the restaurants personally?"

"I'll take the Fifth on that." Sadly enough, the guy she'd been dating at the time hadn't had an adventurous bone in his body. When she'd tried to fondle him under the table, he'd insisted they leave the restaurant.

"I'll bet you did it. Which is exactly what I'd expect of you. You're one gutsy woman."

She was pleased with that assessment. Maybe Dustin would go back to Midland and think about her for another ten years. This time she'd be able to visualize him pining away, and that would be sweet, indeed.

"Here we are—decadence personified." Henry appeared and unloaded three dessert plates, a tall hot-fudge sundae and two iced teas.

"Positively sinful." Erica winked at Dustin.

"Use that in the review," Henry said. "Just say my

sauce oughta be illegal and my desserts are positively sinful. I'll have a line clear down the street Saturday night.''

''I hope you do.'' Erica surveyed the banquet of sweets and decided to put a little more pressure on Dustin. ''Thanks, Henry. You know what else I like about this place?''

''The charming owner?''

She smiled at him. Henry was gay, so she knew he wasn't even remotely hitting on her. ''Definitely. And also the fact that the service is discreet. You don't hover over us while we eat. You leave us alone to enjoy our food.''

Henry flushed with obvious pleasure. ''I try to treat people the way I'd like to be treated. I make sure they don't need anything, but once I'm sure they're all set, I disappear. Most people like a little privacy to enjoy their meal.''

''You're smart to realize that,'' Erica said.

''That said, I'll leave you two to your desserts.'' Henry bowed slightly. *''Bon appétit.''*

Once he was gone, Erica trained her gaze on Dustin. ''Take whatever appeals to you.''

His chest rose and fell rapidly. ''Did you do that on purpose?''

She played dumb. ''Order dessert?''

''Let Henry know that we wanted to be left alone.''

She pulled the hot-fudge sundae toward her and dipped a spoon into the whipped cream. ''You seemed worried about Henry running back here all the time, so I decided to remove that obstacle for you.'' She licked the whipped cream from the edge of the spoon. Then she waved it over the table full of goodies. ''Have some dessert.''

Dustin pulled the cheesecake plate in front of him. ''I'll bet if I came over there you'd freak.''

''Try me.'' She picked the cherry up by its stem and dangled it above her mouth before plopping it inside. She was giddy with power. Dustin was squirming in his seat and wondering if she was as wild as she seemed to be. Sweet.

He grabbed a fork and ate the cheesecake automatically, shoveling it in like a robot unaware of what he was doing. "I should call your bluff."

Pulling the cherry with her teeth, she twirled the stem between her fingers as she chewed and swallowed. Her heart hammered, but she kept her tone casual. "Assuming I'm bluffing." This was the most fun she'd ever had in her entire life. All this teasing was giving her quite a buzz.

"You're bluffing. You might have done something in a dark restaurant at night, but this is the middle of the day." He finished the cheesecake and started on the mud pie. "No way would you go through with it."

"Whatever you say." Digging out some hot fudge, she left the spoon poised over the dish so the warm chocolate dribbled over the whipped cream. "You're the one who said we couldn't be friends if you didn't give me an orgasm. I'm only trying to accommodate you."

He paused, his fork in midair, and watched the hot fudge ooze from the tip of her spoon. In what looked like an unconscious gesture, he ran his tongue over his lips. "Tell me again when you'll be finished with the newsletter?"

"I have to put it to bed, as we say, by noon tomorrow. I got behind this week so I'll probably pull an all-nighter to get it done." She turned the spoon upside down and slid it into her mouth as she held his gaze.

"Will you be free after that?"

She sucked the hot fudge from the spoon and slid it back out of her mouth. "I'll have to check my calendar. I might have a date tomorrow night." She didn't. She'd broken up with Brian two months ago, and nobody promising had appeared on the horizon since then. But she had to protect herself, or she was liable to end up in Dustin's hotel room tomorrow night.

Although she'd been an easy conquest once upon a time, she wouldn't make that mistake again. No matter what he might say to the contrary, this could be all about the chase. Once she gave him what he wanted, he could easily drop her again. Fool me once, shame on you. Fool me twice, shame on me.

His voice was husky with leashed tension. "You're torturing me on purpose, aren't you?"

She gestured with her spoon as she leaned toward him. "I'm trying to show you that this is an impossible situation you're trying to set up. You can't ride into my life after ten years and expect me to fall into bed with you so that you can have a perfect record with the ladies."

"So you won't see me tomorrow night?"

"I might, if I don't have a date. But we have to have an understanding that I won't go to bed with you. That would put way too much pressure on both of us." *And might leave me open to another painful rejection.*

"All right."

She was a little disappointed that he'd give up the campaign that easily, but she smiled as if pleased with his decision. "Good. Then we understand each other. I think eventually you'll see that—" She paused as he eased out of the booth. "What are you doing?"

"Move over. I'm taking you up on your earlier offer."

"Uh…" The spoon dropped from her fingers and clattered to the table.

He sat on the edge of her seat, his thigh brushing hers, his arm over the back of the vinyl seat. His mouth was inches from hers, his scent surrounded her, bringing a surge of memories. "Lost your nerve?" he murmured.

"No," she lied, looking into eyes blue as the center of a flame. "You just…took me by surprise." *Do the unexpected, gain the advantage.* She'd seriously miscalculated, and if she backed down now, she'd lose all the ground she'd won. Her reputation as a sophisticated, savvy chick would be seriously damaged. Then she realized with a jolt of awareness that *she wanted to let him do this.*

"You didn't expect me to come through, did you?" His voice was soft, his touch even softer as he trailed warm fingers up the inside of her thigh. Only his quick, shallow breath and the intensity of his gaze revealed his excitement.

She could barely breathe, herself. "Seriously, no." Her voice was choked with tension.

"You thought a clodhopper cowboy from Midland wouldn't rise to the challenge." He slid his hand under her short skirt and brushed the hem of her organic cotton panties. "But the way you're throwing roadblocks in my way, this looks like my only option to change your mind about giving me a second chance."

His warm hand on her inner thigh made her heart race, but she met his gaze, determined not to flinch. "I won't change my mind. I'm still not going to bed with you."

"Then this will have to do, won't it?" He nudged her with his thigh. "Ease over a little and give me more room to work."

She was so excited she thought she might pass out. "Have you...ever done something like this before?" She had visions of creating a scene that she'd never live down, but she was too aroused to care.

"Can't say that I have. But I figure you'll coach me."

She swallowed and scooted further into the booth.

He followed, his hand wrapped around the inside of her right thigh. Then he angled his torso so that he blocked her from view and cupped his other hand around her shoulder. Holding her gaze, he stroked her thigh. "Last chance. Want to back out?"

Not bloody likely. Not when she was burning like this. She shook her head. A woman of the millennium should be able to take her satisfaction whenever and wherever she wanted. And he was right—he owed her. Taking her pay-back this way, wild as it was, didn't scare her as much as the bedroom scene.

He rubbed his knuckles over the damp cotton crotch of her panties. "I think you want this."

"Maybe." She gripped the edge of the table with both hands.

"No maybe about it." He worked his fingers through the elastic leg opening. "Damn. You're so wet."

As if he had to tell her. The minute he'd laid his hand on her thigh she'd become drenched. She caught her breath as he slid two fingers inside. Her muscles automatically tightened around them.

"Oh, you're ready." His lips parted as he stroked slowly back and forth, curving his fingers upward to ride along her G-spot. "This will be easy."

She held back a moan and closed her eyes.

"Better open your eyes." His voice was rough and breathy. "Make it look like we're having a serious con-versation."

Her eyelids fluttered upward and she looked into the fur-nace of his gaze. "You want me...to talk?"

"Sure." He brought his thumb into play, brushing it la-zily back and forth. "That gatekeeper of yours is getting real excited. Tell me how this feels."

Her tongue felt as swollen as that gatekeeper he was teasing. "Good," she whispered.

"I thought so. Your cheeks are pink and your eyes are dark, like there's a storm rolling in." He thrust with his fingers as he kept up the relentless motion with his thumb.

"There...is." She clutched the edge of the table and started to close her eyes again.

"Don't close your eyes." He seemed winded. Leaning closer, he subtly increased the rhythm of his fingers as his breath came in ragged bursts. "Come for me, Erica."

In an instant the spasms took hold of her. She clenched her jaw against the cries that threatened to erupt and clamped her thighs tight, holding his hand prisoner. Then she ducked her head, closed her eyes and struggled for breath.

"Incredible," he murmured.

"Not…bad." She drew in one trembling breath after another. He'd taken the edge off, but an insistent throbbing told her that if he started over, she'd come again.

He leaned in close. "You're not even finished, are you?"

She grasped his wrist and pulled his hand from between her thighs. "Yes. Yes, I am."

"I don't believe it. You're still humming like a top."

She looked into his eyes and heat simmered between them. "We need to go."

Eagerness flashed in his gaze. "We sure as hell do. Your place or mine?"

"Mine, but you're not staying." And he would have no idea how much she wanted him to. "I have a newsletter to put out." Thank God for the newsletter. It would keep her from making a complete fool of herself.

His jaw tightened. "Would it be the end of the world if you missed the deadline? You told me yourself that the newsletter isn't all that important. So it's a little late. So what?"

"My subscribers expect to get it Saturday, and they'll get it Saturday. Henry's planning on my review, for another thing. Didn't you hear him say that he'll have a full staff on hand to deal with the rush of customers?"

"Not really. I was thinking of something else."

She didn't have to ask what that was. Now she'd have sex on the brain, too. Putting out the newsletter would be a challenge when all she wanted to do was fool around with Dustin. That would be a dumb move. She was so totally lucky to have an obligation she couldn't ignore.

She put a hand on his arm and tried to sound blasé. "Dustin, that was great. Truly. A peak experience. But I have to go back to my apartment and work." She smiled at him. "And now we're even."

"This wasn't about being even, damn it. We still haven't…you still don't know whether I…"

"Can go the distance? I'm sure you can." She wouldn't mind finding out for herself, but that was too dangerous. "Now I really do need to go home."

He sighed. "Getting out of this booth may take a moment."

"I understand." All in all, things were going very well between them. This little interlude hadn't cooled him off at all. He was even more hot to have her. She wanted him to leave Dallas in that same condition. No way would she be an item checked off his list of things-to-do.

Eventually they left the restaurant. She called out a cheery goodbye to Henry, but Dustin only waved and didn't look cheerful at all.

He remained silent for the first half of the ride back to her apartment. Finally he cleared his throat and spoke. "I didn't realize your restaurant reviews had such an impact. Why do you think that is?"

She'd wondered about that herself. The rush of business after her first review had surprised both her and the restaurant owner. Her girlfriends had helped her analyze it, so now she had an answer to give him.

"The newsletter hits the right market, for one thing," she said. "Single people eat out a lot. And I don't review a restaurant unless several friends tell me it's good, so my reviews are always positive and people trust my judgment. But I've had a good response even before people knew they could trust me, so I've had to conclude something else is going on."

"What else?"

"Sex."

He nearly ran a red light and laid a strip of rubber as he slammed on the brakes. "Are you telling me that what happened today is something you do all the time? And then *write* about it?"

"No. Today was unique. And I won't tell a soul."

His shoulders relaxed.

"Dustin, I'm not *that* uninhibited."

"Anything's possible. You were a rabble-rouser in high school, and I haven't seen you in ten years."

She laughed, happy to have him think of her as a wild woman. "When I said sex, I meant the way I write the review has sexual overtones. I didn't realize I was doing it until one of my friends pointed it out. Now I purposely make the food sound sexy."

"Like sauce that should be illegal and positively sinful desserts."

"Exactly."

"So you realize perfectly well that sex sells, and you're using that to your advantage."

"Okay, maybe I am." She'd barely been willing to admit that to herself. *Dateline: Dallas* was really all about sex, even the date-worthy attractions. Movies were rated as to whether they'd get a date in the mood. She usually recommended nightclubs with dark, cozy corners, and outdoor trip suggestions always included one or two secluded spots for canoodling.

She was promoting places where people could get it on. Then in her column, she helped them figure out how best to do it. Fun and games—that's what she was all about. Instead of seeking social reform, she was immersed in social intercourse. Literally. No wonder her parents hadn't commended her on the success of her newsletter.

"Erica, if you don't bottle this winning formula of yours and export it all around the country, you're crazy. Whether you want to tie in with me or not is up to you. It's obvious we have some issues between us, and maybe I'm not the guy you want to do business with, but you need to find somebody to back you. You've struck pure gold."

"Fool's gold," she said softly.

He pulled into the parking lot of her building, but he kept the motor running. "Then if you really believe that, throw the damn thing together as fast as you can and give me a call."

"I can't throw it together. You know that."

He gazed at her, his expression disguised by his sunglasses. "I dare you to stop writing about sex and come over to the hotel and have some. Call anytime. After what happened at lunch, I'm sure I'll be awake all night."

5

ALL THE WAY BACK to his hotel, Dustin cursed the very quality he admired most in Erica. If she weren't so damned conscientious, she'd be in bed with him all afternoon, all night, maybe for the entire time he was in Dallas. Instead she was putting together a newsletter that she claimed not to care about.

He didn't buy that. She loved what she was doing, and yet she was so hung up on wanting to deal with big issues that she couldn't admit that the newsletter was worthwhile. He couldn't see a damn thing wrong with spreading the newsletter concept all over the country. It would help the local economy in each city and teach couples to have more fun.

But that was his opinion, and he couldn't expect her to listen to anything a guy like him had to say. He was tainted by the oil business that had fed and clothed him for his entire life. From what he could tell, he had only one trump card to play when it came to Erica—she craved his body.

The feeling was entirely mutual. All he had to do was sniff the tips of his fingers and he was in a state of taut readiness. He'd thought he was one bad dude when it came to women, but he'd never experienced anything like those moments in the restaurant booth. Now that he'd seen Erica in the grip of a climax, he wanted a repeat performance.

Ten years ago he'd had a short-but-sweet plunge into her warm, wet body. But darkness had kept him from seeing much and they'd left some of their clothes on, anyway.

Today he'd been able to watch the turmoil in her eyes when she'd climaxed. He'd seen her breasts quiver with each gasp and felt the ripple of her orgasm against his fingers.

Now he wanted it all—the meeting of mouths, the slide of naked bodies, the leisure to explore. He wanted Erica's hands on his penis, and her mouth, too, for that matter. From the way she responded to him, he knew she fantasized about making love for hours, too. If he could overcome her resistance, they'd set the sheets on fire.

He was a tiny bit worried, though. She was such a babe and so incredibly sexy that she'd test the control he was proud of, the control that he wanted to demonstrate thoroughly for her. Still he'd take the risk if he could get her to agree.

Somehow he'd manage that. He was more determined about it now than he had been this morning driving to Dallas. Although he couldn't explain why, he felt that her refusal to go to bed with him and her decision to drop the newsletter were tied together. It would definitely help if she trusted him more, but maybe this was about trusting herself, too. He sure could relate to that problem, considering how he struggled with self-confidence.

Once back in his hotel room, he gazed at the clock on the nightstand and realized he had a hell of a lot of time to kill before Erica put the paper to bed. She'd used that phrase on purpose, along with several other tricks to drive him crazy. If her goal had been to make his tongue drag on the ground, she'd succeeded.

But then she'd left him to stew. He didn't appreciate that, and he didn't intend to hang around the room feeling sorry for himself. His two racing buddies might not be the kind of guys he'd ask for business advice, but they knew how to party. He dug his address book out of his briefcase and reached for the phone.

USUALLY ERICA COULD BANG OUT a restaurant review in an hour. That's all the time she'd allotted herself for this one, because she still had to pull together her main feature article about a day at Six Flags, write a review of a foreign film she'd seen at the beginning of the week and answer three more letters for her advice column.

Then she had to proof the whole thing, figure out her layout and round up some clever fillers. With a sigh she acknowledged that her fillers were always about sex. Anyone would think she was fixated on the subject.

She hoped that wasn't true in general. But today it seemed to be all too true. Admittedly she'd never tried to write a review of a meal that had ended with a man giving her a climax under the table.

No matter how determined she was to get the words down, she'd only type for a few minutes before lapsing into a daydream about her lunch with Dustin. Then a bird outside her window or the chiming of her clock would remind her that she was sitting there motionless, not getting the work done.

If she wasn't reliving their amazing time together, she was wondering what he was doing now that she'd abandoned him. She'd left him in quite a state. Although that had been her intent, now she felt guilty about it. She was still plenty aroused herself, and she'd had a chance to release some of that tension. She could only imagine how frustrated he must be.

Maybe he'd take matters into his own hands. Now that she had *that* picture in her head, she'd never be able to finish the review. Judging from the letters she received for her column, men weren't shy about taking the edge off when they couldn't get satisfaction from the woman they were seeing. She'd even recommended masturbation to guys whose sex drive was greater than their girlfriends'. It was way better than having an affair.

She wondered if Dustin preferred the bed or the shower, whether he took his pleasure fast or slow. Maybe he'd think of her at the time, and maybe he wouldn't. He might picture her hand stroking him…

Damn it, this wasn't getting her anywhere except ready to go find the vibrator in her nightstand drawer. Or call Dustin and ask him to come over. No. She would *not* cave in to these inappropriate urges. And she would get this review written.

Using every ounce of willpower she had, she kept her fingers moving over the keys for the next half hour and was fooling around with the final sentence of the review when her doorbell rang. Her first thought was that Dustin had decided to ignore her wishes and barge in anyway. Her heart began to pound and the dull ache of arousal that had plagued her all afternoon blossomed into full-blown lust.

But a look through her door's peephole quieted her body's response. Her buddy Denise, a short brunette who wrote obits for the *Morning News,* stood outside holding a bag of Chinese takeout. Erica opened the door with a smile.

"I knew this was deadline night," Denise said. She'd pulled her long hair into a ponytail and was dressed in shorts and a Cowboys T-shirt. "And you've been known to go without food, so I decided to bring some over. I won't stay. Unless you could use some help, that is."

"I could use some company, but I won't take the help unless you'll let me pay you." She led the way into her kitchen.

"You've already given me a complimentary subscription." Denise put the bag on the table and began taking out aromatic cartons. "And I get a real thrill out of writing about live people once in a while. I got you vegetables and fried rice, plus we each have an egg roll and some egg-drop soup. But you can have a bite of my Kung Pao Chicken if you want to live dangerously."

"I'm already living dangerously." Erica poured iced tea and took out plates and silverware. She liked eating Chinese with Denise because Denise didn't consider it necessary to struggle with chopsticks.

"How so?" Denise took her usual seat nearest the wall.

Erica sat down across from her and began dishing out her meal. "Do you remember when you, Josie and I got smashed on margaritas for Cinco de Mayo?"

Denise paused with a spoonful of rice halfway to her plate. "And we each told about how we lost our virginity." She rapped the spoon against her plate to dislodge the sticky rice. "Yep, I remember."

"Well, my Virginity Guy turned up today."

Denise looked at her, wide-eyed. "No shit. The overprivileged jock from Midland?"

"Right. And he says he ignored me after we had sex because he was embarrassed about his poor performance."

"It took him ten years to admit that?" Denise ladled some Kung Pao Chicken over her rice. "I'm not impressed."

"Apparently he's been thinking about me all that time, and…he wants another shot."

Denise began to grin. "Outstanding." She dug a fork into her food. "So what's your plan?"

That was just it. She needed a plan. She opened her mouth to explain the complications.

"Wait, don't tell me. Let me guess. You're going to lead him on, and maybe, if he's very, very deserving, you'll let him have sex with you. Then you'll dropkick his butt back to Midland." Denise chewed her food and gazed at Erica with an expression of triumph.

If only she could do that. She shoved her vegetables and rice around her plate. "He's very cute."

"That's a plus. You might as well enjoy yourself while you're getting revenge."

"I'm just afraid—" she paused and glanced up at Denise "—that I'll like it too much. That I'll want to keep him around."

Denise's smile faded. "Have you been thinking about *him* for ten years?"

"Kind of." Erica took a sip of her iced tea.

"You never got over him."

"I don't know." Erica sighed and leaned back in her chair. "I thought I had. Then I saw him again, and realized no one has ever turned me on like he does. But he's totally wrong for me. He's all V-8 engines and juicy steaks. His goals are completely opposite mine. He wants to provide financial backing so I can franchise my silly little newsletter in other big cities, maybe take it national."

"Wow. I can see the problem. The guy may offer great sex and untold riches, but I'll bet he doesn't even recycle his beer bottles."

Erica laughed. "Probably not. Go ahead, make fun of me."

"I'm just jealous. My Virginity Guy is married with three kids. Nobody's ever held a torch for me for ten months, let alone ten years. But I don't want to see you get hurt, so maybe you're right to steer clear."

"I think so."

"But can't you picture yourself decked out in a Victoria's Secret number and turning this guy inside out? Wouldn't you love to show him that the shy little virgin is now one hot babe?"

"Yes, damn it!" She'd already made strides in that direction at lunch today, and she'd spent part of the afternoon fantasizing how she could build on the excellent beginning. Leaning her elbows on the table, she cupped her face in both hands. "I wish I could use him for sex and send him back where he came from. But what if I get all tangled up in this guy? There's every chance he'd drop me before I could drop him. That would be a hideous ending to the story."

"How soon's he going back to Midland?"

"He's here for two nights. And I told him I wouldn't be available until after I took the newsletter to the printer at noon."

"Then you have some time to think about this. Come on, eat up. Then I'll proof what you've done so far. Tell me about your main feature while we eat, so I can help you with that, too. That's always the backbreaker."

They abandoned the topic of Dustin while Erica explained how she wanted to handle the Six Flags article. After they'd finished eating, they put away the extra Chinese food and took their iced tea over to her battered desk, where she printed out the restaurant review for Denise to edit. Then she started on the movie review.

After only a few minutes of reading, Denise glanced up. "Is the person you shared lunch with by chance Virginity Guy?"

Despite a five-year history with Denise in which many secrets had been shared, Erica blushed. "Um, yeah. Why?"

"Your review reads like a page out of a porn novel, that's why. Listen to this. 'The succulent barbecue is moistened with a thick sauce that tickles the palate with near orgasmic delight. Such gastronomic pleasure should be illegal.'"

Erica's cheeks grew warmer. "A little over-the-top, huh?"

"Let's just say this is how I imagine Hugh Hefner might write a restaurant review. Exactly what went on during lunch?"

She'd promised Dustin she wouldn't tell a soul. "I'm not at liberty to say."

"Omigod. You finally found a guy who would fool around in a public place. Listen, sweetie. This man may be a total loss as an environmentalist, but I hate to see you pass up a chance for hot sex. You've dated anemic losers ever since I've known you. Sounds like this guy's tuned in.''

''That's exactly what worries me!'' Erica rolled her chair away from the desk. ''What if he's the best lover I've ever had?''

''Okay, let me get this straight. There is nothing between you two except this incredible sexual attraction, right?''

Erica thought about Dustin's little speech today. He'd implied that he valued her attitude toward life, that he wanted her input during this shaky time in his life. Apparently he needed her for more than just sex. However, she didn't need him for any other reason. In fact, he was trying to lead her away from her life's goals.

''He's recently taken over the company from his father and seems to think I can help him focus,'' she said.

''Really?'' Denise put the review pages on the coffee table and tossed her pen on top of them. ''So he wants you for business purposes *and* sex. Sounds like the guy appreciates your finer qualities.''

''Actually I think he'd like to change me. He thinks I should give up the idea of working on a major daily and throw myself into franchising the newsletter.'' Erica looked at Denise. ''And that's not me.''

Denise gazed at her for several seconds.

''It's not!'' Erica said again. ''I want to sink my teeth into the important issues. I started *Dateline: Dallas* because you and Josie dared me, but it's frivolous fluff, and you know it. I'm sure the hard-news guys down at the paper make fun of what I'm doing.''

''When they're not sneaking a copy and reading it on the sly.'' Denise sighed. ''I love the newsletter, Erica. Why do you suppose I hang around when you're putting it together? I'd rather read it than some of the stories that are candidates for Pulitzers. If that makes me shallow, then call me shallow. I know you plan to quit publishing it someday soon, and I'll be sorry to see it go.''

So nobody was on her side, except maybe her parents.

"But I want you to do what's right for you." Denise stood and came over to wrap an arm around Erica's shoulders. "Don't let me or Virginity Guy influence your decision, because God knows we need people like you fighting the big problems, too."

"Thanks." Erica glanced up at her friend. "Take your red pencil to the restaurant review and tone it down, okay?''

"Will do." Denise gave her shoulder a squeeze and went back to the sofa.

"Oh, and Denise?"

"Yeah?"

"Do you have anything going tomorrow night, or would you like to catch a movie with me?"

Denise studied her. "Gonna book yourself up so you won't be tempted?''

"Yeah. Do you feel used?''

"Uh-huh." Denise grinned. "But what are friends for? I'll see if Josie's free, too. We'll find a chick flick and bawl into our popcorn. I'm sure that'll replace hot sex with a guy who's been saving up for ten years. Ten years he's been dreaming about getting you naked. Can you imagine how eager a lover he would—''

"Stop it!"

Denise shrugged. "I still don't see how a one-night stand with the guy would be such a bad thing. Lots of superficial sex, no talking. But if you insist on spending the last night he's in town with me, I'll accommodate you.''

"I want to see a movie, damn it."

"Then we'll see a movie."

CURTIS AND ROGER TOOK DUSTIN to their favorite bar, and then his two friends proceeded to get sloshed and dance with every available woman in the place. Curtis was short and chubby to begin with, and his beer-drinking life was beginning to give him a paunch, but he was a great dancer. Roger had the advantage of being taller, and he worked out to keep his gut in check, but he had two left feet. After a couple of beers, that fact didn't bother him at all.

Both of them were definitely there to party. Dustin drank enough to give him a nice buzz, but he'd lost the urge to drink until the room tilted. His dad's stroke had seriously crimped his style in that regard. Now that he was the guiding force behind Ramsey Enterprises, a newly discovered conscience told him that getting sloppy drunk was no longer an option.

He'd danced with several of the women, too, and at least one of them had hinted that she wouldn't mind if he escorted her home. From the way she'd wiggled against him on the dance floor, he had no doubt that was an offer of sex. In days past he would have accepted the offer, especially considering how Erica had left him high and dry this afternoon.

"Are you gonna go home with that little filly?" Curtis asked when he and Roger came back to the table to order another beer.

"No."

"*No?*" Roger asked, blinking and trying to focus. "Why do you think we brought you here in the first place?"

Dustin hadn't thought about it, but now that he did, he remembered the drill. Whenever a racing friend came to town for a visit, his buddies were supposed to take him to a bar where he could cruise for women. It was considered the hospitable thing to do.

"Sorry." He looked at his two very smashed friends and decided not to feel guilty. There had been a day when he'd have jumped at any excuse to go out and party, so tonight hadn't been a sacrifice for these two. "I'm sort of...involved with a woman here in Dallas."

Curtis scrubbed a hand over his flushed face. "Then why are you here with us instead of with her? Is she married or something?"

"No, but she had to work on her newsletter tonight, and—"

"Dateline: Dallas!" Roger said. "You're hooked up with her? Man, she must be one hot chick." He leaned closer. "That newsletter has all kinds of stuff about sex in it."

"Um, yeah, I know." Dustin wasn't crazy about having Roger describe Erica as one hot chick, even though the label was accurate. Still, she was classier than Roger made her sound. She wasn't Roger's kind of woman at all. Hell, she probably wasn't even his kind of woman. He didn't know what his type was, come to think of it.

"So she's working on the newsletter and kicked you out?" Curtis asked.

"Something like that."

"Hell, boy, that's a crock," Roger said. "Seems to me you could make yourself useful. You know—" he paused and winked broadly "—give her a back rub and so forth."

Dustin had been thinking about that very thing. He'd allowed Erica to call the shots, which didn't speak well for his dedication to the cause. If the situation was reversed and she was hell-bent on some mission, she wouldn't back off the minute he told her to. He was in Dallas to soak up some of her determination and drive. And initiative. At the moment he wasn't showing any of that.

"You're right," he said to Roger. "I think I'll go over there and make myself useful." Anticipation surged with him. Yes, it was time to take matters into his own hands...literally.

"Attaboy." Roger clapped him on the back. "It sure was nice to see you, though. I can't believe you're giving up racing."

"Aw, he's not," Curtis said. "He'll be back, once he gets this company of his squared away."

"Don't count on it," Dustin said. "Those days are probably over for me."

"Then I guess we'd better start hitting you up for sponsorships," Roger said.

Dustin laughed as he shook hands with both of them. "Let me get my act together. Then we'll talk." He could imagine how Erica would react to that. He didn't even have to ask her opinion on sponsoring auto racing. "No promises, though. I'll be in touch." He'd started toward the door when something else occurred to him. "You guys are taking a taxi home, right?"

"What for? We never take taxis. That's for sissies."

Dustin returned to the table. "Then drink up. I'll drive you home."

"I hate to say this, but you're sounding like some damned straight arrow, buddy," Curtis said. "Never thought I'd see the day."

Dustin smiled, not the least offended. "That makes two of us. Now finish your beer."

AT MIDNIGHT Erica sent Denise home. Other than the layout, some fillers and the advice column, the newsletter was basically done, and Denise had to be at work early. Erica was getting tired herself, so she'd decided to make a pot of coffee before answering the rest of the letters for the column. Then she'd catch a few hours of sleep and do the layout first thing in the morning.

When the doorbell rang close to twelve-thirty, she thought Denise had forgotten something. Maybe she'd changed her mind about taking home some of the Chinese food. Erica checked the peephole, expecting to see Denise out there grinning.

Instead, Dustin stood at her door holding a doughnut bag and two covered foam cups. He wore a loud western shirt and faded jeans.

Adrenaline made her hand shake as she opened the door. From the smell of cigarette smoke, she had to guess he'd spent the evening at a bar. Looking as good as he did, he could easily have found some female company if he'd wanted it. Yet here he was, at her door.

He smiled, as if sure of his welcome. "I thought you might be able to use some caffeine and sugar for the home stretch."

"You're not supposed to be here." But she was so glad he wasn't lying in some strange woman's bed. She hadn't figured on that possibility, but she should have.

"Are you gonna send me away?"

"I should. I have work to do." She was making a token protest and they both knew it.

"Let me in, Erica. You know you want to."

Silently she stepped aside. Something told her that making the movie date with Denise wasn't going to save her, after all.

6

ALTHOUGH DUSTIN HAD BEEN blown away that morning by Erica in full makeup with her sexy city clothes on, he was thoroughly seduced by the Erica who opened the door to him now. She was infinitely more accessible. Dressed in denim shorts and a faded University of Texas T-shirt, she wore no makeup and her feet were bare.

He wanted to tumble her straight into bed. But that wouldn't show any respect for her work, and he wasn't about to undermine her newsletter. He believed in it, even if she didn't.

"How's the writing coming along?" He walked over to the desk and set down the bag of doughnuts and two coffees. Papers were strewn over the sofa and chair and the computer was on. One of her kitchen chairs was pulled up to the desk beside her regular desk chair as if someone had been sitting beside her helping out. He wanted to know who.

"I have the advice column to finish," she said, "and I'll do the layout in the morning. My friend Denise came over for a while and helped out."

That explained the extra chair. He was glad to hear it had been occupied by a woman. Earlier today she'd skirted the issue of whether or not she was dating anyone, and he couldn't take the incident at lunch as any indication of her status.

A liberated woman like Erica might think nothing of playing around in a restaurant booth at noon with one guy and getting it on with a different one that night. Except she'd said she had to work, and Erica didn't lie.

She ran a hand through her hair, which was already tousled. "You must be psychic. I was thinking of making coffee."

That pleased him. "I ordered them black. I thought if you liked cream or sugar, you'd have that here." He didn't think she was wearing a bra. He tried not to look at her bare thighs and relive what had happened at the restaurant, but that was a losing battle. She had terrific legs, and the shorts gave him a better view than her skirt had. He was already half-erect, just standing here in the same room with her.

"I like cream. Or I should say rice milk, which is better for you. How about you?"

Whatever you'll give me. "Sugar."

"I have raw sugar. Will that be okay?"

"Sure."

"I'll be right back."

He watched her walk into the kitchen and somehow managed not to moan out loud. Forcing himself to think about the work she had to do, he turned to the computer. No help there. Sure enough, the answer to Frustrated Franny taunted him with the suggestion of fellatio to cure the premature ejaculator.

"Here you go." She handed him a cute little sugar bowl, sort of peach colored. It took him a few seconds to realize that the lid was in the shape of a woman's breast. Then he glanced at the cream pitcher, and damned if it wasn't even more X-rated. The pitcher's bowl was shaped like a scrotum, which made the design for the spout obvious.

She was apparently hoping to throw him off balance by impressing him with her worldliness. He decided not to comment on the sugar-and-cream set, although he would love to know whether she'd bought it herself or received it as a gift. And whether the giver had been male or female.

"I appreciate this," she said. "I'm running low on coffee, so now I'll have some for the morning." She set down the ultrasuggestive cream pitcher and snapped off the lid on one of the coffee cups. Then she reached into the pocket of her shorts and pulled out two spoons, handing him one with a smile. "Thank you for thinking of it."

"You're welcome, but I'm afraid there's nothing healthy about those doughnuts."

"That's okay. Doughnuts are something I allow myself once in a while. And they smell delicious."

He couldn't tell. His senses were too occupied with the scent of warm, aroused woman. Judging from the way her nipples tented the material of her faded T-shirt, she wasn't particularly calm about being close to him, either.

Although he'd told himself not to pay attention to the cream pitcher, he couldn't help watching in fascination as she poured rice milk out of the erect penis. That had to be a game prize from a bachelorette party, something ordered from a catalogue or picked up in an adult toy store. He must be living a more sheltered life than he'd thought, because he'd never seen anything remotely like it.

After she finished pouring, it was his turn. He snapped off the lid of his coffee, grasped the top of the bowl by the nipple and lifted it to scoop out the caramel-colored sugar inside. Then he set the top back on and ventured a glance in her direction as he stirred his coffee.

She gazed at him in amusement. "You're a cooler customer than I thought."

He gave her a blank stare. "About what?"

She laughed and shook her head. "Nothing. Absolutely nothing. Would you like to sit down?"

"Only if I can sit here and help you finish up."

"You might be able to give me some suggestions, at that.

I've often wondered if I needed the male perspective on the column." She sat in her desk chair and sipped her coffee while she scrolled past Frustrated Franny to the next letter.

"There's an idea. You could answer the question first, and then a guy could answer the same question from his viewpoint," he added.

She looked at him in surprise. "You know, that might work. I don't think I've ever seen anything like that."

"Feel free to use it."

"I just might." She continued to gaze at him as she sipped her coffee. "But to be effective, the guy giving answers along with mine would have to be a real man's man. If he's too evolved, his answers would sound exactly like mine, and that wouldn't create any interest." She grinned at him.

"I get it. A not-so-evolved type like me, you mean." He wasn't entirely unhappy with her assessment. Evolved or not, he could make her quiver with desire. Someone who thought exactly like her might not strike that kind of spark.

"Let's try one," she said. "We'll answer this letter and then reward ourselves with a doughnut. How's that?"

He could think of a better reward, but then they'd never make it to the rest of the letters. "Okay. I'm in." Cradling his coffee in both hands, he read the letter she'd brought up.

Dear Erica,
My girlfriend loves sex toys, specifically all her various vibrators. I don't mean to be a prude, but sometimes I worry that she has more fun with her toys than she does with me. Am I being unreasonable to ask her to put them away sometimes?
Sincerely, Unplugged Paul

"Here's my response." Erica began typing her answer.

Dear Unplugged,
Make friends with her toys! Sounds like she plays and
you watch, which implies that battery-operated good-
ies intimidate you. Why shouldn't your lover enjoy
both you and her vibrator simultaneously? Buy your
own models and get acquainted in private. You might
be surprised at what you're missing.
Sincerely, Erica

Taking her fingers off the keys with a flourish, as if she'd just finished a piano recital, she looked at him. "Got a rebuttal for that?"

"Absolutely. Do you want to trade seats or take dictation?" Coming over here had been an excellent idea. Helping with the letters had been brilliant, too. Talking about sex had to end up with a predictable result.

"I'll type it in. Just tell me what you want to say."

He cleared his throat. "Dear Unplugged, motors belong in cars, trucks and chain saws, not in the bedroom. I would suggest..." He paused as she turned to him in obvious disbelief. "Why aren't you typing?"

"Because your answer is so bogus! I can't believe you're going to agree with him!"

"I thought you wanted a sort of point-counterpoint deal, here?"

"I thought your ideas would be different, not prehistoric!"

He put down his coffee. "What in hell is exciting about a motor buzzing while you're having sex? I'll tell you what I think of when someone switches on a vibrator. I think of going to the dentist!"

"I certainly don't." She set her coffee down, too, and swiveled her chair to face him. "I think of having a wonderful climax, because I associate that little buzzing noise with extreme pleasure."

"You can't tell me it's as good as the real thing. You can talk until you're blue in the face, and you won't convince me of that."

"It's a lot more predictable than the real thing! I don't have to worry whether my vibrator is going to stand me up or go out with other women. My vibrator isn't going to go limp and make apologies while I'm clenching my teeth in frustration."

"That happens a lot with you?" He couldn't imagine any guy with a limp noodle if they had the chance to have sex with Erica.

"Let's say it can happen occasionally, okay? I realize you guys don't always have perfect control, and that's understandable, but have the good grace to accept help from modern science! Good old Unplugged Paul needs to realize that her vibrator gives her security and can be fantastic backup during the times when he isn't up to the task. At least with a vibrator, there's a guarantee that his girlfriend will have an orgasm."

His erection, extremely real at the moment, strained against his jeans. "Are you saying you actually *prefer* having sex with a piece of quivering molded plastic?"

Her chin jutted out. "Sometimes it's a lot less complicated. Sometimes I want to know I'll be taken care of, and that's not always—"

"Who the hell have you been having sex with, guys from the local rest home?"

"Normal guys! But I suppose you think that *you*…" She gulped and her eyes widened. "Forget I said that."

"No, I won't forget it. And yes, I know I can. Better than any damned vibrator." He was relieved to discover she'd been having mediocre sex. That was a huge confidence booster. "I want you to rethink your answer to Unplugged Paul. The guy needs to be given the confidence to perform like a stud, not encouraged to depend on batteries to satisfy his lover."

"You are so arrogant," she whispered. But her gray eyes had darkened the way they had in the restaurant, right before he'd slipped his hand up her skirt.

"And you need some good old-fashioned, unplugged sex." He was on firm ground now. In a contest with a vibrator, he'd win every time.

"Now there's a classic remark." Her breathing grew ragged. "Anytime a man disagrees with a woman's thinking, he's sure all she needs is a good lay and she'll come around."

"Anytime a woman spends all this time and energy praising her vibrator, she absolutely needs a good lay."

She began to quiver. "I most certainly do not."

"We could run an experiment." His heart thudded with excitement. "Have sex with me and then see if your answer to Unplugged Paul stays the same."

"That's crazy. You're just trying—"

"You bet I am, which is what real men do. They pursue. They seduce. They follow through. They don't need no stinkin' battery-operated toys."

"Maybe this idea of you helping me with the column…" She ran her tongue over her lips. "Maybe it isn't such a good one."

"Or maybe you have a chance to write the best column of your career, after you've been fully satisfied by a guy who knows what he's doing."

"I can't believe you're so cocksure of yourself!"

He smiled slowly, holding her gaze. "Perfect choice of words."

"You can't possibly live up to the advance billing." Her chest rose and fell rapidly, broadcasting her agitation.

"Unless we have sex, you'll never know." He could smell victory, smell the scent of her arousal. "And I think not knowing will drive you crazy."

"All right, damn it!" She rolled back her chair and stood. "Let's do it, and I predict the pressure will wilt you like a two-week-old celery stalk. Fortunately for you, I have fresh batteries in my vibrator." With that she stomped down the hallway.

Gazing after her, Dustin grinned. It wasn't the most romantic invitation he'd ever had, but it would have to do. He glanced at the computer screen. "Wish me luck, Paul."

INSIDE HER DARKENED BEDROOM, Erica flung off her clothes, yanked back the bedspread and slid between the sheets. If she treated this episode exactly as he'd phrased it, an experiment and nothing more, she had a chance of staying objective about Dustin. He couldn't possibly be as good as he said he was. Like all men, he had an inflated idea of his abilities.

But he was right about one thing. From the moment he'd told her that he wanted to prove himself in bed, she'd been beyond curious. The concept had kept her in a constant state of arousal. Although she'd vowed not to give him what he wanted, she'd been crazy to find out exactly what it would be like.

Well, he was in the hot seat now. He'd made some tall claims, and now he had to live up to them. He wouldn't, of course, and then she could go back to her regularly scheduled programs.

His boot heels clicked against the hallway's wooden floor as he walked toward her bedroom. She took deep breaths and tried to stop trembling with excitement, but there wasn't much she could do about the wetness between her thighs. He'd already won a partial victory there.

Chances were he'd be able to give her an orgasm, considering she was halfway there already. That wasn't technique on his part, just her natural reaction to him, something that had been going on ever since high school. He couldn't take credit for the fact that she found him incredibly sexy.

His broad-shouldered silhouette filled the doorway. Then the overhead light come on, making her blink.

She'd counted on the darkness to help her maintain some emotional distance. "Why don't you leave that off?"

"Nope." He leaned against the wall and pulled off his boots and his socks.

"Why? Afraid you'll lose your place?"

He began unsnapping his shirt, beginning with the cuffs. "I wouldn't lose my place blindfolded. But I want you to be able to see what's going on and make sure I don't have any vibrators up my sleeve."

As he pulled off his shirt, she really wished he hadn't turned on the light. Now he wouldn't be just some naked man in her bed. He would be a specific naked man with chest hair the color of maple syrup and dusky nipples the size of a quarter lying flat within the thicket of hair.

Some football players turned to flab when they stopped playing, but not Dustin. If anything, he'd bulked up since his days as a star halfback.

He reached in his jeans pocket, pulled out a condom packet and tossed it onto the bed. It landed on the sheet right between her thighs. "Bull's-eye."

She'd never had sex with a man who treated the experience with such nonchalant confidence. It really turned her on. "You couldn't do that again if you tried."

"Usually I'm not working with such a handicap."

"Meaning?"

"Usually I can see the target. And while we're on the subject, I think you're being unfair."

"Why?" She'd never promised to be fair. In this game she'd cheat if she had to.

"While I'm stripping down, you have that sheet pulled up to your chin, almost as if you're dreading this. If that's the way you usually treat your men, I can see why they might feel a little…inadequate."

"I never said they were inadequate!" She also hadn't meant to cower under the covers, but he'd startled her by flipping on the light like that. Now she wasn't sure how to change the dynamics. Throwing back the sheet lacked class.

He unfastened his jeans and eased down the zipper, as if cruising over sensitive territory. "You mentioned that they made apologies while you gritted your teeth in frustration. That sounds like inadequacy to me."

As he shoved his jeans to the floor, she knew that there would be nothing inadequate about this man. His gray knit boxers outlined equipment that made her reconsider throwing back the covers, whether it was a classy move or not. She moved restlessly under the sheet, her body yearning for what was inside those shorts.

He gazed at her with a smile. "Thinking about that noisy piece of cold plastic in your nightstand drawer?"

Not at the moment. At the moment I'm thinking of that hot joystick between your thighs. "How do you know where it is?"

"That's where most women keep them. It's my mission in life to make sure those buzzing little bastards stay in the drawer." Then he tugged down his boxers.

She gaped. She knew she was doing it and couldn't stop herself. If every man walked around looking like that, vibrators would disappear from the face of the earth. Heat sluiced through her and her mouth grew moist.

So this had been the instrument that had ended her virginal state. At least she'd started her sexual life with the deluxe model. And she had to admit that no one since had measured up. Maybe she'd been a little hasty in recommending battery-operated enjoyment to women. Maybe they needed to keep looking until they found a man with top-of-the-line features.

He walked toward the bed. When he sat on the edge of the mattress and reached for the condom packet, she assumed he was going to put the condom on. Instead he tossed it aside and pressed the sheet firmly between her thighs, forcing them apart. "Let's do a test run," he murmured, massaging gently.

She gasped at the unexpected caress, a caress that shot sensation deep inside, letting her know how close she was to a climax.

"You just drenched this part of the sheet." He shook his head, his gaze smoldering as he looked into her eyes. "What a shame that you waste that kind of response on a vibrator."

She had a moment of panic. He could ruin her for anyone else, never mind making her throw away her little play toys. Maybe she should stop him now, before it was too late.

"Don't be afraid," he murmured, leaning down, his mouth drawing closer to hers as he continued to rub his hand over the damp sheet tucked between her legs. "This isn't going to hurt. In fact, it will feel very, very good."

She hadn't really factored in kissing, either. Somehow she'd imagined that they'd just do the deed, hard and fast, and kisses wouldn't be a big part of the equation. Especially kisses like this.

He nibbled at her lips as if tasting a whipped-cream dessert. He was a coffee-flavored treat, a mocha delight. She combed her fingers through his hair and gripped the back of his head, trying to get even more of that sweetness. He resisted, teasing her but never fully settling down.

"I don't want to dive right in and forget myself," he said softly between kisses.

That was a concept, that if he gave in to the kiss he'd lose control. She certainly would. She'd forgotten how good his mouth felt, how sensuous that full lower lip was brushing lazily against hers. And all the while he increased the pressure of his hand between her legs, rocking his fingers right where he needed to.

She began to whimper as the tension coiled tighter within her.

"Did you hear that?" he whispered, dipping his tongue into her open mouth, retreating, dipping in again.

She moaned as he pressed harder with his finger. "Hear…what?" She was barely able to think, let alone speak. Her body quivered in anticipation.

His breath feathered her mouth. "The sound of a woman ready to climax. No buzzing, just delicious moans."

She gripped his head tighter as she began to pant with need. "Dustin…"

"Right here." He vibrated his finger faster.

There. She arched into his touch with urgent little cries as the waves of sensation carried her away.

He splayed his hand over the damp sheet and cupped her heat while he nuzzled her ear. "I love the sound of a woman coming. It's the best sound in the world."

Gasping for breath, she sank back to the mattress. So much for cool, collected and in control. All he'd had to do was touch her, and despite the sheet covering her, she'd erupted into a million pieces. No one had affected her like this. It was embarrassing.

He lifted his head to gaze at her.

She connected with that gaze and decided he looked definitely triumphant. "I suppose you think that proves your point." Maybe now he'd suggest they get dressed and go back to the computer so she could reword her response to Paul.

"Oh, no." He smiled at her. "As they say, you ain't seen nothin' yet."

A new tingle began deep in her belly. "You just proved that you can give me a good orgasm without the benefit of batteries. Isn't that what you wanted to demonstrate?"

"That was a spur-of-the-moment thing. That sheet tucked all around you was an interesting challenge. I decided to see if I could make you come without taking it off."

"Which you did. I'm impressed, and I'll consider modifying my response to Paul." Maybe she could still save herself, if he thought he'd won.

"That was only a superficial test." Sitting up, he reached for the condom he'd thrown to the far side of the bed and tore open the wrapping. "I'm glad you were impressed, but you don't sound thoroughly convinced."

"Oh, but I am."

He rolled the condom over his magnificent penis. "Just to be sure, I think we should probe into this issue some more, don't you?"

She gulped.

"Come on, Erica," he said softly. "Let's take this investigation deeper."

7

DUSTIN THOUGHT he deserved an Oscar for his performance as a totally in-control lover, when in fact he wanted to rip the sheet away and ravish Erica until neither of them could see straight. But giving her a climax first, before they got to the main event, was a nice touch.

She hadn't expected that move, and he was proud of his innovation. But if he didn't get inside her soon, he wouldn't be able to guarantee giving her another orgasm, and this next one was for all the marbles. If he couldn't outlast her this time, thus wiping out his failure of ten years ago, he wouldn't be able to live with himself. This was what the whole exercise was about.

Truthfully he'd have been better off in the dark. He was an intensely visual animal, and he had an imagination that wouldn't quit. Erica slept in an old-fashioned iron bedstead, the kind with lots of handholds and places to tie silk scarves. He wondered if she'd ever used it like that, but actually, he didn't want to know. Thinking of her with other guys bothered him far more than it should have.

Her sheets and bedspread were an earthy beige color, probably organic cotton. Although he'd complained about the sheet covering her, he found it very erotic knowing she was naked underneath it. Because it was a soft, well-worn sheet, it didn't really disguise her all that well. He'd been able to make out the darkened tips of her breasts and the soft triangle where he'd tossed the condom packet.

He'd never tried a stunt like that in his life. She inspired him to be creative. She always had. Ten years ago he'd been too inexperienced to take advantage of that inspiration, but now...now the possibilities were endless.

"So you want to take this deeper?" Erica's voice had dropped to a seductive purr. "I like the sound of that. I think I'll like the feel of it even better."

He studied her expression with a sense of foreboding. Until now, he'd had her on the run, but she must have gotten her second wind, because the sassy light was back in her gray eyes. "I expect you will." Now if he'd said that more forcefully, and hadn't gulped right before he'd said it, the words might have had a stronger effect.

Slowly she eased the sheet down, inch by inch, gradually revealing her breasts. "It's warm in this room, don't you think?"

"Um, yeah." He stared at the show unfolding before him. Kissable plumpness, dynamite cleavage, and finally...finally! rosy nipples peeking above the hem of the sheet.

She cupped her breasts in both hands. "Would these be involved in our experiment?"

"*Oh,* yeah."

She released her breasts and stretched her hands over her head, grasping the scrolled metal rods behind her. Damned if she didn't arch her back, too. "Then knock yourself out."

He didn't want to groan out loud, but he did, anyway. And he might have been less than graceful as he lunged for those incredible breasts, filling his hands and eventually his mouth—kissing, sucking, licking and generally losing himself in all that bounty. Encouraged by the way her moans mingled with his, he climbed astride her.

One quick glance at her face—eyes squeezed shut and lips parted as she gasped for breath—told him that she was having a good time. She was also clutching the headboard so tightly her knuckles showed white. Another good sign.

But he had no more time to observe her reaction. He was too engrossed in worshiping her breasts. Ten years ago he'd been so eager to bury his penis inside her that he'd taken very little time for this. What a young fool he'd been. The joy of stroking and kneading what she offered made his head spin. When he captured a firm nipple between his tongue and the roof of his mouth, he thought he might come right then.

Concern about that was all that drew him from her breasts and made him think of the next step. He was supposed to be seducing her, not winging it on autopilot. Besides, the next part was delicious, if he could manage to live through it.

The sheet was history by now, and he wasn't sure whether he'd kicked it aside or she had. At any rate, he had clear sailing as he moved downward and nudged her thighs apart with his shoulders. "Tell me if your vibrator can do this," he murmured. Then he circled his tongue around that wonderful hot button that announced her eagerness for him.

Her groan was rich with meaning.

"Or this." He sucked gently at the same spot. She thrashed around and he gripped her thighs, holding her steady. "Can it?"

"Nooooo," she moaned.

Victory. He began to lick and nibble, loving every second. From her cries and shudders, he assumed she was loving it, too, loving it more than she'd ever loved a session with her plastic buddy.

But he had to admit that a vibrator wouldn't make the demands his penis was making right now. If he gave her another climax this way, he might be toast when he finally entered the golden gates. He might be toast, anyway, but he'd be wise to stop torturing himself and get on with it.

With one last, lingering swipe with his tongue, he slid back up her sweat-slicked body and got his knees back under him. "Open your eyes, Erica." He braced his hands on either side of her shoulders.

Her lashes fluttered upward as she worked to draw in each breath. She looked dazed and disoriented, exactly the way he wanted her to look. He planned to completely blow her circuits. Maybe it was about the vibrator thing, or maybe it was about the crummy performance ten years ago. Or maybe it was about more than that. He sort of hoped not, but he was beginning to think he didn't completely understand his own motives.

"If you want, you can let go of the headboard and hang on to me for this part." He realized that he'd like that. He'd like that a whole lot.

Slowly she peeled her fingers away from the iron scroll-work. She searched his gaze as she settled both hand on his shoulders. "What…what do you want from me?" she whispered.

In the long run, he wasn't sure anymore. In the short run, it was very simple. "This." Gradually he pushed into her and gave a little hum of delight at how damned good she felt—slick and hot and pulsing, pulsing already.

Her eyes widened and her grip tightened on his shoulders. "I didn't mean to give you this."

"I know." He shoved home. Oh, heaven. "I'm… grateful." He clenched his jaw against the orgasm pounding to be let loose. At last he'd regained enough control to begin stroking, but this would be a very tricky session. His heart sounded like an engine that had thrown a rod.

She began to quiver beneath him. "Okay, you're better."

His brain refused to function. All his attention was on

maintaining his rhythm and not coming, because this was the best sex he'd had in his entire life, and he didn't want it to end. "Better than...who?"

She gasped and wrapped her arms around him. "My vibrator."

If he hadn't been concentrating so hard he would have laughed. Competing with the vibrator had fallen far down the list. "Glad to hear it."

"In fact—" she clutched his bottom with both hands and lifted to meet him "—this is..." She moaned. "Outstanding."

"Uh-huh." He wondered if the top of his head was about to blow off. He tried to gauge the look in her dark eyes. "Are you..." He didn't mean to increase the pace, but he couldn't seem to help it. Instinct was overriding everything.

"Yes." She dug her fingers in. *"Yes."*

He had no more control. Nothing existed but gazing into her flushed face and plunging into her over and over. He felt her convulse around him, but if she hadn't, she would have been on her own, because he was coming, coming, coming, and nothing could stop it.

She cried out and closed her eyes, her body rising, shuddering and sinking back down. With a deep bellow of satisfaction he drove home one more time and locked his elbows so he wouldn't collapse and crush her.

But he was trembling so much he couldn't support himself. Slowly he eased down, keeping most of his weight on his forearms. Then he settled against her breasts and rested his forehead on her shoulder as he gasped for breath.

Good Lord. Sex was supposed to be recreation. It wasn't supposed to turn a guy inside out and make him think that time spent doing anything else was time completely wasted. He'd planned to clear the slate with Erica, not start writing a whole new chapter. But suddenly, leaving in thirty-six hours seemed like a very bad idea, the worst idea of the millennium.

"I think…I think you'd better go back to your hotel now." She sounded breathless but determined.

"Go back?" He'd just gotten started.

Her tone became firmer. "I won't finish the newsletter with you here. You know I won't."

He groaned. The newsletter. He'd forgotten all about it. After promising himself not to interfere with this project he believed in so completely, he'd done exactly that. How had it happened? He'd meant to help her with the advice column, and that had led to…this.

He raised his head to look at her. "I've put you behind."

"I'll just forget about sleeping."

"Damn. I'm sorry."

She cupped his face in both hands. "Are you?"

"No. That was a lie. I'm sorry if you'll go without sleep because of me, but I'm not sorry about what just happened."

Her gaze softened. "What did just happen?"

Good question. "You know, I think we need to talk about that, but not now. Now I need to get my butt out of your bed and out of your apartment. You can heat up both cups of coffee and give yourself a sugar rush with the doughnuts. Maybe you'll power through that way. It used to work for me with finals."

"Maybe."

"Although you're a good influence on me, I think I might be a bad influence on you."

She smiled. "We could blame it on Unplugged Paul."

"Or your sugar-and-creamer set."

She giggled.

What fun, to see a dedicated woman like Erica dissolve into giggles. "You are such a naughty girl." He grinned at her. Watching her laugh had the most amazing effect on him. He wanted to hang around, just so he could make her giggle some more. For a moment he envisioned sitting on the sofa reading one of her *Mother Earth* magazines while she worked. He could run to the convenience store and get her more coffee. If she started to lag, he could give her a back rub.

Sure he could. One massage and they would end up right back here in her bed. Or on the sofa. In fact, he might not be able to sit on the sofa and read a magazine while Erica and her inviting body sat only a few feet away, especially if he remembered she was answering questions about sex.

"Can I see you in the afternoon?" he asked. "After you put the newsletter to bed?"

Eagerness shone in her eyes. Then she took a deep breath and seemed to mentally douse that light. "I'll call you."

He closed his eyes and cursed softly. Those were the exact words he'd used when he'd taken her home ten years ago.

"No, seriously," she said. "I'll call you."

Opening his eyes, he tried to figure out if she was jerking his chain. "That's a pretty standard kiss-off line, Erica. I should know."

"I know you know." She held his gaze. "It might be a kiss-off line for you, but when I say it, I mean what I say. I'm not sure what happens next with us. I have to think about the franchise, and I have to think about you."

"Listen, I don't want what happened just now to screw up the franchise thing."

She chuckled. "If we'd had bad sex, it would have definitely screwed up the franchise thing."

He relaxed a little. "But we didn't have bad sex."

"No." She continued to smile at him. "No, we didn't." Then her smile faded. "But I didn't intend for us to have any sex at all, other than that incident in the restaurant. Events have gotten a little…out of control, and I need to regroup. So give me some space and let me call you after I take the newsletter to the printer. If you'll be in your room about noon, I'll call then.''

"Come by," he said on impulse.

Her voice remained steady. "No, I think I'd better call. Once we're in a room that contains a bed, we both know what's likely to happen."

He tried a wisecrack. "Then how about meeting me in the back booth of the hotel coffee shop?"

"I'll call you."

"Okay." He wasn't used to being the one who waited, but if that's how she wanted to play it, he'd go along. He refused to consider the possibility that she wouldn't have sex with him again.

Originally, as he'd been planning this back in Midland, he'd thought one encounter with Erica might do the trick. This notion only proved that, in some ways, he was no smarter than he'd been as a virginal idiot of eighteen. He still had a lot to learn, and he wanted Erica to teach him everything she knew.

Dear Unplugged Paul,
If you want to reduce your sweetie's dependence on battery-operated love machines, you might want to look into a little self-education.

ERICA PAUSED, her fingers on the keys but her mind and libido totally elsewhere, drifting back to the most astonishingly wonderful sex she'd ever had. She'd suspected that Dustin might be good, but she'd never dreamed he'd outclass all her other partners by a country mile. That was a problem. A huge problem. And speaking of huge…she would never forget the moment when he stripped off his boxers.

Then again, she'd never forget the moment when he massaged her to orgasm while she was still totally covered by a sheet, or the moment when he nestled his head between her thighs and demonstrated how well he could use his tongue, or the moment when he slid that fine-looking penis deep inside her and made her admit that no vibrator made could equal that sensation.

She was ready to be his love slave, and that wasn't good. She'd vowed to have the upper hand this time. Supposedly she had it, because he had to sit and wait for her call at noon.

The way she felt now, she wouldn't be able to keep from calling him. If he wanted to see her, if he wanted to have sex, if he wanted to spend the next twenty-four hours naked in his bed, she'd agree. He could have anything he wanted.

Unfortunately, that was exactly the way she'd felt at eighteen. So what if she hadn't had a climax in the back seat of his Mustang? She hadn't minded. Instead she'd longed for another drive into the country and another session in the back of his car so that she could feel the rush of sexual excitement.

When he hadn't called, when she'd finally given up hope of making out with Dustin again, she'd consoled herself by dreaming that another guy would come along who would produce the same feelings. Just her luck that it hadn't happened.

She'd handpicked her dates, too, looking for those with values to match hers. If she admired their approach to life, then it stood to reason she'd be turned on by their caresses. Faulty thinking, apparently. In each case she'd manufactured enough enthusiasm to fool the guys, and even to fool herself, for a little while.

Until tonight, she hadn't realized how lacking those encounters had been. Tonight had been the real deal. All Dustin had to do was undress and she responded. She'd planned

to take a more active role, to fondle him and make him
beg, to show him that she'd learned a thing or two, herself.

Instead she'd been putty in his hands. One maneuver—
a little topless tease—had been all she'd managed before
he'd taken over and turned her to liquid fire. She still
burned. And the hell of it was, she couldn't go into the
bedroom and pull out her vibrator. It had been a legitimate
substitute for her other mediocre lovers, but compared to
Dustin, it was a joke.

Her screen saver came on, the tumbling blocks reminding
her that she had a newsletter to finish. She'd sent Dustin
away so that she could finish it. If she intended to sit here
and fantasize instead of working, she might as well have
kept him around.

With a sigh, she touched the space key and brought the
letter back. What to tell Paul? She didn't think a book
would help.

*Rent some adult videos, Paul. Study the techniques
used by the participants, and ask yourself if you're
that dedicated to your lover's pleasure. Once you have
new ideas, invite her to a hotel room where she won't
have access to her toys and prove to her that she
doesn't really need them.*
Best of luck, Erica

She had doubts that Paul would be able to compete with
his girlfriend's vibrator, no matter what he did. Dustin was
a rare find, unfortunately. She also knew exactly where that
hotel room scenario she'd suggested to Paul had come
from. All she could think about was returning to Dustin's
rented room for love in the afternoon.

She shouldn't do that. Another session and she'd be begging him for sex on a regular basis. She was even consid-

ering the franchise idea because it would mean more contact with him.

Ugh. She'd discovered amazing sex and immediately wanted to trash her goals so that she could get more of it? Something was seriously wrong with her priorities.

Maybe her thinking was all messed up from lack of sleep. She'd already nuked her coffee and finished that. Now it was time for his. In the kitchen, as she waited for the microwave to finish, she gazed at the sugar and creamer sitting on the counter.

She'd won them at a bachelorette party for a woman at the newspaper, and tonight was the first time she'd ever used them. When Dustin wasn't thrown by her choice of china, she should have known right away that she was in over her head...again.

The microwave bell dinged and she took the steaming coffee out. After pouring some rice milk in it, she headed back to the computer. She hadn't even opened the doughnuts yet. Maybe now was the time. A sugar rush might get her through, like Dustin had said.

When she opened the bag, she laughed out loud. He'd bought two long johns and two raised glazed. What a hoot.

Maybe he hadn't thought of the long johns as phallic symbols and the other two as the perfect female counterpart, but she wouldn't bet on it. She could create an X-rated puppet show with these doughnuts. Smiling, she deliberately chose a long john and bit into it as she scrolled to the next letter.

As she took another bite of the doughnut, she naturally thought about the fact that she hadn't given Dustin any oral sex. How lame was that? He could easily assume that she wasn't sophisticated enough to think of it. That was no good.

Besides, giving a man oral sex put a woman in control. She wouldn't mind being in control of Dustin for a change.

She owed herself that chance, owed herself the opportunity to prove to him that she was as knowledgeable about these things as anyone.

Okay, that was settled. She'd go to Dustin's hotel room in the afternoon, give him a fantastic blow job and leave victorious. It would be a surgical strike, a blatant grab for power. Dustin wouldn't know what hit him. Excellent. Let him dream about that for the next ten years.

Licking flakes of glaze from her fingers, she scanned the next letter.

Dear Erica,
I'm a twenty-seven-year-old guy who's still a virgin. I've been shy all my life, yet I expected to have a sexual experience before now. It hasn't happened, and I'm sure the woman I'm dating is more worldly than I am and might laugh if she discovers I've never had sex.

How can I get past this awkward situation and enjoy a normal sexual relationship with her? I don't want to "save" myself for marriage. I want sex now, with this woman.
Sincerely, Nervous Virgin

Aw, poor guy. Her chest tightened in sympathy. Letters like this made her consider breaking a cardinal rule and sending a personal reply back to the e-mail address at the top of the message. But she couldn't start doing that, or she'd spend all her time in e-mail correspondence with her subscribers. Letters were ignored if they weren't appropriate or interesting, answered in the newsletter if they were.

She thought carefully about her reply. Nervous Virgin needed help, not some flip response that made Erica sound cool. She'd been guilty of giving those a few times, but less and less as she'd settled into her role as advisor.

Dear Nervous Virgin,
If she's the right woman—

The phone rang, making her jump. At three-thirty in the morning it could only be a disaster with family or friends, or…Dustin. She picked up the kitchen cordless on the third ring.

"I can't sleep," Dustin said.

"Try counting condoms." She smiled, thrilled that he'd admit to needing her. Or at least needing her body.

"Are you finished with the newsletter?"

"Almost. I'm going to answer one more letter and then start the layout."

"What did you say to Unplugged Paul?"

She prowled the apartment, wishing his voice didn't get her so hot. "What do you think I said?"

"I know what I would have said, if you hadn't thrown me out."

"The dual answer is good in theory, Dustin. But I could see that in practice it would make this issue very, very late to press." She wanted him. If he suggested coming over in another hour, she might agree. Just thinking of that dampened the material of the fresh panties she'd put on after a quick shower.

"What's your last letter about?"

"Some poor guy who's made it to age twenty-seven without having sex. He's dating a woman who obviously knows her way around, and he wants to have sex with her, but he's afraid of looking like a fool."

On the other end of the line, Dustin said nothing.

"Are you trying not to laugh? Because this isn't funny, damn it. I suppose a stud with your record thinks it is, but I—"

"I don't think it's funny." Dustin sounded amazingly serious. "In fact, I totally relate to his problem."

"Oh, right. You are laughing, aren't you?"

"No, no, I'm not. Be nice to the guy when you answer, okay?"

"I'm always nice." She wasn't sure that was true.

"I mean, go easy on him. No wisecracks. What you say could have a big impact on a guy like this."

She finally accepted the idea that Dustin was in sympathy with Nervous Virgin, and his compassion touched her. "I promise to be careful. And helpful."

"Good. Listen, I know you said you'd call me after you take the newsletter to the printer, but that wasn't exactly a promise that we'd get together. Could we do that?" He hesitated. "Please?"

He was making himself incredibly vulnerable. Being a softie at heart, she melted a little knowing that. Well, she had recently decided to go over to his hotel and give him oral sex. Maybe there was no harm in letting him know she'd decided to see him again. "Yes, we can. I'll just come to your hotel after I drop off the newsletter."

He sighed in obvious relief. "Thank you. Do you remember the room number?"

"Yes." It was probably etched forever in her mind. "But I need to warn you that I have a movie date tomorrow night." Just because she was melting a little didn't mean that she should abandon all the protective barriers she'd put in place and leave herself open to heartbreak.

"Oh." Some of the eagerness went out of his voice. "Okay. Well, see you sometime after noon, then."

"See you then." She pressed the disconnect button on the phone and held it against her chest, where her heart thudded with excitement. That man sure could flip her switches. Returning the phone to its recharge cradle, she went back to her computer and Nervous Virgin.

Dustin should be happy with the opening line.

If she's the right woman, she won't laugh when she finds out you're a virgin. You're offering her a gift and an opportunity. She can teach you exactly how she likes to be treated, and because she'll be your first lover, you'll never forget her.

Oh, God, that was certainly true. Dustin was lodged forever in her heart.

Then she blinked as she realized the significance of that. The sexual pull he exerted was causing her plenty of anxiety, but if he was lodged forever in her heart, she was in a lot more trouble than she'd first thought. She definitely couldn't linger in his hotel room in the afternoon. One quick round of oral sex and she was outta there.

8

THE PROSPECT OF SEEING ERICA again allowed Dustin to sleep a couple of hours, but he was awake early, surprising himself with his eagerness to work on Ramsey Enterprises business. He'd left his laptop under the seat in the truck, but he could bring it up to the room, order breakfast and get a few things done this morning. In the process of retrieving his laptop, he realized he could drive to a fast-food place, get his breakfast to go and forget about room service.

Old habits died hard. He was used to thinking of his cash flow as endless. Maybe someday it would be again, but not today. Today he'd make do with an Egg McMuffin and a large coffee.

Twenty minutes later, he'd set himself up on the hotel room's desk and pulled files out of his briefcase. He'd stuffed quite a few in there, figuring he might have time to continue his project of transferring all the company records to computer disks. It should have been done years ago, but his father hadn't understood or trusted computers.

After Clayton's stroke, Dustin had immediately filled the vacant secretary's job with a young woman who could handle the phone in the small Ramsey Enterprises office. But he'd decided to computerize the files himself and turn them over to the secretary after a trial employment period.

He needed to know everything in those files, and there was no better way to get a picture of the company's assets and liabilities. Unfortunately it wasn't a pretty picture. From the boastful way Clayton had talked, Dustin had assumed his father was a savvy business tycoon. Turns out he was a total business disaster.

Taking a hefty bite out of his egg-and-muffin sandwich, Dustin opened the top file, a profit-and-loss statement for the Houston weekly. The small newspaper had almost no advertising support. Somebody needed to go to Houston and sell ads, and after years of getting racing sponsors, Dustin knew he could do that. Maybe he'd be able to pull off this CEO thing, after all.

Three hours later, he'd run out of gas. Computerizing files wasn't in the same league with answering sexy letters for *Dateline: Dallas,* and it was a hell of a lot duller than getting horizontal with the hot, sassy publisher of said newsletter. Everything about the woman was supercharged with excitement. She even had an X-rated sugar-and-creamer set.

And she would be at his door in less than an hour. Bolting from the chair, he glanced around the room in panic. He'd hung out the Do Not Disturb sign so that he could work, but that meant the room hadn't been cleaned and more important, the sheets hadn't been changed.

Grabbing his card key, he headed out the door looking for a maid. Ten minutes later he found one working on another room. Angela spoke only Spanish, but fortunately he knew enough to communicate what he wanted. The ten dollars he handed her didn't hurt, either. So much for economizing.

He pushed the cart for her, just to make sure she didn't dawdle. As she started stripping the bed, he put away his laptop and files. Then he took them out again. Maybe he'd pretend he'd been in the middle of a project when Erica arrived. Yeah, that would be a good thing. He'd acted too needy on the phone, so he should look engrossed in his work, as if he'd forgotten about her.

But there was the lunch issue. She was coming by after

dropping off the newsletter at the printer around noon. By
agreeing to come straight to his hotel, she'd obviously left
the lunch decision up to him. Jumping her bones and ignoring the possibility that she might be hungry would be
tacky.

But going out somewhere to eat meant leaving the room.
Once he got her here, he didn't want her to leave. He
planned to do his damnedest to talk her into canceling her
movie date with whatever bozo she was seeing. Whoever
he was, he wasn't a sexual wizard, or she wouldn't have
been so enamored of her vibrator. Dustin thought he had
at least a fighting chance of changing her plans for the
evening.

So he needed to keep her right here, preferably naked.
That meant a room service lunch and to hell with the
budget. Grabbing the leather-bound menu, he studied the
selections. Something chilled. For one thing, it was sum-
mer, and for another thing, they might not get to the food
right away. He hoped they wouldn't get to the food right
away, but it had to be here before she arrived. Once she
was inside the door he didn't want interruptions.

Picking up the phone, he ordered a fruit and cheese plate,
a shrimp salad, a grilled chicken salad, a basket of assorted
rolls, two orders of strawberry cheesecake and a bottle of
champagne. That last was the priciest of the entire order,
but he wanted alcohol and he didn't want to look like a
cheapskate. He didn't want to get her drunk, but he wasn't
above making her a little too tipsy to drive home in time
for her date. She could worry about her other men after
he'd left town, but tonight—tonight she was his.

The maid turned out to be a perfectionist. It seemed that
the sheets had to be just so and the blanket hanging at the
perfect angle, because she'd redone them twice. He needed
her to move on and clean the bathroom so he could jump
in the shower before Erica showed up. Finally he shooed

Angela away from the bed and explained in poor Spanish that he'd finish putting the bedspread on if she'd clean the bathroom.

Apparently his Spanish was so bad that she thought he wanted her to leave. He had to physically pull her back into the room, search his limited vocabulary for a few more words and gesture repeatedly toward the bathroom before she finally understood. After making sure that she was spraying and rinsing and whatever hocus-pocus was required, he finished making the bed.

He'd never learned to clean a bathroom, but one of his girlfriends had taught him to make a bed, declaring that she refused to have sex with a man who couldn't tuck in a damned sheet. Sex had always been a powerful motivator for him. Once the quilted spread was secured over the row of three pillows, he decided to unfold it and turn the covers back.

After doing that, he stood in the doorway and studied the effect. Too blatant. Erica would take one look at the bed and know that he'd fixed it in that cheesy way, not the maid. Lunch with champagne was one thing. Turning back the covers was way too obvious. He remade the bed.

Then he paced while the slowest scrubber in the West polished every square inch of the bathroom. He hesitated to hurry her along. She already seemed a little afraid of him, and if he interrupted her before she was finished, she might run out the door with some critical part undone. He would never know the difference, but Erica might. Women picked up on these things, and he didn't want anything to spoil the mood.

At last Angela reappeared from the bathroom and started out the door to her cart. Dustin heaved a sigh and was about to close the door when she marched back in pushing a vacuum cleaner. He groaned. Now that was overkill. Or maybe not. He couldn't guarantee that he wouldn't have

sex with Erica on the floor, and if that happened and she
noticed lint on the carpet...

Wait a minute. He was being paranoid. If she noticed
lint on the carpet, he wasn't doing his job. He decided to
dispense with the vacuuming and take his chances on lint.
Easier said than done. He tried to get Angela's attention
over the noise of the industrial-strength machine, but she
was focused on her task and didn't look up. Eventually he
had to leap in front of her to get her to stop.

That must have been the last straw for the poor woman,
because she screamed and ran out of the room, barely stopping long enough to yank the vacuum plug from the socket.
Dustin didn't have time to worry about it. He raced for the
shower.

A rap on the door and the voice of the room service
waiter interrupted him while he was still drying off. Good.
The room was clean and the food was here. All he had to
do was throw on some clothes and sit down in front of his
computer. Camera, lights, action.

Tucking the towel around his waist, he padded barefoot
to the door. The bellman wheeled in a loaded cart complete
with a carnation in a bud vase. Nice touch.

Right behind him came Erica, an amused gleam in her
eyes. "Looks like someone's having a party."

So much for playing it cool.

ERICA HAD THE JITTERS from too much coffee, too little
sleep and the stimulation of seeing the man who made her
insides quiver draped in a towel. To keep her courage up,
she'd dressed in one of her bad-girl outfits—a shimmery
red halter top and hip-hugging capris that reminded her of
the sleek white football pants Dustin used to wear.

She'd expected him to be wearing something, too. From
his expression, she guessed he'd expected that, too. "I can
go walk around the lobby and come back in ten minutes."

"Uh, no, that's okay."

They both watched as the waiter expertly removed the foil and wire from the top of the champagne bottle before twisting out the cork with a soft pop. Tendrils of carbonation drifted from the bottle.

Champagne was one of Erica's guilty pleasures. She'd been raised to believe it was an elitist beverage, but she'd discovered a taste for it, nevertheless. Dustin had made a good guess, ordering some this afternoon. The surgical strike she'd planned might be in jeopardy, judging from all the covered plates on the cart and that chilled bottle of bubbly.

Besides being sexually on edge and sleep deprived, she was starving. She'd skipped breakfast in favor of some last-minute touches to the newsletter and she hadn't wanted to stop for lunch before coming over to the hotel. She hadn't wanted to stop for *anything*.

Besides, she'd thought Dustin might provide food. She hadn't expected him to dazzle her with such splendor, but then, luxurious touches were part of his background. Although she tried to look at the loaded cart with disdain, she failed.

"Would you care to taste the champagne, sir?" the waiter asked.

"That's okay. I'm sure it's fine." Dustin checked the tuck job on his towel before crossing the room to sign the bill the waiter held in his hand.

"Thank you, sir." The waiter kept his gaze neutral, his smile polite. "Enjoy your meal." Then he left, closing the door softly behind him.

"Wow." Erica gestured toward the cart. "That looks like quite a lunch."

"I thought you might be hungry."

"I am. I skipped breakfast." But as good as the food smelled, she was already becoming distracted by his nakedness. She'd always wondered which appetite was stronger, the one for food or the one for sex. She was quickly discovering the answer to that question.

He smelled as good as the food, come to think of it. She wanted to lick his clean skin and inhale the aroma of soap and shaving cream. Nibbling him sounded better than munching on food.

As her gaze traveled over his bare chest, her nipples tightened with the memory of his soft hair tickling her breasts, brushing back and forth while the equipment hidden under the towel stroked her to a shattering climax. Too bad she didn't intend to stage a repeat of that today.

She wouldn't even undress. In order to complete the operation she'd planned, all she had to do was cross the room, remove the towel, sink to her knees and make him a happy man. Then she'd leave.

But that would mean no champagne, no warm rolls, no tasting whatever decadent delights were hidden under those silvery domes. She hesitated, too tempted by both man and food to decide what to do. The plan to give him oral sex and then leave was excellent, because then he'd go back to Midland with that memory uppermost in his mind. She liked the idea a lot.

But maybe she could postpone the event long enough to have a little bit of food and a taste of champagne. Then she'd do the deed and whirl out of the room while he was still delirious with pleasure.

"Let me put something on so we can eat," he said.

She hated to have him do that when the towel would be so easy to remove. "Don't get dressed on my account."

He drew in a sharp breath. "When you said you were hungry because you missed breakfast, I assumed you meant—"

"I did mean hungry for food." Teasing, sexy words

came so easily when she talked to this man. "But I thought I'd save room for dessert."

The towel quivered. "I like the thought, but if I'm going to have a naked lunch, so are you."

"Why?"

"It's just the way it has to be. Either I put something on or you take something off." He started toward her. "Or even better, let me take it off for you."

She backed up a step. "Okay, you win. Put on clothes if you must. I just thought we could save some time afterward."

"Exactly." He advanced again. "There's a white terry robe in the closet. If you're feeling modest, wear that."

She retreated. "Maybe later. Go on. Put on your pants."

"It's the only way I'll be able to sit here and eat without lunging for you." His glance moved over her. "I'll have to work at not doing it anyway. Did you wear that stuff on purpose to drive me crazy?"

She smiled. "These old things? I got them at a resale shop."

"Yeah, recycled directly from Frederick's of Hollywood."

So she'd made a hit with her outfit. "I take it you find these clothes provocative."

"Do the Rangers play baseball?"

"Sometimes that's debatable," she said with a grin.

"Well, those are strip-me-naked clothes and I'm having a tough time ignoring the invitation. But if you didn't have breakfast, you need food." He rummaged in his open suitcase until he came up with some boxers and a pair of Levi's. "Help yourself to the food and champagne."

"I'll wait for you."

"Suit yourself. I won't be long." He went into the bathroom and closed the door.

So he wouldn't be as conveniently available for her seduction as he would have been with only a towel to strip away. No problem. She ought to have no trouble unzipping those jeans and shoving down his knit boxers. Come to think of it, adult movies usually had the women doing exactly that. Oral sex with an open fly seemed naughtier than oral sex naked, for some reason.

Setting her purse near the door where she could grab it on the way out, she wandered around the room and noticed the laptop and the files on the desk. So Dustin had been working this morning, too. No doubt his work had far more financial impact than hers.

As she stood by the desk gazing at the flashing colors of his screen saver, she allowed herself to imagine what it would be like if she had the money to book expensive hotel rooms and order champagne from room service the way Dustin did so easily. He obviously thought her newsletter would bring in that kind of money eventually or he wouldn't be bothering with it.

The prospect lured her more than it should have. Yes, putting out the newsletter for the next several years would be fun, but life wasn't supposed to be all about fun. It was about making a difference.

A file lay open, and she glanced at it. Although she wasn't much of an accountant, even she could see that there was a lot of red ink involved. She wondered if there was any chance Dustin's company was in financial trouble. Then again, he could be using losses on one hand to offset gains on another. Her father had lectured her about the creative bookkeeping the fat cats used to avoid paying a dime in taxes.

"Pretty boring stuff, huh?" Dustin said as he came out of the bathroom. There was an edge to his voice, as if he wasn't happy to find her snooping in his business.

She wanted to set his mind at ease. When she went after big business someday, she'd start with bigger fish than

Ramsey Enterprises. "Accounting was never my strong suit." She waved a hand over the files on his desk. "This kind of work would confuse me, not bore me."

"I'll confess I had more fun working on your advice column with you." He was wearing the jeans, but he'd left his shirt off and his feet were bare.

"And how long was that, five minutes?" Erica soaked up the view of Dustin standing there looking like a calendar model. Once she left his room this afternoon, it probably would be the end of their relationship, both business and personal. She might tease herself with the idea of accepting the franchise deal, but she knew that in the end, she'd have to turn it down.

"I made a significant contribution to your column," Dustin said.

"You did."

He walked toward the dinner cart. "I thought for sure you'd have poured yourself some champagne by now."

"I didn't want to get ahead of you."

He grinned as he pulled the green bottle from the ice bucket with a liquid swoosh. "There goes my plan to get you drunk so I can have my way with you."

Exactly. She couldn't allow that. "If I'm not mistaken, you've already had your way with me, and I'm thoroughly convinced you're better at sex than you were ten years ago. Mission accomplished."

He poured the champagne into the flutes sitting on the cart and plopped the bottle back into the ice before picking up the glasses. Coming toward the desk, he handed her one. "You still think I want to check you off some master list, don't you?"

"That's the way it seems, but that's okay. I am so checked off."

"It was more along the lines of righting a wrong." He

lifted his glass and touched the rim of hers. "Here's to good sex."

"I'll drink to that." The gleam in his eyes sent delicious shivers through her. She took a sip of the champagne. Maybe her taste buds were as supersensitive as the rest of her, but the champagne seemed about five hundred times better than the brand she could afford. She took another mouthful, to see if it tasted as good as the first. Yep. Terrific stuff.

"To be accurate, great sex."

"You won't get an argument from me." The champagne was marvelous. She'd have to go easy on it, though. With no sleep and no food in her stomach, it could go right to her head. Still, she couldn't resist another sip.

Dustin turned back to the cart and began pulling off covers with his free hand. "We have a fruit and cheese plate, a shrimp salad, a chicken salad and two servings of cheesecake. Where do you want to start?"

Slowly she was coming up with a game plan. "It all sounds wonderful. Let's roll this cart over by the bed and sit there to eat."

"I like the way you think." He moved the cart into position at the foot of the bed, leaving room for them to sit there. "How's that?"

"Perfect." She took another sip of her champagne so she wouldn't be in danger of spilling it as she eased down on the bed. She surveyed the beautifully presented food in front of her—crisp greens, pink shrimp, tender pieces of chicken breast, plump rolls and two of the most luscious pieces of cheesecake she'd ever seen drizzled with raspberry sauce.

Then she realized that Dustin hadn't come over to sit beside her. She glanced up and found him standing on the other side of the cart staring at her, his gaze hot. The temptation provided by the food began to fade as she looked into his eyes.

"You know what I want to do?" His voice was husky.

"Forget lunch?"

"No. I want to mix you and lunch up together. Come play with me, Erica."

She took a big gulp of her champagne. This wasn't going at all according to plan. But oh, how she wanted to turn him loose and see what he had in mind. No man had ever showed this kind of sexual daring with her, and she loved it.

Maybe she could modify her plan a little more. She could have a naked lunch with him and hold off on the oral sex until a little later. Then she could get dressed and make that the last item on the agenda before she left.

She took one more mouthful of champagne. She'd have to stop drinking it soon or risk getting mildly drunk. "I assume you mean for us to play without our clothes on."

His eyes glowed with heat. "Yes."

"You're a naughty man, you know that?" She set down her champagne and reached for the front fastening on her halter top.

"Yeah." He unzipped his jeans. "And all my life I've been looking for a woman who would be naughty with me."

Interesting choice of words—*all his life*. Then she forgot about that as he stripped away his jeans and boxers in one smooth movement, and his erect penis sprang forth, mesmerizing her yet again.

"You're falling behind." He pushed the cart aside and reached for her, peeling off her capris and panties while she laughed and weakly, very weakly, protested. Ah, the pleasure of feeling his hands on her. She sizzled everywhere he touched.

He kissed her soundly. "Now stop squirming and lie still," he murmured. "We're going to have food sex."

9

So far, so good, Dustin thought. Erica was naked and drinking champagne. Soon she'd start having orgasms, and after that he couldn't believe that she'd want to leave for a movie date.

As for him, he didn't want to be anywhere but right here. Erica inspired him to say and do things he'd never thought of before. *Food sex.* He had no idea where that phrase had come from, but he was ready to find out where experimentation would lead him.

Once he'd come up with the concept, he'd pulled the cart around to the side of the bed so all he had to do was reach across Erica to snag whatever items he wanted. He started slow, feeding her shrimp, taking the juicy pink morsels between his teeth and making her work to get her half.

Meanwhile he stroked her breasts and her thighs, but he stayed away from operation central, not wanting her to get excited enough that she choked. In between bites he dipped his finger in his champagne and she licked it off. Before the afternoon was over, he'd know what her tongue felt like on his penis, but he needed to delay that if he wanted to prolong the pleasure, and he definitely wanted to do that.

Yes, he throbbed and ached. Sometimes he had to stop everything and take a few deep breaths. But that was part of the fun—testing himself to see how long he could play before he was forced to get serious.

After the shrimp, he went for the chicken pieces, offering her tender breast meat as he caressed her nipples.

"Symbolic," she murmured.

"Mmm." He loved the way she managed to kiss him at the same time she maneuvered the chicken into her mouth. But then her hand started to wander in the direction of his penis and he caught her wrist. "Uh-uh."

"But you're touching *me*."

"Not there."

She grinned at him. "You don't have the same kind of *there*. Mine's tucked away, but yours is so accessible and inviting that I can't seem to avoid it."

"Wouldn't you like this to last all afternoon?"

Her eyes darkened. "*All* afternoon?"

"Sure. A little food, a little sex." He cupped her breast and teased her nipple some more. "Take it slow and see how long we can make the anticipation last."

"How long we can hold off coming, you mean?"

"For me, yeah. For you, not so important." He slid his hand down over her stomach and into her blond curls, stopping short, taunting her a little. "Feeling the urge?"

"Not a bit."

"Cool customer, huh?" He didn't sink his fingers into her and prove that she was fibbing. Playing along was more fun. "Since you're not particularly aroused, I have an idea that might help." He withdrew his hand from her curls and reached for the purple plum nestled on the fruit plate. "Do you like these?"

"Yes. But if we start eating that together you'll get juice everywhere."

"Good point." He brushed the plum over her breasts. "Maybe we'd better keep the skin intact."

"Then you can't taste it."

"Oh, I don't know about that." While he kissed her gently, he stroked her breasts with the smooth plum. Then he gradually moved the caress lower, to the valley between her ribs, the indentation of her navel, the thicket of curls leading to his destination.

She gripped his head and forced his mouth a fraction away from hers. "What are you going to do with that?"

"Play."

Her breath caught as he rolled the plum over her most sensitive spot. Reaching lower, he dipped the fruit into her juices and dragged it back over her flash point.

Her breathing roughened. "That feels…different."

"No motor buzzing," he whispered. He settled the plum a little deeper this time and wiggled it as he drew it out.

"Mmm."

He lifted his head to gaze at her as he used the silky surface of the fruit to drive her crazy. Her nostrils flared and her pupils widened as her excitement grew. Yes, this had been a good idea. She was becoming very wet.

Dipping the plum into her moisture again, he raised the glistening fruit to his lips. "Now I can taste it." He swiped at it with his tongue. "So can you," he murmured, touching it to her mouth. He drew the plum away.

Slowly, holding his gaze, she ran her tongue over her lips.

He nearly climaxed just watching her. "Good?"

"You…are a wild man."

"With you I am." He reached down again and rotated the plum gently at the entrance to her vagina.

She moaned and pulled his head down for a deep kiss.

Thrusting his tongue into her mouth, he teased and caressed her with the plum until she arched her back in surrender, her cries of release muffled by his kiss.

As she sagged panting on the mattress, he eased his mouth from hers. He waited until her eyes fluttered open before he lifted the dripping plum and took a bite. The skin of the plum broke and juice that was part plum, part Erica, trickled down his chin to drip on her heaving breasts.

Keeping her gaze locked with his, she ran both hands down the side of his face and rubbed her fingers over his juice-covered mouth. He offered her a bit of plum and she took it. His attempt to lick the juice as it leaked from the corner of her mouth turned into a tangle of lips, tongues, fruit and lust.

He tossed the rest of the plum on the cart and rolled over her, mindless with need. She matched his frenzy, reaching for his penis, opening her thighs. He had to be inside her, had to— With a groan he thrust quickly. Unbelievable pleasure coursed through him at the sensation of his unsheathed penis sliding deep.

Then he froze. Raising up to stare down at her, he shook his head to clear the red haze from his eyes. "What…are we doing?"

She stilled, looked into his eyes and gasped.

He cursed softly and withdrew. Trembling both from passion and the shock of knowing he'd put them both at risk for pregnancy, he flopped to his back on the bed. As he struggled for breath, he searched for what to say. "I'm sorry," he finally managed, wincing at how lame that sounded.

"So…so am I."

He rolled to his side and looked at her. "It's not your fault."

"It's as much mine as yours." Her rapid breathing slowed and she turned her head to meet his gaze. "I should have stopped you."

"I shouldn't have started in the first place. And we're not totally out of the woods, you know. There's still a chance that—"

"A very slight chance. Statistically, we should be fine."

He reached for her hand. "I may be a business major, but in this case I don't like relying on statistics."

Her gray eyes gentled as she threaded her fingers through his. "Don't worry, Dustin. It's not going to happen."

"I hope not." But even as he said the words, he was having the strangest reaction to this discussion. Once the moment of panic passed, he'd started wondering what it would be like to have a baby with Erica.

No doubt she'd handle motherhood the way she did everything else—beautifully. And the kid would be very smart. It would be fun, watching a smart kid grow up. Of course, she'd probably fill the kid full of tofu and teach it to be suspicious of making money, but that's where Dustin would come in, to give the baby a balanced approach.

Erica squeezed his hand. "Dustin, are you okay?"

"Um, yeah." He brought himself back to reality. Chances were she was right, and there would be no child. But he was amazed at how quickly he'd warmed to the concept of a baby created by him and Erica.

"You seemed to be lost in space."

"Just thinking." He smiled at her. "For a few seconds, there, it felt damned good, didn't it?"

"Uh-huh."

"I've never had sex like that. How about you?"

She shook her head. "I don't react well to birth-control pills, so even when I was in a relationship…" Her voice trailed off, as if she didn't think it was appropriate for her to be discussing past lovers while she lay there naked in his bed.

But he was curious. "Ever been serious? I know you said you'd never been engaged, but did you ever come close to being engaged?"

"Maybe. Not really, though." She cleared her throat. "Nobody should get married before they're thirty, anyway."

"Yeah, you're probably right about that. If you're a little older, you might be a better parent, too."

''You want kids?'' That seemed to startle her.

''Well, sure, someday. I want two, though. Being an only child has some advantages, but I've thought about it and I'd like to give my kid a brother or sister.''

''Me, too. My parents were into population control. I'm a little surprised they had me.''

He brushed his thumb over the back of her hand. ''I'm glad they did.''

''Thanks.''

He'd never quite lost his erection, and now his body stirred, awakening again. ''What do you say we start over, and this I'll time remember to use a condom?''

She studied him for a long moment. ''No, I think maybe I should go.''

''Go?'' Panic set in. ''Hey, we still have tons of food, and we've barely touched the champagne.'' Well, damn. He'd not only risked making her pregnant, he'd ruined the mood. And now she was thinking of keeping her movie date. He hated that.

''The champagne might be what got us into trouble in the first place.'' She squeezed his hand again and smiled. ''Listen, Dustin, whatever you were worried about regarding our sexual history isn't a problem anymore. Believe me, when I think of you, I won't be thinking about that night back in Midland. So maybe we should quit while we're ahead.''

He didn't feel he was ahead. The thought of her leaving this room and going out with someone else tonight made him feel decidedly behind. ''But—''

''Seriously, it's for the best.'' She released his hand and shoved the cart away so she could climb from the bed. ''If I can use your bathroom, I'll wash up a bit and get dressed.''

''Erica, we need to talk…'' He racked his brain. ''About the franchise. We need to talk about the franchise.''

"I'll be right back." She snagged her clothes, hurried into the bathroom and closed the door. The lock clicked into place.

Damn. Just because he'd gotten carried away and started to make love to her without a condom, his entire plan was shot to hell. No doubt he'd scared her to death with that move. She could be scared of herself, too, because she hadn't thought to stop him. No matter how great they were together in bed, she didn't see herself getting involved with him. And that was too bad, because...

He sat up with a start. *Involved?* Since when had he decided to take this beyond a brief and totally satisfying affair? He was already more tied down than he'd ever been in his life now that Ramsey Enterprises was his responsibility. A relationship was the last thing in the world he needed right now.

Scrambling for his underwear and jeans, he managed to pull on both before she walked out of the bathroom. Good thing he'd come to his senses before he said or did something crazy. Erica was exactly right. They'd had some great sex, put the past behind them, and all he had to do was convince her to go along with the franchise plan.

She came out of the bathroom dressed in her tight little pants and halter top. Her makeup was scrubbed off, but he liked her like that. He liked her just about any way, come to think of it. He liked her too much for his own good, and once the franchise deal was in his pocket, he would get out of town.

"So, did you look over the papers I gave you?" he asked. "It's a sweet deal, if I do say so myself."

"I didn't look over the papers because I'm not going to franchise the newsletter."

The food they'd eaten with such sexual abandon turned to lead in his stomach. "Why not?"

"I've told you all the reasons, Dustin." Her tone softened. "Believe me, if I thought it was a good idea, you'd be the first person I'd contact. Now that you're heading up Ramsey Enterprises, I'm sure the company will be run more responsibly than it has been in the past. But I just don't want to go in that direction. Franchising would set me on the wrong course. I want to be free to accept the right job when it comes along."

He hadn't realized how much he'd counted on her going along with his plan. Now that she'd officially turned him down, disaster seemed to loom on the horizon. Sure, he had other options for diversifying, but none of them gave him the same burst of excitement or optimism.

"I'm sorry it won't work out," she said.

"So am I." He gazed into her eyes, unable to believe this was the end of everything. No more business, no more pleasure. He'd run out of excuses to be with her. "I want to see you again." Somehow his thoughts had ended up coming out of his mouth before he could censor them.

"You do?" She seemed surprised. "Why is that?"

He had no good answer. He just couldn't accept the fact that she'd disappear from his life.

She stepped forward and put her hands on his shoulders. "Dustin, you're thinking with the wrong part of your anatomy."

He let out a bark of amazed laughter. "I'm *what?*"

"You know what I mean." She smiled gently. "You want more sex from me, but let's be honest. That's really all you're after, isn't it? Your dad's company has landed in your lap, and that will keep you busy for a long time. If you want to talk on the phone about anything to do with that, feel free to call me. Goodbye, Dustin." She kissed him quickly, walked over to the door and picked up her purse.

As she left, he noticed for the first time where she'd left her purse. All along she'd planned to make a quick getaway. And he needed to let her go, because she was right. When it came to Erica, his brain was on vacation.

As ERICA PULLED HER ten-year-old Geo Metro into her parking space, she realized she'd been oblivious to her surroundings during the entire trip from the Fairmont. Her mind had been totally occupied with Dustin.

She shouldn't have gone over there today. She'd known that, but her stupid ego had stepped in and taunted her with the idea of giving him oral sex as a parting gift. Well, she hadn't managed to do that, had she?

No, instead she'd allowed herself to be seduced by good champagne and wonderful food and…incredible sex. Sex so amazing that she'd lost all her inhibitions, all her good sense in an orgy of sensation.

Although she'd dreamed about sex like that, she hadn't really believed that she, Erica Deutchmann, would ever experience it. Well, now she had, and she'd discovered that in the grip of total sexual abandon she forgot everything except the need to mate. That's really what this afternoon had turned into, a primitive mating session.

Dustin seemed to trigger that urge in her, and judging from his reaction, she did the same for him. In that case, they needed to stay far away from each other before she ended up pregnant and miserable and he ended up obligated and guilty. If harnessed, their combined sex drive was strong enough to provide electrical power for all of Dallas.

This afternoon it had been decidedly unharnessed, and she couldn't let that happen again. She'd been lucky to get out of there with her uterus unoccupied and her pride intact. In fact, Dustin was so potent she wondered if there was any chance that one of those little swimmers had escaped and made a beeline straight for one of her all-too-eager eggs.

The thought should have filled her with horror. When it

didn't, *that* filled her with horror. Surely Dustin's testosterone-drenched presence hadn't corrupted her thinking so much that she'd begun wishing for babies. Babies were for later. *Much* later. She had so much to do before she started producing babies.

Eventually the heat building up in the closed car reminded her that she was sitting in the parking lot under a hot August sun with the windows rolled up and the motor turned off. If anybody saw her, they'd assume she had a few cubes missing from her ice tray. They could be right. The way she felt right now, the whole damned tray had melted.

Two hours later, after some girly indulgences like a soak in the tub, a facial, manicure and pedicure, she felt more in control. Dustin hadn't called or come by, and she was glad. Or at least relieved. Every minute that passed without having to deal with him would make her stronger. Not that she was counting the minutes.

As she drove to the little café and deli where she always met Denise and Josie, she wondered what Dustin was doing for dinner tonight. Maybe he'd hook up with his racing buddies again. Or maybe he'd decide to take one of the single women at the bar back to his hotel.

But she didn't think so. He might be highly sexed, but he wasn't a sleaze. Bringing another woman into his bed so soon after she'd climbed out of it would be icky. Besides, from little comments he'd made, she had the impression that this bonfire they created together was unusual for him, too. After this experience, he might have as much trouble finding a satisfying bed partner as she would.

Leaving her car in a parking garage near the café and movie theater, she walked through the crowded streets to the café. Denise and Josie were already there holding down their favorite table by the window. With a sigh of relief she plopped into the metal chair they scooted toward her.

Josie, a redhead with a burr haircut, pushed her iced latte aside and leaned toward Erica. "I understand we're the distraction so you won't be tempted to go out with Virginity Guy."

"A girl uses whatever crutch she can find." Erica grinned at Josie. "Thanks for coming along."

"Hey, Denise said that because this is for a good cause, I can buy Milk Duds and the calories won't count."

Erica thought of the feast Dustin had ordered for lunch, and then deliberately shoved the thought away. Tonight was about forgetting Dustin and any memories connected with him. "Then I suppose you don't want any of the organic chocolate I have in my purse."

"Nope. I want my chocolate the way I had it as a kid, loaded with preservatives."

"We ordered you a veggie sandwich on seven-grain bread and an iced latte," Denise said. "We told them not to make the latte until they brought over all our sandwiches."

"Thanks." Erica could feel Denise studying her. "So what's going on at the *News?*" she asked to deflect a little of the scrutiny.

"The usual," Denise said. "Ted asked Cindy for a date again today, and she turned him down. Again. Meanwhile Cindy's lusting after some guy in production."

"And don't forget the stuff going on in the ad department." Josie rolled her eyes.

For the next half hour the three ate their sandwiches while Josie and Denise filled Erica in on the latest gossip at the newspaper. Because it was nearly time to leave for the movies, Erica thought she'd escaped having her relationship with Dustin analyzed. Someday she'd talk about him with her friends, but right now she didn't know what to say.

"Either you're breaking out in a rash or you have a little whisker burn on your chin," Denise said.

Erica felt her face begin to glow. She'd thought makeup would cover up the evidence, but it was warm inside the café and apparently the makeup job was fading. "Uh, it might be whisker burn."

"Ah-*ha*." Denise leaned closer.

Josie set down her latte with a sharp thump. "You mean we didn't save you from Virginity Guy? He must work fast!"

"He, um, came over with coffee last night."

"Last night?" Denise eyebrows lifted. "I didn't leave until almost midnight. There was no night left, only early morning."

"Okay, early morning, then."

"Persistent." Josie's green eyes sparkled. "That's exciting."

"So I'm assuming you got it on." Denise's gaze turned sympathetic. "Aw, honey, was it terrible? Is that why you're here with us tonight instead of in his hotel room?"

"I'm here because I made a date with you guys! I wouldn't just break that."

Josie patted her hand. "I'm sorry it wasn't any better than the first time. You'd think in ten years he'd have improved a little, but some guys are slow learners. The hell of it is that Denise said the guy still turns you on. It's not fair that he's gorgeous and worthless in the sack."

Erica swallowed her laughter. "He's not worthless in the sack."

"He's not?" Denise and Josie said together.

Denise gripped Erica's arm. "Listen, you don't have to carry this girlfriend solidarity that far. If he's amazing, go back to the hotel. We totally understand, right, Josie?"

"Totally. We'll sit in the movie and be jealous as hell, but we'll so understand."

"That's just it." Erica finally managed to put it into words. "He's so completely amazing that if I don't keep far away from him he's going to ruin my life."

10

DUSTIN THOUGHT seriously about canceling his second night at the hotel and driving back to Midland or down to Houston, where he could try selling ads. He wasn't getting anywhere sitting in Dallas. He had no urge to go out and party with his buddies again, and since Erica had told him the franchise deal was off, he had no excuse to hang around.

Yet he couldn't seem to leave. He wanted to know what kind of schmuck she was out with tonight. Although he couldn't believe that she'd take the bozo back to her apartment afterward, he wanted to know for sure. Yes, it was juvenile to obsess about it, but he couldn't seem to help himself.

Sitting in his hotel room surfing through channels, eating cheesecake and drinking champagne, he became more fixated on Erica's date by the minute. Damn it, he didn't care what she did tomorrow or the next day, but to go out on a date with another guy hours after having food sex with him was humiliating.

If she took the guy back to her apartment and made out with him, that was even worse. But if they ended up in bed, the same bed Dustin had occupied with her in the wee morning hours, that was beyond terrible. That was atrocious.

If she was that kind of woman, he needed to know. Hell, yes, that was exactly what he needed to know, so that when he went back to Midland he could put Erica Deutchmann right out of his mind. Any woman who could pull a stunt like that wasn't worth losing sleep over.

If he had more time, he could hire Jennifer Madison to investigate, maybe even get some incriminating pictures. But he couldn't expect Jennifer's P.I. firm to swing into action that fast. Not when she had a baby to contend with.

Besides, he'd seen enough movies to know how a stake-out worked. All he had to do was drive over there, find a dark corner of the parking lot, and wait for Erica to come home with the bozo. If she took the guy upstairs, he wouldn't know exactly what was happening, but he could judge by how long the idiot stayed in the apartment. Come to think of it, he could interrogate the creep when he came back out.

Yes, this was sounding like a plan he could live with. He stopped drinking champagne and ordered a pot of coffee. After he drank that, he'd head for her apartment. He'd pick up more coffee on the way, too. One thing he knew for sure, stakeouts always involved lots of coffee.

FORTUNATELY, once Erica explained to her friends that she was afraid Dustin's sexual magnetism would sabotage her goals, they supported her decision to give him a wide berth. All three women laughed their way through the movie and went for coffee and dessert afterward.

Erica couldn't have asked for a better way to distract herself, and she did a convincing job of acting as if Dustin had been banished from her thoughts. He hadn't been, though. While she was giggling about the antics of the actors on the screen, Dustin's smile would flash through her mind. During the love scene she remembered the moment when he'd slid deep inside her…minus the condom. She'd loved the feeling and wanted it again. Naughty girl.

Erica had been the one who'd suggested that they all go out for coffee and dessert. She didn't want to be alone with her longing for Dustin and didn't trust herself to stay away from the phone. But eventually she had to let her friends go home because they both had to get up for work the next day.

Driving back to the apartment, sailing on a hefty dose of caffeine and chocolate, Erica planned how she'd manage to keep herself from contacting Dustin for the next few hours. First of all she'd get into her ugliest nightwear—a short-sleeved button-up top and baggy boxers that were decorated with the most grotesque cabbage roses she'd ever seen.

Next she'd get out the kit she'd bought and never used for highlighting her hair. Although she'd never attempted anything like that, she'd watched Josie do it, and the process wasn't pretty. Once she'd put on the tight bonnet and pulled a bunch of strands through the tiny holes, she'd look like a doll that some kid had been carrying around by the hair for years.

Then she'd wet the strands down with a silver-blond highlighting solution. No woman would pick up the phone and invite a man over to her apartment when she was in that condition. Not even a woman who could think of nothing but naked lunches and food sex and the glories of a condomless penis.

Parking in her usual spot, she quickly exited the car and started toward the apartment building before she could change her mind and drive to the hotel. She only had a few more hours of temptation to endure. Tomorrow morning she had to pick up the copies of the newsletter by nine and get the edition mailed out.

By the time she'd handled that, Dustin would probably be on his way back to Midland. He might be on his way now, but she didn't think so. Crazy as it sounded, she thought she'd know when he was gone. She'd lose the feeling of electricity that seemed to hang in the air. So far, the feeling was still very much with her.

"Erica."

She spun around, hoping she wasn't so far gone that she'd imagine his voice in the darkness. But if it was her imagination, it was the complete package, because Dustin stood in the parking lot a few feet from the shadowy outline of his big silver truck. Dressed in snug black jeans and a black silky shirt rolled up at the sleeves and open at the neck, his Stetson set at a jaunty angle, he was the sort of fantasy that had haunted her dreams for years.

"Dustin?" Heart beating wildly, she started toward him. He didn't shimmer and disappear, so apparently he was real. And she was much too glad to see him. Nothing good could come of this, but she continued to walk toward him, anyway.

The moonlight fell softly on his silky shirt and shadowed his face. He walked with an easy grace that had always made her stomach do flip-flops.

"What…what are you doing here?" she asked.

He ignored the question. "How come your date didn't bring you home?"

"My…" She had to think for a minute to figure out what he was talking about. Then she remembered that when she'd told him about her movie date she hadn't clarified that it was with her girlfriends. She hadn't wanted to clarify it, actually, so he'd jumped to the conclusion she'd intended.

He paused about two feet from her. "Where I come from, if a guy asks a woman out, he makes sure she gets home okay."

She'd been willing to mislead him. She wasn't willing to tell him an actual lie. "I went out with my girlfriends."

"What?" He seemed to find that more unbelievable than a date who'd neglected to bring her home.

"My girlfriends." She swallowed, aware she was trembling and unable to stop. She wanted his arms around her, wanted his mouth on hers, wanted the brush of his naked body as he plunged into her. "We had plans to see a movie together."

He stood, feet planted and arms crossed. "You gave up the chance for us to be together tonight so you could go out with your girlfriends?" He seemed completely baffled.

The plan didn't make nearly as much sense now as it had an hour ago. But she defended it, anyway. "I cherish my friends!" she said. "And just because a man suddenly shows up, doesn't mean that I desert them. If I say I'm meeting them for dinner and a movie, then I—" She stopped abruptly, aware that she was painting an inaccurate picture, trying to disguise her intense need for him behind a wall of feminist outrage.

"I get the idea," he said softly. "You didn't want to see me tonight, or any other night, for that matter. If you hadn't had plans, you would have made some." He tugged at the brim of his Stetson. "Good night, Erica. Sorry to have bothered you." He started back to his truck.

Her whole body vibrated in protest. He couldn't be walking away, and not like this, not with that dejected slope to his broad shoulders. She'd hurt him, and that bothered her more than she would have believed possible. This afternoon he'd been so excited, so sexy and wild. She'd taken that away from him. "Dustin, wait."

He paused but didn't turn around. "I thought you might be using another man to put me in my place. I kind of wish that had been the drill. My ego could have dealt with that a whole lot better." Then he continued around to the driver's side of the truck.

"Dustin, I made the date with my friends on purpose, because—"

"Just shut up, Erica." He reached for the door handle. "Just shut the hell up."

"Because I wanted you too much!" *And I still do. I want you upstairs, in my bed.*

He hesitated, his hand resting on the door handle. Then he glanced over at her. "What does that mean, exactly?"

She crossed the blacktop to stand beside him. Her nostrils flared as she picked up his scent, and her skin prickled. "It means that I find you so incredibly desirable that I'm afraid I'll throw away all my plans in a frenzy of lust."

He stared at her for several seconds, and then he began to grin. "A frenzy of lust? Really?"

"Dustin, something primitive happens when we…when we get…"

"Naked?" he offered helpfully.

"Well, yes, to put it bluntly." She didn't know if she'd be able to control this runaway desire, but maybe talking out her worries would help. "Like this afternoon, for example, when we were both ready to forget about birth control. I don't want to have children right now. I don't even want to get *married* for several years, let alone tie myself down with kids, and obligations, and—"

He released the door handle and turned to her. "Neither do I, so what's the problem?"

"The problem is that we seem to forget all that when the fever takes over! I mean, when you bit into that plum after you'd been using it to give me a cli—"

"Do you suppose any of your neighbors in the apartment building sleep with their windows open?" he asked mildly.

She gazed at him, heart pounding, trying to make sense of the question. "Why?"

"Oh, I just wondered if you really wanted everyone in the general vicinity to hear about our adventures with fruit."

"Oh." She supposed not, but she was so hot and achy she really didn't care much about the neighbors.

"Come on." He rounded the truck and opened the passenger door. "I really want to hear what you have to say on this topic. Let's continue the discussion in my truck."

She eyed him warily. He was like the loaded dessert tray waiters brought when she was trying to lose a few pounds. With heat sizzling through her veins every time she looked at him, climbing into the truck with him was risky. "I'm not going back to your hotel with you," she said. *Talk me into it.*

"Fine." He pulled the keys from his pocket and tossed them to her. "Now you're in control of that."

She caught the keys and tucked them in the pocket of her loose clam-diggers. Because she hadn't set out to look sexy tonight, she'd worn a pair of drawstring pants and a cropped cotton tee. Easy-on clothes. They were also easy off.

"Or would you rather go up to your apartment and talk?"

She was weak, weak, weak. No matter how much she wanted to drag him upstairs and have her way with him, she'd hate herself in the morning. She'd have enough trouble forgetting him after only one episode in her bed. If he spent tonight there, too, she might have to move to get rid of the memories.

She should refuse to spend any more time with him. Sending him back to his hotel and going upstairs to highlight her hair would be the safest move she could make.

"Are you really that afraid of me?" he asked.

Her head came up with a start. Now there was a challenge if she'd ever heard one. She'd wanted to send him back to Midland thinking of her as a fearless sex goddess. A fearless sex goddess wouldn't worry about climbing into that truck. She'd climb in there with him and keep control of the situation. She might even give him a mind-shattering experience with oral sex, something Erica had yet to accomplish.

"Of course I'm not afraid of you," she said. Marching past him, she grabbed the dash and lifted herself into the seat before he had a chance to help her. "Let's talk."

"Okay." He closed the door and came around to the driver's side. Once he'd settled himself behind the wheel, he closed his door, and there they were, in a cozy spot again. He took off his hat and laid it brim-side up on the dash before turning toward her.

The floor shift created a small barrier between the two leather seats, but not an insurmountable one. She gazed at him in the shadowy light and wondered if she had the nerve to make the first move.

Maybe not. He'd start something sooner or later. With a highly sexed man like Dustin, that was a given. So instead she asked the question she'd begun with, the one she wanted to know before he left Dallas. "What are you doing here?"

He rested his left arm across the steering wheel and cleared his throat. "The way you talked as you were leaving my room today, I figured the fun and games were over."

Almost. Maybe not quite. She might still give him a little going-away present. "That seemed like the best plan to me. You and I are on very different paths." She mentally traced the row of buttons down to the waistband of his jeans. A definite bulge rounded the line of his zippered fly. Moisture pooled in her mouth, and she swallowed slowly.

He reached over and traced his finger along her forearm. "I was afraid I'd have some trouble forgetting you."

She liked the sound of that. She hoped he would remember her for a long, long time, but she wanted to be able to forget about him, and that seemed unlikely. His light touch on her arm put her whole system on red alert.

"So I thought if I came over here and saw you take some guy up to your apartment so soon after we'd been together, that would make me mad enough that I could put you out of my mind."

"Good grief!" She jerked her arm away from his touch. "Even if I'd had a date with a guy, I wouldn't have had sex with him! I just climbed out of your bed a few hours ago! Give me some credit for a little discrimination. Sheesh."

"Well, what do I know? Maybe for you, that would be normal. You're a big-city woman. For all I know, you could have shoved that experience with me aside and moved on to the next guy."

She was highly insulted. "I can't imagine being able to do that. I'm not the sort of woman to have that kind of hot sex with a man…" She stopped herself before she incriminated herself any further.

"It was hot, wasn't it?"

"Yes."

"Please tell me you had a good time. I deserve that much."

"I had a good time. But just because I enjoy something doesn't mean it's good for me," she added, almost to herself.

"Do you still want me?" He began stroking her arm again, lazily brushing his finger back and forth.

Oh, yes. She'd wanted him for years. More than ten, to be exact. "Yes, but only for the sex." That was her story and she was sticking to it. "And I don't think having sex for the sake of sex is a good idea. Especially for women. Good sex seems to screw up their inner guidance system and they make decisions that aren't right for them. The letters women send to the newsletter bear that out."

"That's a switch. Usually its the guy who's accused of only wanting sex." He flicked his finger softly against her skin as he gazed into her eyes. "But I want more than sex from you. I also want friendship and a business partnership. Apparently you see no use for me other than my services as a stud. Was sex the only reason you went for that drive in the country with me back in high school?"

"No." The word came out before she could consider the consequences. Then she decided that she might as well be honest with herself and with him. "I liked you. I still do."

He sighed in apparent relief. "Good. I like you, too. And I didn't ask you to go on that drive just because of sex. Sure, I wanted you, but there was more to it than that."

"Like what?"

"I…" He hesitated. "I wanted the first time to be really special."

She was stunned to think that he'd known it had been her first time. The shy types she'd dated wouldn't have engaged in locker-room talk. They wouldn't have been in the locker room, period. And what an ego, to think that his expertise would make her first time special. Maybe she'd be able to forget Dustin faster than she'd thought.

She leaned back against the door. "Thanks for taking on such a worthy project."

"What do you mean?"

"You know, teaching me the ropes, and all. Initiating me into the magic world of sex. How noble of you. But how in God's name did you know I was a virgin? What did you do, interview my girlfriends?"

He blinked. "You were?"

"Of course I—" Her breath caught as she figured out the truth. "Don't tell me *you* were a virgin, too!"

"Wait a minute." He sounded upset. "That couldn't have been your first time."

"Why the hell not?"

"Because I slid right in—no barrier, no blood. I thought there had to be—"

"Every woman's different." Her brain continued to whirl with the knowledge that she'd been the first girl he'd had sex with. Unbelievable. "My mother took me to a women's clinic when I was sixteen, and the nurse practitioner wondered if I was sexually active. When I told her I wasn't, she said that I'd apparently torn my hymen somehow, because it was no longer intact."

He stared at her without speaking for several long seconds. When he spoke, his voice was subdued. "You were such a rabble-rouser, such a free thinker. I was sure you'd had lots of sex."

"Me? What about you? The campus flirt? Everybody knew how the jocks carried on. I can't believe that you never—"

"I pretended I'd had sex because I was afraid the other guys would make fun of me if they knew the truth."

One stunning revelation after another. She was having a tough time assimilating this new version of Dustin. "But you must have had dozens of chances. Girls were always hanging around you."

"The party girls. All that laughing and joking around was fun, but I never had a serious discussion with any of them. They didn't expect it, so I didn't even try. When you and I were in chemistry lab together, it was the first time I'd ever really talked to a girl."

"We talked about homework."

"And...other things. You're the one who told me about cosmetics companies testing on rabbits and why we shouldn't eat things with a lot of red dye in them."

"Wow, I can see how that would make you really hot."

"Come on, Erica. You know what I'm talking about. You cared about something besides who won the game on Friday night and what was the top tune on the charts." He smiled. "I used to watch how hard you concentrated on getting the solutions just right in the test tubes, how you pursed your mouth and made sure nothing was even a milliliter off. You didn't even know how sexy you were."

Her body tightened with a tension she couldn't totally identify. It had a sexual edge, no doubt about it, but something else was going on, something deeper and more frightening, as if a crevice yawned in front of her and she didn't know how to keep from tumbling in. She was beginning to see things from Dustin's angle, and the more she understood, the closer to the crevice she came.

"I didn't want to have my first sexual experience with someone who tossed it off as nothing," he said. "I wanted somebody who took life a little more seriously than that."

"And you expected me to know what to do, to be experienced enough to make it wonderful." She sighed, wishing she'd been the sexual goddess he'd thought. The poor guy got a dud his first time out. "I let you down."

"Hell, no, you didn't let me down! I loved every minute of being in that back seat with you." He shook his head. "Or I should say every second."

"That was my fault. I should have made you wait. We should have fooled around more."

"I didn't want to wait." His voice grew huskier. "Once we were in the back seat, I barely took time to play with your breasts. I was bursting, needing to bury myself in you. But then I also wanted to make it last so that you would come, too."

"Dustin, most women don't climax the first time they have sex."

"But you were so wet, so ready. I'll bet if I'd held on a little longer, you would have. I knew enough to realize that should be happening, and I was somehow supposed to help you get there. But once I was inside you, the sensation was better than I'd ever dreamed it would be. I couldn't stop thrusting. I went a little crazy.''

Her tension became more centered, setting up a deep throbbing between her thighs. When she shifted in the seat, the damp material of her panties massaged her gently. Outside the truck a cricket began to chirp. If she closed her eyes, she could imagine they were back on that country road.

"Turns out I have the same reaction now that I had ten years ago," Dustin said softly. "Get me alone with you in the dark and all I can think about is being inside you." He paused and cleared his throat. "I know we've had good sex, and you said we've wiped out the old memories. But I can't really agree."

She opened her eyes and looked at him. In the shadows he could still be the eighteen-year-old boy she'd had such a crush on. Without her knowledge he'd given her his virginity. What she'd imagined was only a notch on his belt had been a watershed moment for him, too.

"I'm not asking you to go back to my hotel," he said. "I'm not even asking to come up to your apartment. I realize now that what I've wanted all along is for you to climb into the back seat of this king cab with me and recreate one of the most important moments of my life. Only this time, I want us to do it right."

11

"YOU'RE REALLY CRAZY, you know that?" Erica murmured, never taking her eyes off him.

"Yeah." He reached behind him to open his door and let in the warm night air. It wasn't a lonely country road, but it would have to do. He could hear crickets in the bushes lining the parking lot. They'd had crickets on that night ten years ago.

"Be crazy with me," he urged softly. He thought there was a slim chance she might if he didn't give her too much time to think about it. Jumping down from the cab, he hurried around to her side and opened the door.

She gazed down at him. "Did you bring—"

"Yes." While downing his coffee and deciding what to wear to a stakeout, he'd thought to stick a couple of condoms in his pocket. Just in case.

He held out his arms. "Come on down and I'll pull the seat forward so we can climb in back." The bench seat wasn't roomy, but he would manage somehow.

When she hesitated, he stepped up on the running board, ducked his head inside the cab and cradled her head for a long, probing kiss. "For old time's sake," he whispered against her mouth. Then he kissed her again, teasing her with his tongue until she began kissing him back.

Yeah, he had a chance. With one hand holding her head, he had the other one free to try a little extra persuasion. He found the end of the drawstring tie securing her pants and pulled it slowly until the bow came undone. She hadn't noticed, or if she had, she wasn't going to stop him.

Good deal. In one continuous movement, he slipped his hand inside her slacks, found the elastic of her panties and breached that barrier, too. In no time he was deep in pleasure territory.

She gasped and grabbed his wrist as she pulled away from his kiss. "Did I say you could do that?"

He lifted his head and tried to read the expression in her eyes. The play of shadows made that difficult. "I—"

"I've heard about boys like you." Her lips curved in a saucy smile. "Bad boys trying to get away with something. You're trying to fool around below the waist, when I didn't say you could."

His heart raced. That was language borrowed from make-out sessions back in high school, which meant that maybe, just maybe, he'd get lucky. He slipped into the roll of teenager on the prowl, although he'd never really played that game.

He could sure as hell fake it, though. "Aw, Erica, please." He tried to slide his hand inside her panties again.

"No." She pulled his hand free and gave it a little slap. "Naughty boy."

"Come into the back seat with me," he murmured. "We'll just kiss for a while, okay? Nothing else. Just kiss."

"That's what you all say. Just a little kiss. Then before I know it, you're trying to take off my bra." She heaved a big sigh and stuck out her chest. "I just don't know if I can trust you."

He rubbed his thumb over her lower lip. He was so hard he wondered if the rivets on his jeans would hold. "You can trust me. Let me show you how much you can trust me."

"Well, maybe for a little while." She sighed again, and

this time she moved forward enough to rub her nipples against his forearm. "But remember, kissing only."

He was willing to bet she'd never teased a guy like this as a teenager, any more than he'd ever pressured a girl for sex. They'd both missed a hell of a lot of fun. "Kissing only," he promised. That covered a lot of territory.

As he helped her down, she rubbed her breast against his arm again. "Are you *sure* I can trust you?"

"Absolutely." She wanted his hands on her bare breasts, and soon he'd be happy to oblige. He had the seat pulled forward in record time. Then he boosted her into the back and followed as quickly as possible, considering the handicap of a throbbing erection. He closed the door firmly behind him, hit the lock and sat on the bench seat next to her. Close quarters, but that was part of the challenge.

Funny, but he'd never bought a two-seater. When he'd inherited his father's job, he'd traded in his latest Mustang convertible for this truck, but he'd never considered anything but a king cab. Although he'd only had vehicular sex once in his life, he'd always wanted to keep the possibility open for a second time. This looked as if it could be the moment.

Maybe. Erica was eyeing him with suspicion. "I think you have *ideas*," she said.

"Ideas of kissing you." He made his voice deliberately innocent as he put his arm across the back of the seat and leaned toward her. Although he'd always loved the feel of her lips on his, the anticipation seemed greater here in the back seat. He was conditioned to expect wonderful things to happen here.

"Dustin, you seem out of breath."

He cleared his throat and tried to breathe normally, but he was so excited he had trouble doing that. "I'm fine."

"And what's that large bulge in your pants?"

"Never mind about that, now." *We'll explore that matter later.* He cupped her face in his hand.

"But my mother said to watch out for—"

"You know mothers." He ran his tongue over her bottom lip. Velvety and plump, perfect for kissing. "They never want you to have any fun."

"Are we going to have fun?"

"Oh, yes. More fun than you can imagine." Heart pounding, he settled his mouth over hers as he stroked her face and combed his fingers through her hair. Damned if he didn't actually feel like an eager teenager parked out in the boondocks. A randy, oversexed teenager about to fondle a girl for the first time. A kid who would go as far as the girl would let him.

She tasted so damned good—chocolate and coffee blended with the taste of Erica. He could almost swear there was a trace of plum juice in there somewhere, too. Maybe he'd always imagine plum juice when he was kissing her.

But this Erica wasn't his plum-juice wild woman. This one kept her legs together and her hands on his shoulders. She'd make him work for every inch of surrender, and he was loving the game.

Delving deeper into her mouth with his tongue, he rubbed his hand casually down her back, locating the catch of her bra. Two hooks. He trembled in anticipation, as if he'd never unfastened one of these before. Although he hadn't made out with a lot of girls in high school, he'd caught up with the program during college.

By then he was more experienced and so were they, but he'd learned that being able to unfasten a bra without taking off the shirt could be a useful skill. Women didn't like to be aware it was happening, either, so he had to make it fast and efficient.

He hadn't tried this maneuver in years, so he might be out of practice. Rubbing her back, he lifted his mouth from hers and nuzzled her ear. Tonight her earrings weren't as big as the ones she'd worn earlier. He took the small gold hoop between his teeth and tugged gently.

"You're so pretty." He ran his tongue around the inner curve of her ear and felt her shiver. "I'm such a lucky guy. I could kiss you all night." *And all over.* As he continued to caress her ear with his tongue, he honed in on the twin hooks and neatly unfastened her bra. Must be just like riding a bike. Once you learned, you always knew.

"Dustin?"

"What, sweetheart?" Heart thundering, he eased his hand around until his fingers rested under the loose hem at the front of the cropped tee. He was so close to the moment of fondling her breasts that his fingers quivered in anticipation.

"You said we'd just kiss."

"Erica, please. Please let me." He slid his hand slowly upward and encountered the unfastened bra. Touching her breasts became an end in itself, the forbidden treasure he had to have. If she wouldn't allow it, he'd go insane.

"I don't know." Her voice was breathy.

"Please."

"Oh, okay." She sounded bored and nonchalant, as if she'd only be indulging his silly obsession. "For a little while."

Swallowing the moisture gathering in his mouth so he wouldn't literally drool on her, he reached under the bra and cupped the warm weight of her breast. Squeezing gently, he closed his eyes and listened to her soft hum of pleasure. Before long he'd slipped his other hand under her shirt, unable to stop himself from caressing both sides. Ah, heaven.

She leaned against the window and arched her back.

"Feel good?" Being allowed to have both hands under her shirt gave him an enormous sense of privilege. He watched the shifting fabric of her tee as he massaged and stroked. Her heart thudded rapidly against his palm.

"I guess it feels good." She gazed at him from heavy-lidded eyes. "You can keep doing it if you want. I don't mind."

Oh, but he wanted more. "Please let me kiss you there."

"Why?"

His tongue grew thick and his chest tightened. He'd never been so turned on in his life. "Because I think you'll like it. My mouth will feel really good there. You'll see."

"What if I don't like it?"

"Then I'll stop."

She shrugged, as if it meant nothing to her what he did. "I suppose you can, then."

Slowly he pushed her bra and her shirt up to her neck, exposing those silky breasts. Although the view wasn't nearly as clear as it had been earlier today, he appreciated it more. Leaning toward her, he brushed his lips over her nipple.

She gasped softly.

Then he took just the nipple between his lips and pulled gently.

"Ooh."

Releasing her nipple, he looked up. Her eyes were closed and her lips parted. "Do you like that?" he murmured.

She nodded.

"Want me to do that some more?"

She nodded again.

This time he flicked her nipple with his tongue and she moaned. By the time he gave in to temptation and took her fully into his mouth, she was gasping for breath. Dear Lord, she looked like she might come with only a little more encouragement. Caressing her other breast with firm strokes, he hollowed his cheeks and sucked vigorously.

As her cries grew louder, she grabbed at her tee and

brought the material up to her mouth to muffle the sound. At last she shuddered and sank back against the frame of the truck while she gulped in air.

Dustin took a deep, appreciative breath, drawing in the scent of the love juices he knew were drenching her.

As her breathing slowed, her eyes fluttered open. "You're a bad boy. You said we'd only kiss."

He swallowed. Holding himself back was becoming painful. "All I did was kiss you."

"Yes, but you kissed my…my, you know."

"I kissed your beautiful breasts. I sucked on your nipples and rolled them against my tongue." The light wasn't good, but he could still see the moisture on her skin where he'd licked her.

Her nipples quivered as her breathing quickened again. "Yes, and you made me…do things."

"What things?" How he ached. If he didn't break his buddy out of prison soon, no telling the consequences. But torturous though her teasing was, he was having more fun with sex than he could have believed possible.

"Something came over me, like a giant sneeze," she said, sounding shy. "Only…down there. And now, the thing is, after that sneezy kind of effect, I'm all…wet."

"Can I see how wet you are?"

She licked her lips. "I don't know if I can trust you."

"You can trust me." *You can trust me to make you come again.*

"All right, you can touch me there. On the *outside,* only. No funny business, now."

"Right." The funny business would come later. He placed his hand between her legs, and sure enough, she'd soaked both layers of material. He rubbed gently. "How does this feel?"

"Kind of good. Kind of nice and squishy. Are you going to make me do that again?"

"Would you like to?"

"I don't know. Maybe."

"Then let me kiss you there, too."

She eyed him for several seconds, obviously making him wait, making him burn. "With my bottoms still on?"

"I can't kiss you very well with them on. Let me take them off, Erica."

"Then I'd be bare."

"Yes." His blood sizzled in his veins.

"Oh, *okay,* if you *have* to."

He really, really had to, for his sake. As he peeled her drawstring pants and panties off, she kicked off her shoes and lifted her hips to help him. He resisted the urge to bury his nose in those fragrant undies before he tossed everything in the front seat.

With the windows up, it was getting warm in the truck, but the warmth seemed to go with what he wanted to do. Vehicular sex was about challenge, not comfort. It was about risk and intrigue, about claiming a moment, about coaxing a girl to let you take off her clothes and enjoy her body in a confined space.

After throwing Erica's slacks and panties in the front, he turned back to discover her sitting with her thighs pressed together and both hands covering the prize. She was so classic he grinned.

Cupping her face in both hands, he began his seduction all over again. "Come on, Erica, honey." He dropped kisses on her mouth. "This will feel even better than before."

"So says you."

"I promise." Trailing kisses down her throat, he pried her hands away. Although he could feel the heat of desire coming off her in waves, she played the timid virgin and kept her legs together.

He stroked his knuckles over the downy curls springing

up from the tight vee of her clenched thighs. "I promise you'll like this," he whispered. Then he eased his forefinger down, making sure that the knuckle rested against her trigger point. Looking into her eyes, he pressed his knuckle inward.

Her eyes widened.

"Good?"

"Mmm."

He wiggled his knuckle back and forth, and she caught her lower lip between her teeth.

"Open up for me," he begged. "Please."

Gradually her thigh muscles relaxed.

"Yes, like that." He rotated his finger and pushed inside, then crooked it so he could stroke her G-spot with the tip.

She moaned and leaned her head back against the window, her breathing ragged. "It's happening again. That feeling."

"I hope so." He stroked her again. "Wider, honey. That's good." As she spread her legs, he reluctantly withdrew his finger so he could get into position. It was damned awkward, but he'd do anything for the chance to taste her. Resting his knees on the carpeted floor, he guided her legs over his shoulders.

Then he was golden. Hands under her firm bottom, he lifted her slightly and nuzzled his way to the ultimate kiss of all. He was in heaven, soaking up the scent of leather upholstery mingled with the aroma of sex, the sound of Erica's muffled cries blended with the chirping of crickets, the flavor of arousal mixed with the taste of the forbidden.

She gripped his head in both hands, and he knew her response well enough to know that she was very close. Her thighs trembled and she was so hot he thought his tongue might be steaming. He would give her this, and then—

"Stop," she said, gasping. She tried to pull his head up, tried to close her thighs.

"No. Let me—"

"No." She struggled against him. "Take your pants off, Dustin. I want everything this time. You. Buried to the hilt. Now."

He wasn't about to argue with a demand like that. "Don't move." Keeping her legs propped on his shoulders, he drew back enough to reach down and fumble with his jeans. Silently he cursed the denim and wished he'd gone for nylon running shorts instead of macho wear.

"Hurry."

"Don't worry. I'm hurrying." He shoved down his jeans and briefs and groaned with relief once his penis was released. Digging in his pocket, tearing open the package and rolling on the condom took aeons, and all the while he vividly remembered the moment he'd plunged into her without benefit of latex. He'd never forget the sensation and wouldn't be satisfied until he'd experienced it again. But now was not the time.

She moaned again. "Dustin, *please.*"

Music to his ears. The timid virgin was gone, and that was good, considering he was out of patience for coaxing her to let him in. "Okay." He slid his hands under her bottom again, angling her, hoping he'd have thrusting room. Then he probed gently, glad she was slick with need. For this move they needed all the lubrication they could get.

"Right...there," she murmured, reaching down to guide him in.

He loved her hands on his penis, hated the thin barrier preventing him from direct contact with her exploring fingers. Still, he nearly lost control as he glanced down and watched as she helped him dock. Even in dim light it was one of the most erotic things he'd ever seen.

Once he was centered in, he gazed into her eyes. Maybe he couldn't read her expression very well, but he wanted to look at her while he pushed home. Maybe she could see the expression in his eyes and understand the gift she was giving him by acting out this fantasy.

Gripping her bottom, he eased forward, sinking into her heat. He deliberately took it slow, wanting to savor the slide into bliss. For years he'd kidded himself that being inside Erica the first time hadn't been anything special. She'd been his first, so naturally he'd glorified the moment of penetration.

He couldn't expect to recapture the feeling because the sensation of becoming fused with another human being didn't exist except in his imagination. Yet he'd felt it last night, and again this afternoon. And now. Now he was delirious with it.

"It's good." Her voice was thick with passion.

"Very…good." He was up to the hilt, just as she'd asked, and he didn't think anything in the world could be more perfect than this.

His balls, tight and full, brushed her bottom. Like a safe-cracker who finally hits the right combination, he heard the click as the mental tumblers rolled into place. Something more powerful than pleasure was driving him to seek this woman's heat. She'd called them primitive urges, and she'd been right. He wanted to mate.

But he wasn't in a cave lit by an open-pit fire. He was in the back seat of his king cab, in a parking lot in the bustling city of Dallas. And mating was the last thing either of them needed to do right now.

So he went for the pleasure, easing back and rocking forward again. So sweet. If pleasure was all they could have now, this was top of the line.

She clutched the backrest with one hand, the edge of the seat with the other. Lips parted, breath coming in quick little pants, she met his gaze. "Oh, Dustin…I…love this."

"That makes…two of us." He stroked rhythmically,

clenching his jaw against the orgasm that threatened to shatter his fantasy. Even though he'd given her a climax once tonight, as well as several times in the past thirty-six hours, he wanted this one more than any of the others.

She gasped. "Like old times."

"Only better." He felt her tighten around him.

"Much better." She groaned. "So *much* better."

"Ever come in the back seat?"

"Once."

He paused, wishing he hadn't asked, not wanting to know about some other back seat Romeo.

"About ten minutes ago." Her voice had an edge to it. "Dustin, don't stop! Please don't stop!"

That pause was all he'd needed to keep from blowing the program. "Wouldn't dream of it." He picked up the pace, shifted the angle slightly.

"*There*," she said, her voice rich and throaty. "Oh, yes, right *there*."

"Come for me, Erica," he murmured, stroking faster. "Come for me now."

"Yes…I'm coming…coming….oh, *yes!*"

He'd imagined himself under control, but hearing her announce her climax and feeling the contractions surging around him smashed his restraint. With a loud groan he plunged deep. Gulping for air, he slumped over her as the pulsing spasms shook him and his sperm battered against the thin wall of latex.

Despair gripped him. Making love to her tonight, wonderful though it had been, still wouldn't be enough. But it might be all he'd ever have.

As he was contemplating the significance of that, someone rapped on the window of the truck.

12

STARTLED BY THE KNOCKING on the window, Erica's first instinct was to cover herself, and Dustin was handy. She locked her ankles behind his neck and grabbed him around the waist at the same time he struggled to get away.

The knocking came again. "Everything okay in there, folks?"

Erica groaned. "The cops."

"Turn me loose, Erica," Dustin muttered. "I'll deal with it."

She put her mouth next to his ear. "If I turn you loose, I'll be lying here half-naked, with no way to cover up. My pants are in the front seat."

"Well, mine are down around my knees, so I'm not in a whole lot better shape than you are."

"Okay, folks," the man called. "I need you to come on out of there so I can be sure everybody's okay."

Dustin managed to lift his head a fraction. "Can you give us a minute?"

"Yes, I can do that."

"Thanks." Dustin tried to pull away from Erica.

"Wait." She held on tight. "Do we really have to go out there?"

"If that's the cops, we do. If it's not the cops, we still have a problem and need to handle it. Erica, your finger-nails are—"

"Oops." She unclenched her fingers and hoped she

hadn't made him bleed. "Isn't that invasion of privacy, demanding that we come out?"

"Not if he's legit and heard all the noise we were making. Good sex doesn't sound a whole lot different from assault. For all he knows I'm a mad rapist and you're my victim. But I can't tell if he's a cop or not while you have me in a hammerlock."

Reluctantly she uncrossed her ankles. "Do you suppose he's watching this?"

"You couldn't really see much. I have tinted windows." He eased away from her.

She hadn't noticed the tint on the windows. "Heavy tint or light tint?"

"Light, but—"

"Oh, jeez. I'll bet he can see everything. Grab my pants from the front seat."

Dustin fumbled for her pants with his right hand while using his left to dispose of the condom. He tossed her pants at her. "I hate these damn things."

"My pants?" She didn't bother trying to locate her underwear. The pants would be enough for now.

"No, condoms."

"Me, too." Erica turned the pants right side out and shoved her foot into the leg opening.

"When sex is that great with a condom—" Dustin paused and zipped his jeans "—I can't help wanting to try it without one."

"Yeah," Erica said wistfully.

"Okay, I'm ready to get a look at this guy." Dustin peered out the window. "Hmm. Seems like a rent-a-cop. Young guy, short hair, maybe Hispanic. He looks harmless, but I'm going to make him show us some I.D. through the window before we unlock any doors."

Then Erica remembered. The apartment complex had recently decided to have a security guard patrol the parking lot a few times each night. "Does he have a truck that says Allied Security on the side?"

"Yep."

"Then it's a rent-a-cop. The patrols started about a month ago. So if he's not a real cop, do we have to go out or not?"

"We should go out. The guy could probably have a squad car here in no time if we acted uncooperative. I'll go first. You come on when you're ready."

"I won't ever be ready." She lifted her hips and pulled her pants up. "I feel like a kid busted by her parents for breaking curfew. This is humiliating."

"Erica."

"What?" She looked at him and noticed his teeth flash in the dim light. He was grinning. "So you think this is funny?" she asked.

"I think this is perfect. We decided to act like a couple of teenagers tonight, and we got busted like a couple of teenagers. It's the icing on the cake."

She refused to be appeased. "No, it's a cockroach in the punch bowl."

Dustin leaned toward her and stole a quick kiss. "Just think," he murmured. "The rent-a-cop could have showed up five minutes earlier. Now *that* would have been a disaster."

She shuddered to think what that would have been like. "One of us might have broken something important."

"Yeah." Dustin chuckled. "That's for sure. Well, I'd better go out and talk with our friend." Because the passenger seat was still shoved forward, he left through the passenger door.

As Erica fastened her bra and hunted around on the floor for her shoes, she heard Dustin talking to the security guard as if they were buddies. They even started laughing about something. She felt irritated and outnumbered, positive that although she couldn't make out what they were saying, they were sharing sexual war stories.

Why else would they be having such a jolly time? The security guard certainly knew by now what had been going on in the back of the cab, so he'd probably kidded Dustin about it. And Dustin, the cad, was making light of what they'd shared.

She glanced out the window and saw them standing next to the guard's truck, which was parked under one of the pole lamps scattered around the parking lot. The guard was short and well-built, obviously a guy who worked out. He nodded and laughed at something Dustin said. Dustin faced in her direction, so she could see the big grin on his face. The rat.

The longer she listened to the tone of their voices, the more irritated she became. Maybe her original judgment of Dustin ten years ago had been right, after all—just a superficial type out for a good time.

When he'd admitted being unhappy with his performance that first night out in the country, she'd decided he was more vulnerable than she'd thought. His latest confession that he'd been a virgin had really softened her attitude and made her think that she might...well, might be falling a little bit in love with him. Maybe. Despite their different goals in life.

Well, she'd just made the classic mistake that she'd mentioned to him not an hour ago—thinking that good sex was the basis for a relationship. Good sex was good sex, period. Dustin was able to look at it that way, which was why he was out there this very minute yukking it up with the security guard.

She, on the other hand, had expected him to treat their sexual encounter with solemn respect, as if they were bonding, as if they were embarking on an actual romance. Bull. Dustin had laid out what he wanted from her and she hadn't been listening. He wanted sex, friendship and a business relationship, but he'd identified them as separate categories and had made it clear one wasn't supposed to have anything to do with the others.

In a romance, those things had everything to do with each other. They were so closely intertwined they couldn't ever be separated. Now instead of being irritated with Dustin, she was upset with herself.

She'd nearly stalked out there and told him off, as if she had a right to do that. No, she had two choices. If she really didn't like the rules of the game, she could quietly decide not to play and then stick to her guns. No more of these juvenile plans to distract herself from the temptation of Dustin.

The second choice was to play the game his way, by his rules. She'd told him she didn't believe in marriage before thirty. Now she realized the vow had been simple to keep when no man in her life made her tremble with desire. When her sex life was mediocre it was easy to think she wasn't ready for a permanent relationship. The real test was whether she could have dynamite sex with a guy and still not push for a commitment.

She'd whined to Denise that she couldn't continue to see Dustin because great sex with him would make her abandon her goals. What a weak sister she was turning out to be! She should be able to enjoy great sex *and* continue toward her goals.

Drawing in a calming breath, she ran her fingers through her hair and climbed out of the truck. She picked up her purse from the floor of the front seat and shoved her panties into it. Then she squared her shoulders and walked toward the men. Time to be a real woman and claim her full sexuality.

DUSTIN WATCHED Erica coming toward them and his groin tightened. From the way she'd acted when the security guard showed up, he'd expected her to approach hesitantly, as if she had something to be embarrassed about. He'd hoped that his joking around had filtered back to the truck and helped her see this wasn't a serious situation. He'd wanted to put her more at ease.

She'd gone miles beyond feeling at ease. She looked like a lioness on the prowl. He had trouble believing that less than twenty minutes ago she'd been playing the part of the timid virgin, and less than ten minutes ago she'd been clutching him close, afraid to expose her nakedness to this stranger. There was nothing timid about her now, and her glance at the security guard was filled with confidence.

"I'm glad you're on the job," she said to him. "Several single women live in this building, which is why the management decided to step up security in the parking lot."

"That's right, ma'am." The young guy puffed out his chest. "We don't want to give predators a chance. Now, if I could see some I.D...." He asked apologetically, as if hating to bother her.

"Certainly." Erica reached into her purse, pushed aside her panties and pulled out her wallet, extracting her driver's licence from it. After handing it to the security guard, she came over beside Dustin and linked her arm through his. "But I want you to know that Dustin isn't a predator. If anyone deserves that label, it's me."

Dustin stared down at her in amazement. She'd brought his arm in direct contact with her breast and she was practically purring.

The guard glanced up from studying her license. "Erica Mann? Aren't you the one who puts out that newsletter thing? I can't think of the name of it, but—"

"*Dateline: Dallas,*" she said smoothly. "Yes, I am. Are you a subscriber, Mr.—" She peered at his name badge. "Mr. Alvarez?"

"No, but down at the gym where I work out, somebody always has a copy. It makes the rounds, I can tell you that."

Dustin's immediate thought was all the wasted revenue when subscribers shared their newsletters.

Apparently that wasn't Erica's first reaction. "Cool." She seemed surprised and pleased. "I never thought about that. What you're telling me is that for every subscriber I might have several more readers."

"From what I see at the gym, absolutely." The guard handed her license back. "I've tried some of the restaurants you write about." He gave her a thumbs-up. "Excellent."

"That's great." Erica smiled. "I'm glad you liked them."

"It's come to the point where if you say it's good, I know it will be. The guys I know trust you on that, when they're taking a date out for dinner." He winked. "And then there was the time you recommended restaurants where you could get away with fooling around. That was a kick."

Erica snuggled closer to Dustin. "Sounds like you tried one of them."

The guard laughed. "Actually, I did. What a rush."

Dustin wasn't entirely comfortable with the direction the conversation had taken. He'd worked hard to draw the guard's attention away from the sexual angle of this situation by asking if he thought the Cowboys would make it to the Superbowl this season.

Because nobody really believed that, the topic had been good for a few laughs. But now the guard would surely make a connection between fooling around in a restaurant and fooling around in a parking lot.

He did. "The difference between a restaurant and a parking lot," he said, turning serious, "is that in the restaurant, there's no chance a woman could be raped. But out here we have to check anything suspicious. I wouldn't advise making a practice of doing it in a parking lot. If there's security, and there should be, you'll get hassled.''

Erica smiled. ''Dustin tried to tell me it was a bad idea, but I insisted we give it a shot. Sorry if we caused you any trouble.''

''Just doing my job, ma'am.''

''Well, we'll make your job easier by taking our activities up to my apartment, right, Dustin?''

Dustin nearly swallowed his tongue. He'd thought their escapade in the back of the cab might very well be the last. After all, she'd deliberately made a date with her girlfriends in order to steer clear of him. He'd gotten away with luring her into the truck, but he hadn't expected to set foot in her apartment again.

However, he wasn't a stupid man. ''Right, Erica,'' he said. ''Just let me lock up the truck.'' He hurried over to do that while Erica and Alvarez stood chatting, probably about sex.

He wouldn't doubt that Alvarez read Erica's advice column. He was just the kind of highly sexed guy who would gobble up that part of the newsletter. At this very moment he might be asking her which positions most women preferred. Or whether they liked music while they were doing it, or—

Damn, it was time to get Erica away from that young stud. He'd ceased looking like a helpful security guard and was beginning to look like sexual competition. Now Alvarez knew that Erica lived in this apartment building. If he ever discovered Dustin wasn't a permanent fixture in her life, he'd probably beat a path to her door and ask her out. The guard already knew Erica liked to fool around in restaurants.

Dustin ground his teeth and swore under his breath. Time to get the truck locked and leave this damned parking lot. Although he could lock the vehicle without the keys, he'd made a habit of using them so he wouldn't accidentally lock himself out. But when he shoved his hand in his pocket, it was empty.

Where the hell were his keys? He checked the ignition and felt around on the floor of the back seat in case they'd fallen out while he was having sex with Erica.

Erica. He'd given her the keys so that she had control over whether they drove back to the hotel.

Maybe they'd fallen out of her pocket when he'd thrown her pants into the front seat. He sure as hell hoped so, because he really didn't want to go back over there and ask her for the keys, not when Alvarez stood there oozing machismo.

Even under the best of circumstances, asking a woman for the keys to your big muscle truck wasn't a manly thing to do. A real guy kept track of his own damned keys. Briefly he considered locking the truck and taking a chance the keys were in Erica's pocket.

If he was wrong and they were still inside, he'd have to call a towing service when he wanted to leave. Not smooth. Or he could leave the truck unlocked, but having the truck stolen during the night wouldn't be his favorite way to end his visit to Dallas, either.

Another search of the floors and seats came up empty, so he had no choice. He had to find out if Erica had the keys before he locked the truck. All this extra time had allowed her to get better acquainted with Mr. I'm-wearing-a-uniform-and-you're-not. The guy had probably mentioned the gym on purpose so that Erica would notice his muscles.

With a sigh he started back toward Erica. Maybe that newsletter of hers wasn't such a damned good idea if it brought horny guys to her doorstep. He hadn't thought of that before. She should have put the newsletter out under a false name, but she hadn't, and now the problem would be hard to fix. Still, maybe he could find a way.

He'd covered half the distance when he thought of a way to minimize the effect of this embarrassing situation. "Erica," he called. "Toss me the keys, babe."

She turned, her mouth open as she stared at him.

Right away he knew he'd miscalculated. Being called *babe* in public, especially with that particular tone, might not be her favorite form of address. "Uh, just throw them over, okay?" He held up his hand, palm out. He thought of spreading his fingers in the peace sign, to see if that would diffuse any of the indignation he could read in her expression, even from twenty feet away.

Slowly she closed her mouth and he watched nervously as she smiled sweetly. The smile didn't look particularly sincere. He might have just screwed himself out of going upstairs with her.

"Why, Dustin, my little love bug. Did you forget where your keys were, again, honey bunch?"

He winced. This conversation was not improving his manly image. "Um, temporarily."

"You are *such* an absentminded boy." She took the keys out of her pocket, held them up and jingled them. "Good thing you asked me to keep them for you, isn't it, my little sweet potato?"

He ground another millimeter off his back molars and refused to make eye contact with Alvarez. Nevertheless he could see the security guard trying not to laugh. "Just toss them over, please."

"Certainly, my sweet stud muffin." She threw them fast, right at his head.

He managed to get his hand up and catch them, compliments of many years on the football field. The serrated edge of one key bit into his palm, but he forced himself to smile. "Thanks."

As he stalked back to his truck, he tried to tell himself that it was a good thing he'd ticked her off. He was becoming fixated on her, and she was too quick for him. One little slip on his part, one tiny misstep, and she'd flattened him worse than Doogie Hildebrand, the biggest lineman he'd ever faced.

Of course, Erica had a much more appealing body than Doogie. A very appealing body. He found himself getting hard again thinking about what might happen if they actually made it up to her apartment. And most of the time he liked knowing she was so smart, but not when she turned all that brainpower against him.

He shouldn't have tried the *babe* line, though. Chastising himself for being terminally stupid, he quickly locked up the truck. He knew better than to talk to a woman like that. Seeing her acting so chummy with Alvarez had brought out the worst in him, making him extremely territorial. Come to think of it, he'd never *been* territorial before.

Huh. Thinking about that, his steps slowed as he headed back to Erica. He'd always assumed he wasn't the jealous type. His other girlfriends had told him how refreshing it was to be with a guy who didn't get uptight if they hung out with other men. He'd congratulated himself on being so easygoing.

But there was nothing neutral about his feelings as he watched Erica enjoying the company of the security guard. They were standing too close together and looking too happy. He didn't appreciate how Alvarez was glancing at Erica and covertly checking out her rack. If Dustin had been a male cat, he would have walked over and peed on the security guard's shoes.

"Truck's locked," he said. "So you can be on your way." He held out his hand to the security guard. "Thanks for your help."

"No problem." He shook Dustin's hand. "Have a safe trip back to Midland."

Dustin's head snapped around toward Erica. "You told him I was from out of town?" He hadn't wanted Alvarez to know that and think he could move in. But maybe Erica had told him so that he'd know the coast was clear.

"Your address is on your license," Alvarez said, his tone dry as he surveyed Dustin.

"Oh. Right." Apparently sex with Erica had fried every one of his brain cells.

Alvarez turned back to Erica. "Anyway, like I was saying, it's a terrific gym. Good staff, excellent equipment. I think you'd be happy there."

Holy catfish, the guy was inviting her to join his health club. It was a baby step from there to asking her out. Erica asked a question about the hours, but Dustin was finished with this nonsense.

He cleared his throat. "I hate to interrupt, but Erica and I need to go upstairs and discuss a business venture I'm considering. There's an organic brewery she wants me to check out, and I need some more information before I go back to Midland. So if you'll excuse us."

"You're really thinking of doing that?" Erica looked slightly more pleased with him than she had seconds ago.

"I'm really thinking of doing that. Do you have someone I can contact?"

"Actually, I do." She studied him, as if trying to decide if he meant what he was saying. " I was so impressed with the beer that I got in touch with the company, which is how Henry happens to be serving it at his restaurant. I've hooked up the brewery owners with a couple of other places in town, too."

"Then let's go find that information before we forget." He hadn't given the organic brewery another thought until this moment, but if Erica wouldn't franchise the newsletter, maybe he'd look into the brewery. It might even be a decent business idea, but he didn't kid himself about his motivation for mentioning the subject.

"Okay." Erica smiled at Alvarez. "See you later, Manny."

Now they were on a first-name basis. Great. Just great. Dustin started off toward the apartment building, a scowl on his face.

Erica maintained a couple of feet distance between them as she walked along beside him. "I don't know if you're really interested in the brewery or if you think it's a good way to get back in my good graces."

"All of the above." Dustin figured he had no choice but to eat crow. "I was way out of line calling you *babe* in front of Alvarez, and I'm sorry."

"You'd be way out of line calling me *babe* in front of anyone, including my neighbor's Pekinese. I suppose that's what you're used to, though. I'll bet the guys you know do it all the time, as in *Yo, babe, bring me a beer,* so maybe I shouldn't be so hard on you."

"Some of the guys I know do talk like that, but I don't. I never have."

"Until tonight?" She looked very skeptical.

"Yes, damn it! Until tonight I have never addressed a woman as *babe.*"

"Which brings us to the next question." The apartment building's entrance door was locked, and she fished in her purse for the key. "Why did you do it tonight?"

"God only knows." Dustin had an idea, though, and he wasn't pleased with the reason that kept coming to him. He'd tried to stake his claim.

"I don't think any man's ever called me *babe.*"

"Well, if it makes you feel any better, you managed to completely humiliate me in front of the security guard. I think *love bug, honey bunch, little sweet potato* and *sweet stud muffin* trump *babe* any day."

She opened the door and he held it for her. She smiled at him as she walked through. "You started it."

He wanted to argue that she'd started it by being too damned nice to the security guard, but he had a feeling that wouldn't be the wisest course of action, not if he wanted to improve his odds upstairs. "You're right, I did. And I'm sorry."

"I know why you're sorry." She gave him a coy look as she started up the stairs. "You're sorry because you think you've ruined any chance of more sex."

Honesty was the best policy. She could see right through him, anyway. "That, too."

"Are you going to invest in the brewery?"

"Yes." He was doing it to stay in good with her, but he also valued her judgment. If she thought the brewery was a good investment, then it probably was.

"That's nice." She came to the landing and headed for the stairs leading to the second floor. "I also know of a good start-up company that's marketing a dynamite water filtering system."

"I'll be happy to look into it." He followed a little behind for the sole reason that he loved watching the action of her tight little butt. From the way she kept glancing at him, he figured she knew exactly what he was doing and she was showing off for his benefit. He knew she was capable of teasing him and then shutting him down. He sincerely hoped that wasn't her plan.

"Great. But your interest in those companies isn't why we're going to have sex again tonight, in case you think that's the reason."

"It isn't? We are?" His words came out sounding like a bullfrog's mating call. A desperate bullfrog.

"Yes, we are." She flashed him another smile over her

shoulder as she continued to climb the stairs. "Even though you had a chauvinist lapse in judgment, you still turn me on. So we're having sex again because I want to."

Dustin didn't care for her tone. He didn't care for it one bit. When they got to her apartment, he planned to help her lose the attitude. Fortunately he could do that in bed as well as anywhere.

13

AS SHE CLIMBED the stairs to the third floor, Erica wanted to punch her fist in the air. Dustin was jealous! *Jealous!* That was the only explanation for why he'd suddenly turned into a possessive, arrogant jerk. Apparently he'd never considered that any guy would give him a run for his money, let alone the security guard for her apartment building.

She wasn't really interested in Manny, but flirting with him under Dustin's nose had been highly educational and empowering. The nervous woman who had paced the floor of her apartment yesterday morning waiting for the great Dustin Ramsey to appear was gone. In her place was Erica Mann, sex goddess.

Dustin might have thought he could joke with Manny about the episode in the back seat of his king cab, but she would have the last laugh. She would soon have Dustin so sexually captive that he'd be gasping for breath and begging for mercy. Once she had him cross-eyed with lust, she'd give him the best climax of his life. Then she'd send him back to Midland to fantasize about her, while she proceeded to find other men as sexually adept as he was.

She could see now that she'd expected too little of the men she'd dated. From now on, if they didn't make it happen for her, she'd move on to someone who could. Dustin had given her a benchmark, but there had to be other men out there besides him who were capable of floating her boat. She'd have to look a little harder, that's all.

Opening the door to her apartment, she felt like the spider welcoming the fly. Dustin had no idea what was about to happen to him. Up until now, he'd had the upper hand, sexually. That was about to change.

After closing and locking the door, she turned to Dustin. "Can I take your hat?"

"Uh, sure." He looked hopeful, but not entirely sure of himself.

Exactly how she wanted him. She laid his hat on the coffee table in front of the sofa. "Sex in the back seat was fun, but I think we could both use a shower, don't you?"

Eagerness gleamed in his blue eyes. "Great idea. Let's take one together."

She shook her head with a smile of regret. "The shower's too small for both of us. You go first." She leaned toward him and ran a finger down the front of his shirt. "And don't bother getting dressed afterward. I like my men wearing only a towel."

He swallowed. "Okay." He started down the hall, but he turned halfway to her bedroom. "What are you going to do while I shower?"

"Oh, not much. Maybe check my e-mail. Get us something cool to drink." *Figure out the best way to blow your circuits.* "What would you like?"

"Anything."

Excellent. She needed him to be suggestible. "I'll go see what I have in the refrigerator." As he continued down the hall, she went into her kitchen to find something fizzy but non-alcoholic. The champagne earlier today had helped pave the way for her to be extremely foolish and vulnerable. She wasn't taking that kind of chance again.

Moments later she had two glasses of club soda sitting on coasters on the coffee table and a small jar of microwave-warmed honey placed inconspicuously beside the sofa, within reach. She'd pulled the coffee table a little farther away from the sofa to give her room to maneuver. Yet it didn't look particularly obvious.

She liked the idea of staging this seduction in her living room instead of in the bedroom. They'd done the bedroom scene, and Dustin might feel too much at ease in there. She wanted him off balance.

After closing the drapes and lighting every candle in the room, she turned off the lamps and surveyed the effect. Nice. The thought of driving Dustin crazy right under the erotic flower painting by Georgia O'Keefe really appealed to her. And her rattan sofa would work in ways she'd never imagined before tonight.

Taking her copy of the *Joy of Sex* from the bookcase, she laid it next to the glasses of club soda. Dustin might as well have some reading material while she showered. Picking up the book, she flipped through the pages to make sure that he'd be able to see it in the flickering candlelight.

The words might be a little tough to read, but the pictures were clear, and the pictures were what she wanted him to focus on, anyway. In her experience, women liked erotic text but men preferred visuals.

He walked into the room, one of her white bath towels wrapped around his hips. "I didn't know if you wanted me to wait in the bedroom, but it looks like you have something planned in here."

Oh, she certainly did. "I thought we could relax on the sofa for a while."

"Okay." He gazed at her as if trying to decide what she might be up to.

She swept a hand toward the coffee table. "I fixed us each a glass of club soda."

"What, no glasses in the shape of a penis?"

She laughed. "The sugar and creamer are my only X-rated items." She'd thought they'd shock him enough to give her an edge last night, but she'd underestimated him.

Tonight would be a different story. "Have a seat. I'll only be a moment, but I left you some reading material so you wouldn't get bored."

He sank down on the sofa cushion and picked up the book. "Are you saying I could use some instruction?"

"Not at all." Now that she was running to meet this powerful attraction instead of hiding from it, she felt so in charge. "I thought you'd enjoy a trip down memory lane. Enjoy."

She left him peering at couples in various sexual poses. As she walked down the hall, she imagined his state when she returned. She thought the candlelight and the anticipation of what was to come would stoke his fire almost as much as the naked people in the book. By the time she reappeared, she expected him to be aroused and ready under that towel, but she didn't think he'd ever be ready for what she had in mind.

DUSTIN HAD ONE CONDOM LEFT of the two he'd brought along tonight, and he tossed it into his hat once Erica left the room. He wondered if she had any stashed away somewhere. Women in this day and age often kept some around, and he was hoping she was one of those who believed in being prepared.

He wanted a good supply of condoms, because tomorrow he was going back to Midland, which meant he wanted to make use of every minute that he had left with Erica. If the sex was good enough, and if he could override that unfortunate incident when he'd addressed her as *babe,* then maybe he could set the stage for his next visit.

There had to be a next visit. A guy would be stupid not to want more of what Erica had to offer. But his needs went beyond sex, and he'd had a feeling about that all along. He simply liked being with her, talking with her.

When he was with Erica, he knew everything would be okay.

But he couldn't get a handle on how she felt about continuing their association, more specifically their sexual association. By getting involved with the brewery and this water-filter deal, he could keep a business connection with her. If those investments worked out, he could consult her about other things. But he wanted those consultations to be in person. Preferably naked.

He knew he was running his company by using his johnson as a sort of water witching tool, but while taking his shower, he'd come to terms with that and decided it was okay. If Erica were some airhead, it would spell disaster for Ramsey Enterprises. But she was a very smart woman. She had good business instincts, whether she wanted to acknowledge them or not.

Taking the cool glass of club soda in one hand, he leaned back against the sofa cushions and sipped the carbonated drink while paging through the book she'd left for him. Nice pictures. *Very* nice pictures. He liked the look of that one, a graceful doggie-style pose.

He and Erica hadn't tried that one yet. Maybe he should put a bookmark there. The way his penis was rising to the occasion, he'd be able to use it to hold his place while he glanced through the rest of the book.

She'd meant to get him aroused, of course. She might not realize that sitting in this room waiting for her to finish her shower would have done the trick without the benefit of this book. The book just made it happen sooner.

The sound of rushing water stopped, and his heart beat a little faster. He'd thought about ignoring her instructions and joining her in the shower. The stall wasn't huge, but he thought they'd both fit. She had a shower massager, and he could imagine doing all sorts of fun things with that.

But he'd hesitated, deciding to give her some rope.

Maybe she had a little too much attitude to suit him right now, but he probably had that to thank for her decision to have sex again. Earlier today she'd been determined to run away from him. She could have used the excuse of his chauvinistic behavior in the parking lot to ditch him if she'd still been worried that he'd somehow sidetrack her from her goals.

She didn't seem worried about that anymore. He wasn't sure why, but if the end result was more time in bed with her, he couldn't very well argue. Of course, it didn't look as if they were headed immediately to bed. That was okay, too. The first time he'd sat on this sofa, he'd envisioned its excellent makeout potential.

"I'm back."

"Oh!" Her appearance in the candlelit room startled him. Then he realized that her bare feet hadn't made any noise as she came down the hall. For some reason, he'd expected her to show up in the other bath towel, but instead she was wearing a silky red robe tied loosely around her waist. Very loosely. He had no trouble seeing the shadowy temptation of her breasts.

Beneath the towel, his penis twitched. "I like your book, especially this page." He turned it to show her the doggie pose.

Her voice floated around him, soft and seductive "A lot of men like that position."

The pressure in his groin grew more insistent. He wanted that position *now*. "Want to sit here and read to me?" He patted the cushion next to him.

"Not right now." She untied her robe.

His heart thundered as the lapels of the robe parted slightly. They caught on the tips of her breasts, but he still had an excellent view of cleavage and the downy triangle between her legs. The candle flame on the coffee table reflected on a drop of moisture clinging to her curls, making it sparkle like a tiny diamond suspended in paradise.

Mesmerized by the quivering droplet, he ran his tongue over his lips. He'd developed quite a taste for her, and it hadn't been nearly satisfied. "Come here," he murmured.

"That's what I had in mind." She walked toward him. "See something you like?"

"Yes." He seemed to have tunnel vision. What he wanted was exactly at eye level, or more accurately at mouth level, and he couldn't focus on anything but the soft curls that quivered when she walked. The closer she came, the stronger his hunger grew.

She stepped around the coffee table, making the bathrobe flare away from her, stirring the air as an erotic, spicy scent wafted toward him. Erica's scent. His mouth watered as he reached for her, sliding his hands under the robe and cupping her smooth bottom. With a groan he pulled her forward and buried his face between her thighs.

Heaven. He could stay here forever, filling his nostrils with her aroma, sliding his tongue over the sweetest confection he'd ever discovered. If he gave her pleasure in the process, so much the better, but this was for him, not her. He felt as if he could easily come simply by plundering her bounty to his heart's content.

Yet she'd be the first. He could tell by her rapid breathing and trembling thighs. Maybe he'd give her several orgasms like this—see how many she could manage before he erupted with her. Yes, she was nearly there. She clutched his shoulders and moaned softly as he sought his prize.

Then he no longer had to seek. Gasping, she thrust herself toward him, silently asking for more. He pressed his mouth tight against her and quickened the motion of his tongue.

She came in a rush and he lapped greedily, wanting her

to come again, wanting more, and even more. But she drew away. He tried to pull her back toward him, but she grasped his wrist.

He wasn't going to force her, but he was sure that he could make her come again in seconds. "Let me—"

"No." She struggled for breath and locked her fingers around his wrist. "Let me go."

Reluctantly he did, but his brain swirled with sensory overload and he closed his eyes to bring himself back under control. Vaguely he realized she was still holding on to his wrist, and her silky robe teased the sensitive skin over his pulse. No, it wasn't her robe. It was the tie of her robe.

"Move your arm over here," she whispered, guiding his arm to the back of the sofa.

He opened his eyes and gazed up at her in confusion. "What?"

"Let's have some fun," she murmured.

That's when he realized the tie of her robe was snug around his wrist and she was looping the silky strip of red material through the latticework of the rattan sofa. "B-bondage?" he stuttered.

"Mild bondage. Just your wrists."

"So that you can…"

She slowly ran her tongue over her lips. "So I can return the favor."

"Oh." He nearly passed out from excitement. Never in a million years had he envisioned being tied to her sofa while she gave him oral sex. But with an imagination like Erica's, a guy never knew what might happen next. He began to wonder how he'd ever be happy with someone else after these days and nights with Erica.

When she leaned forward to weave the tie through the lattice behind his head, her robe hung open and her breasts swayed temptingly in front of his face. He reached for one trembling plaything, but she grabbed his hand.

"I need your other wrist."

He let her pull his arm to the back of the sofa and tie it there, because in the process her nipples brushed against his cheeks, his eyes, his open mouth. He took advantage of every opportunity. But when she finished her work and stood back, he realized that now he could only have what she chose to give him.

As if to underline his helplessness, she took hold of the robe's lapels and pulled them back. Then she let the red garment slide from her shoulders and puddle on the floor at her feet.

Lust raged through him. He wanted to slide his hands from her slender ankles up her long legs, pause to stroke the moist lips between her thighs, then continue up her flat belly to fondle her full breasts. If ever a woman was made to be touched, it was this one. By standing naked in front of him when he couldn't do any of those things, she'd created a sweet torture different from anything he'd experienced.

"Ever let a woman tie you up before?" she asked in a tone dripping with sexuality.

"No." He wouldn't have allowed it, not with the women he'd known. He wouldn't have trusted them that far.

"How does it feel?" She ran her hands from her stomach up to her breasts, lifting them in her cupped hands before releasing them so they settled gently back into place.

"Wild." His voice was thick with need. "I want you so much I hurt." He thought of asking if she'd ever tied a man up before, but if the answer was yes, he didn't really want to hear it.

"I'd hate for you to be in pain." Her gaze locked with his, she came toward him again, slipping between his knees and the edge of the coffee table. Then she sank down in front of him and licked her lips.

He moaned. He wasn't proud of that, but a guy could

only take so much. Talk about building the suspense. The blood roared in his ears as he waited for her to reveal an erection so hard and hot he was surprised he hadn't caught the towel on fire.

"What do you want?" she asked quietly.

He gritted his teeth. "I think you know exactly what I want."

"Then tell me…exactly."

He began to shake in the grip of a desire that dwarfed anything he'd ever known. "I want you—" he paused to swallow "—to unfasten this towel."

Soft fingers tugged at the place where he'd wrapped it around his hips and tucked in the end. His breath caught and sweat dampened his skin. Slowly she opened the towel, and as the soft terry tickled his rigid penis, he moaned again.

Laying the two ends of the towel against the sofa, she contemplated the sight he presented. "I do think you're ready."

"Could…be." His wrists hurt, and he figured out he was straining against the silk tie. He forced himself to relax against the cushions, but there was no way his buddy would relax until she… Thinking about what she would do next made his ears buzz and his head swim.

"Now what do you want?" she asked.

He felt as if someone had him by the throat.

"Tell me," she coaxed.

"I want you…to touch me."

"How?"

Oh, God, he would come right there, before she ever laid a hand on him. He fought the urge. "With your hands." He swallowed. "Touch me with your hands."

"Like this?" Curving her fingers loosely around him, she stroked him from base to aching tip. A drop of moisture gathered there.

"Yes. And…I want you to use…your mouth."

"Ah." Her smile was lazy, the gleam in her eyes filled with sensuality. "I thought you might enjoy that." She leaned sideways and reached for something sitting on the floor beside the sofa. "So I've decided to add a little extra touch."

He stared at the jar in her hand. "Honey?" he croaked.

"Mmm. Do you like honey?"

"Uh." He was speechless as she brought the jar close to his stiff penis and began to tip it.

"I like honey," she murmured.

A small ribbon of gold liquid oozed from the lip of the jar and headed downward. He held his breath. *Warm.* Oh, God, it was warm, and felt like…like he'd already come and his warm juices were sliding down his quivering shaft. He groaned in desperation, sure he would erupt at any moment.

She set the jar on the floor. "I wonder how you taste…"

"Erica…" He began to pant and pull against the silk tie. "Erica…please…"

"Want me to lick you clean?"

"Yes, oh, yes. Please…I can't…hold on much… longer."

"Poor baby." She leaned forward, her breasts touching his knees. For one agonizing moment she hesitated, looking up at him with sparkling eyes. "Let me help you." Then she lowered her head and began to lick him with deliberate swipes of her tongue.

He'd never wanted to come so much in his life. But he had to wait, had to be in her mouth when he finally let go. Time became meaningless as he delayed, delayed and then…she stopped.

Reaching behind her, she picked up her glass of club soda and took a sip. Through eyes glazed with passion, he watched her swish the liquid in her mouth without swallowing. Slowly she put down the glass and leaned toward him.

He cried out as she closed her lips over the tip of his penis and began to suck gently. The club soda fizzed and he thought he would go out of his mind with pleasure. At last she paused, swallowed and took all of him in one swooping motion.

The last thread of his control snapped, and he surged upward. As the convulsions racked him and he moaned with the intense pleasure, she pressed him gently back to the cushions as she drank the liquid fountaining from his body. She swallowed, then swallowed again. Hollowing her cheeks, she continued to suck, milking him of every last drop.

At last he lay sprawled against the cushions—eyes closed, semiconscious and quivering from the impact of an orgasm he would never forget. Vaguely he realized she'd untied his wrists because his arms flopped down as if they were made of straw. He would have believed they were, and that nothing remained of him but a hollow husk of a man with no bones, no blood and, most of all, no brain.

She crawled up on the sofa next to him, and when she drew his head down and pillowed it on her breasts, he sighed in relief. It was exactly where he wanted to be, but he didn't have the strength to make it happen.

Stroking his hair, she leaned down and placed an almost sisterly kiss on his cheek. "I'd intended to make you leave now," she murmured.

He groaned, knowing that if she wanted him to leave, she'd have to have him hauled out on a stretcher.

"But I don't have the heart."

"Good." He didn't have the ability to question, only to accept. "Good," he murmured again, and snuggled closer.

She sighed. "Ah, Dustin, I don't know what to do about you."

He wrapped his arms around her and closed his eyes. "This is fine."

She sighed again. "Easy for you to say."

14

ERICA HELD a sleeping Dustin and stared at the flame of the blue pillar candle on the coffee table. The breeze from the air conditioner made the flame dance and the candle burn erratically. Unless she moved it, the wax would break through and spill down the side.

Usually she was more cautious and made sure the candles weren't in a draft. Well, caution hadn't been her strong suit lately, and now she'd landed herself in a real mess. In an attempt to show Dustin who was the boss, sexually, she'd outfoxed herself. She hadn't realized that his surrender would touch her so deeply.

He'd willingly made himself vulnerable, more vulnerable than she'd ever been with him. If their positions had been reversed and he'd wanted to tie her up, she'd never have agreed to it. Too risky. But he'd agreed. He'd trusted her.

And by trusting her, he'd started working his way into her heart. That didn't mean she planned to throw away her dreams or make him a part of her life. But now it would be harder to let him go.

She hadn't meant to have him drift off to sleep in her arms, either. Having sex with a man was one thing. Holding him while he slept seemed far more intimate, and the longer she stayed here doing that, the closer she and Dustin would bond.

Time to shake him awake and send him back to his hotel. Yet she hesitated, knowing he must be exhausted. If she pushed him out the door and forced him to drive, he might fall asleep at the wheel.

The very fact that she was worried demonstrated how totally screwed she was. Instead of claiming her sexuality and then cutting all ties with Dustin, she was cuddling him and allowing him to sleep over. Yet he was the same guy who had probably joked with the security guard about the incident in the back seat and had most definitely addressed her as *babe* in front of that same security guard.

She had trouble holding on to her anger about the comment, though. He'd only been a guy marking his territory. Not that she was *territory* to be marked, but in Dustin's world… She stopped stroking his hair as an unbelievable thought occurred to her.

Was Dustin falling for *her?*

If so, like most guys he'd be the last to know. He'd just stumble along, thinking this was all about sex, with maybe a little business thrown in. But if in the process he'd begun losing his heart in the same way she'd begun losing hers, then she had the power to hurt him.

Correction, they had the power to hurt each other. Saying goodbye to him wouldn't be a picnic for her, either, but no way could she see herself permanently attached to Dustin Ramsey, a product of the establishment. And she was all wrong for him, too, but of course he wouldn't see that. He'd let lust blind him to their obvious differences and assume they'd get along fine. It was a common story.

Because he was clueless, she'd have to do the thinking for both of them. The first step was making sure they didn't have sex again. Once they stopped having sex, Dustin might begin to see how unsuitable they were.

Cuddling naked on the sofa was going in the wrong direction, but that could be fixed easily enough. She'd just slip out of his arms and ease him down to the cushions.

Then she'd go into her bedroom and put on those ugly pajamas of hers and bring a blanket to cover him up.

Slipping away from him turned out to be tougher than she'd thought. The minute she moved, his arms closed around her. Thinking he was doing it in his sleep, she gently tried to ease away, but his grip tightened even more.

"Where're you going?" he mumbled.

She checked and his eyes were still closed, but he wasn't asleep. "To get a blanket."

He nuzzled her breasts, his lips soft against her skin, but his arms were like a vise. "Are you cold?"

"No. Yes." She didn't know the right answer. "Dustin—"

"If you're cold, you should have said so." He rubbed his cheek against her breasts.

"You were asleep." She registered that his cheek was smooth, and yet she distinctly remembered feeling a little stubble when they'd made out in the truck. He must have used her razor while he was in the shower. She didn't want to know that he'd been that considerate and eager to please.

His eyes opened. "And now I'm not asleep."

Okay, he wasn't asleep. He'd had a little nap, and now this was the moment when she should suggest that he get dressed and head back to his hotel. "Dustin, maybe it would be a good idea if—"

"I'll bet I can warm you up."

"I think—" She gasped as he moved with amazing speed. One second she was sitting beside him on the sofa. The next she was stretched out on the cushions beneath him. "How did you do that?"

His grin was full of self-satisfaction. "Wrestled in the off-season." Then he kissed her.

That's what she got for fooling around with a jock. And, damn it, now she had to fight her own response. Nobody kissed like Dustin. Nobody. When you threw in the added attraction of his dynamite body poised over hers and his talented hands caressing her here, there—oh, especially there—he was lethal.

She automatically wrapped her arms around him as if she'd been programmed to do that. She might never get over the thrill of running her hands up a back so sculpted and solid. Feeling those muscles flexing beneath her fingers stirred her in ways she was embarrassed to admit. It seemed she was susceptible to beefcake, after all.

After stroking her breasts and arousing each nipple to aching awareness, he slipped his hand down between her legs. She knew what her condition was, what her condition always seemed to be with this man. She was, once again, embarrassingly wet and ready for him.

Lifting his mouth from hers, he nibbled at her lower lip. "Getting warmer?"

"I think you should go back to your hotel." She caught her breath as he shoved two fingers deep. Then he found her G-spot and began working his magic.

There was laughter in his voice. "Now?"

"Soon." But she had a feeling it was too late. Much too late.

"You tell me when." He used his thumb to rub her pleasure point. "I wouldn't want to overstay my welcome."

"After…after this."

He leaned down and ran his tongue around the inside of her ear. "After I make you come? Then I should leave?"

"Yes." She began to pant as he thrust his fingers rhythmically into her drenched channel.

"After I make you come this time? Or the time after that?"

She groaned. How dare he taunt her with an image of nonstop pleasure? "No fair."

"I never promised to be fair." He moved his fingers faster. "How's that?"

"G-good." Incredible. She was nearly there.

"I thought so. Now, tell me," he whispered into her ear. "Tell me when you want me to leave."

"Not...yet."

He chuckled, his breath warm on her neck. "No, I wouldn't leave you like this, lifting your hips for more, making little sounds deep in your throat, quivering, wanting...ah, that's good. Take what you need, Erica. That's it. There we are. Now. *Now.*"

His soft command pulled her response from her, and in a rush of sensation she came, shuddering and moaning as he stroked her. She continued to tremble even after he drew his hand free. Dazed, her body humming as if hooked up to an electrical circuit, she listened to him rustle around with something on the coffee table. She could guess what he was doing, and she tried to remember why she'd wanted to avoid this very thing, having sex with Dustin.

Before she could figure it out, he lifted her hips and pushed inside her, locking their bodies together. And heaven help her, she loved the feeling. Logic told her that he was all wrong for her, but he felt so very right.

"Erica."

She opened her eyes and found him gazing down at her.

"I was really dumb to call you *babe* tonight."

She didn't want to talk about it. She only wanted him to make love to her. *Make love to her.* Apparently she'd slipped over the line and what they shared was no longer just *having sex.*

His smile was gentle. "It won't happen again."

"I know."

He began a slow, easy rhythm. "I was embarrassed that you had the keys."

"Yeah." She could really learn to like this lazy kind of

loving. "And I was mad because you were joking with Manny about us having sex."

He stilled. "No, I wasn't."

"No?" She gazed up into his eyes. You had to believe a man when he looked at you that way, especially when he was locked deep inside you.

"No. I'm sorry if you thought that. We talked about the Cowboys."

"Oh." She'd staged her entire bondage scene in reaction to a misunderstanding. "I'm...sorry I called you chauvinistic. You're not."

"No."

She pressed against the girth of him, enjoying the tension building within her. "I wouldn't have...I wouldn't have tied you up if I'd known you were talking about the Cowboys."

His blue eyes glowed. "Then I'm glad you didn't know," he said, his voice husky. "I loved it."

"You know what I love?"

"What?"

"What you were doing before. But now you've stopped."

"Mmm. Then maybe I'd better start doing it again." He eased back and pushed home. "Because I like it, too."

"Good." With every thrust she became more convinced this feeling was rare. She might hunt for years and never find a man who brought out this kind of response in her. "*Very* good."

"The best." The casual sound of his voice matched the unhurried motion of his hips.

She would have thought that the slow pace wouldn't do much for her. To the contrary, each smooth stroke tightened the spring within her another notch as another climax hovered near.

"That whole deal with the honey, and then your

mouth… I thought I'd keep coming forever," he murmured. "And afterward, I was so wiped out." The gradual slide of his penis continued its steady pace. His breathing stayed measured and even.

But hers didn't. She was starting to gasp for breath. He must have located exactly the right spot to apply friction, because she was going to come, again. "I thought…you'd be out for the night."

He laughed. "Not likely. A healthy twenty-eight-year-old male, naked with a woman like you, is not going to be sidelined that easily."

"I can tell."

"But you did give me some stamina for this next round. That hair-trigger reaction is gone for now. I feel as if I can do this for a long time."

"And I'm…" She gulped for air. "I can't believe that I'm…"

"Good. I love that you're going to come again. I love watching your eyes get dark, and your skin get all rosy, and then you lick your lips. Did you know you lick your lips right before it happens?"

She shook her head, her heart thundering, her body quaking. She couldn't seem to drag her gaze from his. The light in his eyes fueled her excitement almost as much as the thrust of his penis.

"There. You just did it."

Sure enough, she erupted, crying out and rising to meet those firm, steady strokes. He didn't change his rhythm as the shock waves rolled over her, and as she lay panting and looking dazedly into his eyes, he continued the long, easy thrusts. She felt as if her body had liquified into a warm, creamy substance that parted silkily before his smooth invasion, closed around him, then released him only to welcome him back.

Nothing existed except the glide of his penis—insistent,

arousing, coaxing still another unbelievable climax from the depths of her womb. But this time, as she felt the tension build, she heard a subtle change in his breathing. Then she felt, very slightly, a difference in his thrust.

She cupped his bottom in both hands. "Your turn?" she murmured.

"I wanted to go on until morning, give you as many orgasms as you could take." He swallowed. "I can't. When I look down at you and watch your breasts shimmy, and then I look down lower, to where I'm pushing into you, I...I can't...wait."

"Then come," she said, urging him closer.

"Will you?"

"Yes."

His muscles bunched as he drove into her, faster and faster. Yet he continued to look into her eyes this time. He gasped. "Erica...oh, yes...Erica!" With one last shove his body grew rigid. Only then, as the shudders began, did he close his eyes.

Her own climax surprised her, rising up and mingling with his. Her moans joined his as she wrapped him in her arms and held on as they both quivered in the aftermath.

When he finally sank down and rested his head in the curve of her neck, she stroked his back and closed her eyes, too.

He sighed and nestled closer. "Want me to go back to the hotel, now?" he murmured.

"No, that's okay."

"Are you sure?"

She caressed his warm, damp skin. "I'm sure. It's too late, now, anyway."

SOMETIME AFTERWARD Dustin managed to leave the sofa long enough to take care of the used condom. When he returned, Erica was asleep. Deciding the sofa wasn't the best place to spend the rest of the night, he scooped her up and carried her into the bedroom, where he tucked her under the covers. Then he slid in after her, gathered her close and went immediately to sleep himself.

He awoke to sunlight and the shower running. By the time he'd thought about joining her and swung his feet to the floor, she was back in the bedroom, one towel around her body and the other around her hair.

She glanced at him and hurried toward her dresser. "I'm late."

"And good morning to you, too."

"You don't understand. I have to pick up the newsletters and get them in the mail." She jerked open a drawer and pulled out underwear. "If I don't get them in the mail on time, they won't get to the subscribers by Saturday, and Henry won't have his review."

Dustin glanced at the radio alarm on her bedside table. Nearly ten o'clock. They'd slept in, all right. Great sex could do that to you. "Is there anything I can help you with?" he asked.

"No, but thanks for asking." She whipped off the towel and started putting on her panties.

He glanced away, but he was too late to save himself from the beginnings of an erection. "Would I be in your way if I grabbed a quick shower?"

"No, but I need to be out of here in less than ten minutes. Can you be ready to go by then?"

"Sure." He headed for the shower while his mind scrambled to find the best course of action. He didn't want to leave Dallas without establishing that he'd be back, and that he and Erica would pick up where they left off.

He didn't see how she could object. They'd had a helluva time together, even considering the rocky parts. As he finished in the shower, he heard the whine of a hair dryer. He stepped out and found her in front of the bathroom mirror dressed in shorts and a snug red tee.

She was using a brush and the dryer on her hair. He noticed how her breasts lifted beneath the shirt when she raised her arms, and how they quivered as she manipulated both instruments at the same time. He could spend quite a bit of his time watching the Erica show and never be bored.

The coziness of sharing a bathroom struck him for the first time in his life. He'd never thought he'd care much for getting in each other's way first thing in the morning. To his surprise, he liked toweling off while Erica dried her hair. He liked being surrounded by the scent of her soap, her shampoo and her perfume, with all the associations those aromas had for him.

Being there while she got ready for her day made him feel as if he knew something about Erica that everyone didn't know. He was an insider. That made him smile. Yeah, a *real* insider. That long, lazy session on the sofa had made him feel exceptionally tuned in. He'd never experienced a connection quite like that before.

The previous night, he'd left his clothes hanging on a hook on the back of the bathroom door, so he was able to grab them and start putting them on without leaving the area. He continued to watch Erica style her hair, although she seemed to be making a point of avoiding his gaze in the mirror.

He wondered if she might be bothered by his nakedness in the same way he'd been bothered by hers. That would be nice, and it would certainly help the cause.

She switched off the dryer and finger-combed her hair into place.

"Looks good." He shoved his arms into the sleeves of his shirt.

"Thanks." She pulled open a drawer next to the sink and took out a bunch of stuff that looked related to makeup.

Pouring a small amount of creamy beige liquid into her palm, she began smoothing it on her face.

He thought of the warm honey she'd used on his penis. Next time he might try the warm honey trick on her. She didn't need flavor enhancement—she was plenty delicious all by herself—but he wanted her to experience the sensation of honey oozing over her as if she'd already climaxed. It had been wilder than wild.

She leaned toward the mirror and parted her lips as she concentrated on the mascara brush in her hand. Woman always opened their mouths a little bit when putting on mascara, he'd noticed. Right now he wanted to walk over there and take advantage of her open mouth by sliding his tongue inside. But she wouldn't appreciate that, so he didn't.

He zipped up his jeans and sat on the closed toilet lid to pull on his boots. "Maybe after you mail the newsletter we can have lunch."

She paused, the mascara wand in midair. Then she lowered the wand and turned to him. "Dustin, I hate to say this, but—"

"Whoa." He stood. "I'm not crazy about sentences that begin with *I hate to say this, but.* If you hate to say it, save yourself some grief and don't." He couldn't believe she'd dump him now, but she sure looked like that was on her mind.

Trouble lurked in her gray eyes. "I've had a great time being with you. I think you know that."

"I'd have to be blind and deaf not to know it. Listen, Erica, I'm not asking for a personal commitment. I'm not even asking you to reconsider the franchise, although I wish you would. If you're too busy to have lunch today, I'm fine with that. But I'd love to drive back here weekend after next and spend some time with you."

"You mean have sex with me."

That was certainly part of his plan, but he didn't like the sound of it when she laid it out like that. Yet he wasn't sure exactly what to say, instead.

"That is what you mean, so don't think you have to deny it." She screwed the cap back on her mascara. "And there's nothing wrong with that. I'm just tapped out on the sex-for-sex's sake. Been there, done that for the past forty-eight hours."

"Okay, I get your point. We've probably overdone it. You don't want another two days of nonstop sex, and I can understand that." Actually, he couldn't. He'd love another two days of nonstop sex with Erica. But maybe she was the kind of woman who liked her lust in smaller doses. "We'll do other things—go dancing, see a show, whatever you like. What do you like?" How strange that he didn't know, considering how intimate they'd been.

"Art galleries."

He did his best to look enthusiastic. "Then we'll go to art galleries."

"Dustin, you're not into that. You'd be forcing yourself for my sake."

He shrugged. "Maybe I'd learn something." If he had to wander around staring at pictures for a few hours in order to get the warm honey and bondage treatment, he considered the price more than reasonable.

"More likely you'd be hideously bored."

"So name something else."

"The Dallas Symphony. And don't you dare say you'd love to take me, because I saw the expression on your face when I said the word *symphony*. Dustin, we're not compatible! You're into making money and I'm not. You're into guy stuff like NASCAR and football. You eat meat all the time. You probably don't even recycle."

"I do, so!" When he thought of it, which wasn't always. But he'd been known to toss his beer can into the recycling container at the county fair. "And we're damned compatible in bed!" On in the back seat, or on the sofa.

"We're back to having sex for the sake of sex. We've done that already. And it was terrific. But carrying it beyond a couple of nights seems like a very shallow exercise in self-gratification."

He winced. Put that way, he sounded like a superficial jerk only interested in getting laid. Maybe he was. Maybe Erica outclassed him, as he'd always suspected. That was the general message she was giving him, whether she realized it or not.

Her gaze softened and she walked toward him. "That was too harsh. You're a very considerate lover, and I'll never forget what we've shared." She cupped his face in both hands. "Thank you, Dustin." Then she kissed him gently.

With a groan he gathered her close. He might not measure up to her standards, but he couldn't help wanting her, anyway. He'd thought good sex would convince her to let him hang around, but apparently she needed more. He was willing to attempt pleasing her in other areas, but she was already convinced he couldn't do it. She'd indicated she didn't even want him to try.

But he could make her body hum, and she couldn't deny that. As he plunged his tongue into her sweet mouth, she wrapped her arms around his neck and arched her pelvis into his. He cupped her bottom and fit his erection into the space between her thighs. When she moaned, he slipped his hands under the hem of her shorts and squeezed her sweet, silk-clad cheeks.

As he was beginning to consider propping her up on the bathroom vanity and unzipping her shorts, she broke away from him and staggered backward. "I can't do this. I have to go."

Hands on his hips, he drew in a ragged breath. "So you

don't want to continue this, then?'' He gulped in more air. ''Because in spite of what you said, I don't think you're *tapped out* on having sex with me. I think you still want it as much as I do.''

Her smile was sad. ''As I said before, just because I want it doesn't mean it's good for me.'' She cleared her throat. ''I never gave you the information on the organic brewery or the water-filtering company. I'll send all that to you if you still want it.''

''I still want it. And I still want you. If you change your mind about…about anything, you have my number in that envelope of franchise stuff.'' Then he left before he lost all dignity and started to beg.

15

ERICA STOOD completely still until she heard her apartment door open and close. Then she touched her fingers to her mouth and closed her eyes. What had she done? He'd been gone two minutes and she already felt as if someone had stolen a part of her.

But continuing this sexual relationship would end in disaster eventually. She could choose to deal with it now, when she only had forty-eight hours of Dustin to get over, or deal with it much later, when the cost would be enormous. That last time they'd made love—and that had been the right term, even if Dustin wouldn't have used it—she'd known the connection was becoming too strong.

She had herself to blame for that. Inviting him back up to the apartment after the incident with the security guard had been a mistake. She'd only dug herself in deeper. First she'd stripped him of all his defenses, and then she'd discovered he hadn't deserved her aggressive sexual treatment. Oh, yes, he'd liked it, but that was beside the point.

She'd uncovered the tender, vulnerable part of Dustin Ramsey, the part that would cause her to fall in love with him if she didn't watch herself. She had to prevent that if she intended to proceed with any of her goals. She might not even be living in Texas six months from now.

For the time being, she had a newsletter to mail, and a life to lead. Dustin had only been a moment of madness, a fantastic roller-coaster ride that was over. If she felt a little dizzy and queasy, that was only natural.

BEFORE HEADING HOME to his condo or checking in with his new secretary, Dustin drove to Jennifer and Ryan Madison's house. He'd spent the hours between Dallas and Midland considering his options, and they were precious few. The bottom line was that he couldn't lose track of Erica. With Jennifer on the job, that wouldn't happen.

Reason dictated that he should forget Erica and get on with the task of running Ramsey Enterprises. But without Erica, he felt adrift. He hadn't decided what the hell to do about that. She'd said she didn't want him around, but that story changed the minute he started kissing her.

She was right about one thing, though. They couldn't spend all their time in bed, and she was convinced that out of bed they'd never make it as a couple. Dustin wasn't even sure he wanted to make it as a couple. His preference would have been a little sex, a little business, a little friendship and no forecast of exactly where that would take them. Wait and see.

Erica wasn't a wait-and-see kind of woman, obviously. If a guy didn't fit her vision of the future, fit it *exactly*, then he was out on his ear. Dustin had spent the first part of his drive fuming about that, but hours cruising along a hot Texas highway eventually calmed him down.

He couldn't see himself charging back to Dallas with a ring in his pocket. A guy had to work up to something like that, and besides, she wouldn't accept a ring from him. She'd liked the sex, but beyond that she wasn't much interested.

Funny how things worked out. He'd gone to Dallas to prove to her that he was a stud. She believed that, now, but that was the *only* thing she believed about him. Maybe he'd overstated his case.

Parking in the driveway of Jennifer and Ryan's spacious home, Ryan made the hot trip from his air-conditioned truck to their front door in record time and waited, sweating, for entrance into the cool interior. When they didn't answer the door right away, he hoped he hadn't interrupted dinner. He'd been so focused on talking with Jennifer that he hadn't thought about that.

Finally Ryan came to the door, and Dustin noticed the strangest thing. Ryan's shirt was buttoned up wrong, and it wasn't completely tucked into his jeans. He was barefoot, too, and seemed slightly out of breath.

Dustin's recent escapades helped him guess what had been going on before the doorbell rang. He grinned. "Sorry, man. I can come back."

"No, no." Ryan looked sheepish as he tucked his shirt in a little better. "Jennifer would kill me if I turned away a client because we were—"

"I should've called." Dustin envied Ryan at that moment, even if the guy had been interrupted in the middle of a good time. At least Ryan knew he'd have another chance. That's how it was when you were married. Dustin had never considered that angle before.

"Not a problem. Come in." Ryan stood back from the door.

"I feel like an inconsiderate jerk. I didn't even think about the cell phone. I just drove over here on my way back from Dallas."

"Hey, it's a reasonable time to be doing that. It's just that Annie was sleeping, so—" A high, thin wail echoed through the house. "And now she's not."

Dustin was astounded by the volume. "How does such a little kid make so much noise?"

"Baby monitor. We have one in her room, and speakers all over the house, because we never know where we'll be."

And they still liked to have spontaneous sex. Dustin figured if he were married to Erica, not that such a thing would ever happen in a million years, he'd always want to have spontaneous sex. He took note of the baby monitor idea.

"So how was Dallas?" Ryan asked.

"Hot." Dustin thought that covered all the bases.

"Yeah, the whole state's in the middle of a heat wave. We don't take Annie out much, and Jennifer's constantly dabbing ointment on her so she won't get a rash."

"How's Annie?" Dustin wasn't much into babies, but with new parents, you needed to ask.

Ryan's whole expression changed. His smile was tender and his face glowed. "Awesome," he said in a tone Dustin might have used while standing inside the Brickyard at Indianapolis. "You have no idea until you get a kid of your own, but Annie's the best thing that's ever happened to me, except for meeting Jen, of course."

Dustin listened as Ryan continued talking about what had obviously become his favorite subject. Although Dustin would have thought he'd be bored, he found himself following right along and even thinking that maybe he was missing something because he didn't have a kid of his own. First you had to locate someone who would like to be the mother of that kid, though. Erica didn't want to be a mother. She wanted to save the world.

"Hey, Dustin!" Jennifer started down the stairs carrying a now-peaceful little cherub sucking on a pacifier and wearing only a diaper.

"Hi, Jennifer. Sorry to barge in on you like this." Annie's diaper had little ducks printed on it, and for some reason, that made Dustin's heart lurch. Her dark hair stood out in tiny wispy curls, and she had the biggest brown eyes Dustin had ever seen.

"That's okay." Jennifer handed the baby to Ryan. "Would you see if she'll drink a little juice while I talk with Dustin?"

"Absolutely." Ryan took Annie as if accepting the

crown that would make him the king of England. Then he nuzzled the baby's tummy. "How's my princess? How's daddy's pretty girl?"

Dustin took it all in. So this was what happened when sex and love came together—a beautiful little girl like Annie. Instead of looking ridiculous talking nonsense to a baby, Ryan looked…nice. Dustin wouldn't mind having a chubby little kid to nuzzle. But he wasn't married. Not even engaged.

"Come on in the office," Jennifer said. "And forgive the mess. I'm in the middle of opening an outside office and I really have to hire another detective soon so I can catch up on the paperwork. The agency can't function with me doing everything."

"I almost hate to be bringing you another job, then."

She waved a hand as they walked down the hall and into her office. "Don't worry about that. I want the business, especially now that I'll be paying rent on an office."

"So you won't work from home anymore?" Dustin couldn't help thinking about Erica's newsletter. If she'd make a career out of that, she could continue to work at home. So much could be handled over the Internet these days. She could work at home, have a baby…oh, God, he was really in fantasyland, now.

"Whenever I can, I'll stay home. But when meeting with clients, I need another office." Jennifer sat at her cluttered desk and motioned Dustin into the chair beside it. "Oh, wait." She grabbed a squeaky toy before he ended up sitting on it. "Case in point. Sorry about that."

"Don't apologize," Dustin said. "I think how you're managing everything is very cool."

Jennifer smiled. "It will be, once I get more personnel and the new office is up and running. Now, what can I do for you?"

"First of all, I told you that you could trash the remaining issues of *Dateline: Dallas* while you let the subscription run out.''

"I know you did, but I'll confess I plan to keep reading them before I pitch them. Even though I'm not single and I don't live in Dallas, I love that advice column. She has a good thing going, there."

"Yeah, I know." He saw no point in telling Jennifer that the newsletter might be abandoned at any time. "Anyway, instead of throwing them away, would you send them to me? And let me know immediately if they stop coming, or you get a notice saying publication will be suspended."

"I can't imagine why she'd do that, unless she can't afford to keep it up. She should look for some backers and expand the concept. It's a dynamite idea."

"I completely agree. But she's not interested in that, so she may give up the newsletter in the near future. If she does, I want to know about it. And also, if you could...kind of keep tabs on her. Nothing heavy-duty, but just...keep tabs.''

Jennifer's gaze was sympathetic. "I can arrange for that."

"What will it cost me?" Dustin hated to have to ask, but he was trying to hold expenses down.

Jennifer named a figure, and he nodded. He could justify that for a few months, at least until he came to grips with this situation and either thought of a plan or gave up. At the moment, when he felt hollow inside and a million miles away from Dallas, giving up didn't seem like an option.

ERICA SPENT SATURDAY NIGHT at Henry's restaurant with Denise and Josie. Technically it was Erica's turn to be the designated driver, but Josie stepped into the rotation because both she and Denise agreed that Erica needed to get sloshed on organic beer and forget about Dustin.

Unfortunately, Josie's generous offer went to waste. No

matter how much beer Erica drank, she couldn't totally forget about Dustin. Although it was great for Henry when the restaurant reviewer herself showed up, Erica was swamped with memories of the lunch she'd shared with Dustin. Consequently she drank more than she should have and stayed out extremely late.

She didn't even stir from her bed until nearly one in the afternoon. Her mouth tasted as if she'd been licking the inside of a garbage can and her head felt as if somebody was in there putting up drywall with a nail gun. But she needed to start work on the next issue of the newsletter. Sunday was the beginning of her week, and she was already behind.

Three cups of coffee and a couple of ibuprofen later, she was shaky but able to face the idea of turning on her computer. She might not have the energy to start on the feature story, but she could edit a few letters for her column. She was surprised by how many had accumulated since she'd last checked this e-mail address. She opened the first one and started to read. Oh, dear. The guy wanted to start a correspondence. She simply couldn't do that, but she'd finish reading the letter before deleting it.

Dear Erica,
I wrote to you last week and signed myself Nervous
Virgin. Something I didn't mention in my letter, be-
cause I didn't want the pity vote, is that I'm in a
wheelchair.

Erica gasped and pressed her hand against her chest. Maybe she'd have to break her rule and write back to this guy. A wheelchair. Thank God Dustin had been around to soften the edge of her sometimes wicked prose. If she hadn't made fabulous love to him before answering this letter she might have said something flip to this guy. She'd like to think she wouldn't have, but it was possible.

I'm writing to you this morning to report that I had a wonderful night with a beautiful woman, and, just like you said, she considers it a privilege to be my first. Without your encouragement I might have been scared to take a chance. I can't thank you enough. Your advice changed my world.
Sincerely, No Longer Nervous or a Virgin
  P.S. I shared your comments with some wheelchair-bound friends who are in the same situation. If you're disabled at a young age, it can be a real problem.

Erica stared at the screen for several minutes. She'd had fun with her column, but she'd always considered it sort of a lighthearted, racy piece of entertainment. Nothing serious. Yet she'd changed this young man's world. That would take some thinking about.

Saving the letter to answer later, she opened the next one.

Dear Erica,
I'm not writing to be included in your column, but to thank you. My friend shared your comments about being a virgin with me. In a way it's better he didn't mention the wheelchair. Your comments work great with or without that factor. But I am in a wheelchair, and I am also a virgin. Thanks to your perspective, I don't plan to be one much longer. You may have no idea what a service you've done.
Sincerely, Rejuvenated

Erica's headache vanished in the glow of knowing she'd made a difference to at least two men who had obviously needed to hear what she'd said. Or maybe they'd simply needed to hear her say it, because they could have gotten the same message elsewhere. But *Dateline: Dallas* was considered a trendy newsletter that young singles had begun to trust for restaurants and attractions. Apparently they trusted her sexual advice, too.

Elated and yet humbled, she continued to read letters and found six more from wheelchair-bound men, some who had borrowed the newsletter from a friend of a friend. Apparently Nervous Virgin had told some people, who had told some other people.

Interspersed with those letters were others from both men and women who were also virgins and now felt better about seeking that first sexual partner. Erica knew there were still people out there who treasured virginity and planned to wait until they married, but for most singles over twenty, being a virgin could develop into an embarrassing handicap. A sign of the times, perhaps, but true from the standpoint of Erica and most of her friends.

Her phone rang and she jumped. Every damned time she heard the noise, she thought it might be Dustin, and this was no exception. She forced herself to walk slowly to the kitchen and pick up the cordless receiver. Clearing her throat, she pushed the talk button. "Hello?"

"Are you alive?" Denise asked.

"Yeah, barely." Erica felt guilty for being disappointed. Denise was a great friend and Erica was glad to hear from her. Dustin wouldn't call, anyway. She'd practically told him to get lost.

"I've never seen you drink so much," Denise said. "Are you sure sending Virginity Guy away was such a good idea?"

No. "Yes. It wouldn't have worked out. But Denise, I have the most amazing thing to tell you. Remember the letter from Nervous Virgin? Last night you and Josie were talking about it.''

"Sure I do. He sounded sweet. Why? Gonna give me his phone number?''

Erica forced herself to sit on the sofa while she talked to Denise. For the first day after Dustin left she'd avoided it, but now she was determined to sit there. She couldn't stop using a major piece of furniture because of its associations with a former lover.

"I don't have his phone number," she told Denise, "and you know I couldn't give it to you even if I did have it. But he wrote back, and guess what? He's in a wheelchair."

"Wow. That puts a new spin on things—no pun intended.''

"I know! And there's more.'' Erica described the rush of letters, all of them praising her comments.

"That's great," Denise said. "Really great. Y'know, this newsletter of yours is changing lives.''

"Kind of scary, isn't it?''

"Maybe, unless that's what you want to do in the first place.''

The comment shocked Erica into temporary silence. "I'm not trying to do that," she said at last. "The newsletter's one of those crazy ideas that I decided to try for the fun of it until a real job came along.''

"Define a real job.''

Erica knew that one by heart. "Where you can take satisfaction in what you're doing because it makes the world a better place.''

"Case closed," Denise said.

"Denise! So I helped a few people. That's not much of a contribution.''

"You might want to ask them how they feel about that. I think they'd disagree with you.''

"Yeah, but—''

"Never mind. I know you, and you have to think everything to death. Want to go out for Italian tonight with Josie and me?"

"Yes, but no drinking."

"Not a drop. We all have work to do. You had your wild night to forget your problems, so now you have to go cold turkey. By the way, have you heard anything from Virginity Guy?"

"No, but I told you I wouldn't."

"Just asking. See you about six. We'll meet at Josie's."

"Sounds good. See you then." Erica pressed the disconnect button and replaced the receiver before walking back to her computer. When Dustin had said her newsletter provided a service, she hadn't been willing to listen. But now Denise was saying the same thing, and Denise had no ulterior motive other than wanting Erica to stay in Dallas.

Erica's head began to ache again. If she really considered sticking with the newsletter, then Dustin's idea of franchising to other cities was the right thing to do. Dustin's motive had been increased profits, but Erica didn't care about that. If the newsletter helped people, then she wanted to help more than one city's worth.

But she didn't know how in the world she'd be able to work with Dustin on a regular basis. The sexual temptation was huge and overshadowed their differences enough she might make a serious mistake and think they had a future. Franchising without Dustin's help seemed unfair, though, because it had been his idea. He should share in whatever rewards came along.

Because she had no answer to her latest problem, she decided to read a few more letters. So far they'd all been thanking her for the answer to Nervous Virgin. She needed some letters asking for advice or she wouldn't have a column this week.

The next one wasn't that kind.

Dear Sweet Erica,
I'm lying here in bed alone with nothing for company
but my laptop...

Heart beating wildly, Erica scrolled up to make sure the
e-mail was from Dustin and not some sleazoid who'd decided to write her an X-rated fan letter. Yes, Dustin was
writing the X-rated fan letter.

For all I know you'll delete this the minute you find
out it's from me....

Not bloody likely.

But I had to reach out and touch you, even if I'm only
touching the keys so that I can write you this letter.
Just thinking of you, I'm getting hard, which poses
something of a problem with a laptop. So far the
weight of the computer is taming my erection, but if
the laptop suddenly flips over onto the bed, I'll know
I'm in trouble....

Erica pressed her fingers to her mouth to hold back a
giggle. Of course the mere mention of his penis brought on
her own response, and she squirmed in her seat.

The laptop is warm like you, but not nearly as soft.
As a masturbation aid it lacks a lot, and besides, you
know how I feel about machines in the bedroom. Still,
I thought lying in bed was the only way to compose
this letter.
 I'm wearing a pair of running shorts because later,
I plan to get some exercise. But while I'm writing to

you I feel naked. Maybe that's because we've stripped
ourselves bare for each other in more ways than one.
I think you know exactly what I mean....

She did, and that was the problem. During sex, especially
the last time, she'd allowed him in, given him a good look
at the real, lusty, uninhibited Erica. She couldn't take it
back. He'd always have that knowledge of her. And she
had the same knowledge of him.

But she was a little surprised that he'd come to the same
conclusion. Maybe she hadn't believed that his thoughts ran
that deep. Shame on her.

Despite that, you seem to think we don't have enough
in common to share any more time together, in or out
of bed. If I understood you right, you think sex is all
we have between us, and powerful though that is, it's
not enough.

So I had an idea. We could e-mail each other for a
while and see if we have anything in common besides
sex. Forgive me if I talk about it, though, because I
can't help myself when I'm thinking of you. You get
me hotter than any woman I've ever known....

She moaned and pounded her fist on the desk. She
wanted Dustin here, and she wanted him here now. Sure,
she could go find her vibrator, but thanks to him, she
wouldn't be satisfied with that anymore.

We need topics of conversation, obviously. If you're
right and we have nothing going for us except sex,
we'll run out of things to say very quickly and that
will settle that. But I've already thought of something
to talk about—world population control.

I'm for it. I support providing birth control infor-
mation to everyone old enough to need it. I use it all

the time myself, except for one glaring exception, when I got so carried away with your hot, wet vagina that I thrust right into you without thinking. Ah, Erica, it was so damn good.

I'll never forget that feeling, but I'll have to wait until I'm ready to make a woman pregnant before I have that feeling again, because I am definitely in favor of population control. Personally I'd like two kids, but that's the limit. Okay, your turn. How do you stand on the question?
Dustin

Adrenaline pumped through her as she contemplated what to do. She could delete his message and ignore any future ones. If the rest turned out to be like this, social discussions laced generously with sex talk, they'd only make her hot and bothered.

Oh, hell, she knew herself. She'd no more be able to ignore his e-mails than toss a bag of trash out the window of her car. If she was right, they would eventually run out of things to say to each other. But in the meantime, she was too fascinated to resist. She hit Reply and began to type.

16

DUSTIN HEADED HOME after a long day at the office, eager for a private moment to read his latest e-mail from Erica and dream up a seductive reply. For three solid weeks he'd engaged in Internet foreplay with her, and he believed he was making progress in his campaign to see her again.

They'd covered many subjects and even he was surprised that they agreed on many things, even the big-ticket items like politics and religion. Sure, he wasn't as informed as she was about some issues and she continued to chide him about that. He loved sports and she didn't. But he thought she was beginning to see that they weren't complete opposites, after all. She was becoming more friendly by the day, more daring in her own e-mails.

He desperately needed her to soften toward him, because he was ready to explode from the exquisite torture of talking with her intimately every day at least once and sometimes twice, all without benefit of any skin-to-skin contact. Yes, he'd resorted to solo sessions in the shower in a bid for survival. They were a poor replacement for sliding into Erica's warm, pulsing vagina, but he required some relief.

His goal was an invitation to Dallas. He thought he might get one soon. In the meantime, he'd thrown himself into Ramsey Enterprises, using his unspent sexual energy to search out promising ventures. Two of the most exciting were the ones Erica had told him about, the organic brewery and the company making water filters. He'd decided she had an instinct for commerce, whether she'd ever admit it or not.

Even more amazing, he'd made a quick trip to Houston and another to San Antonio, and he had ad campaigns in place for both weeklies. The staffs were fired up and he was beginning to think the newspapers might survive. Ironically, Erica might have done him a favor by rejecting his franchise idea. Without that—or her—to lean on, he was forced to get the job done by himself

And he was getting it done—wheeling and dealing, taking risks and using Ramsey's vast acreage as collateral to float loans and invest for the future. Besides the brewing company and the water-filter operation, he'd found a start-up software company that had tremendous potential. He was working a couple of other options, too.

In the back of his mind lurked the thought that he was proving himself. Maybe if he could run the company effectively and carry on a constant conversation with Erica, he'd become worthy of her. He still wasn't sure what form he wanted a relationship to take, though. She'd said flat out that she wouldn't consider marriage until she was thirty.

The more confident Dustin became in the new life he was building, the more restrictive that seemed. He carried a mental picture of Jennifer and Ryan Madison as they'd appeared three weeks ago. He could be happy in a setup like that.

But he needed the right person to create that sort of golden dream, someone intelligent, sexy, warm and funny. Erica was all those things, but he was afraid to want her too desperately, afraid to put a label on the emotion that swamped him whenever he thought of her. He'd never been in love before, and if Erica was going to shoot him down, he didn't want to be in love now.

So he seduced her through the modem of his computer and didn't think about love, only about making a connection. Every night he looked forward to the moment when he could reach out to her again. Whether in a hotel room while he was on the road or at his condo in Midland, he composed his letters in bed. That was where he conducted this Internet affair with Erica because it seemed the appropriate place to send and receive messages from the most exciting lover he'd ever had.

His evening routine had been the same for three weeks. While he turned on the laptop and accessed the Internet, he started peeling off his clothes, getting down to basics. Then he pulled on running shorts before he settled down on his bed to read her latest message, in case he decided to take a run after answering it. It was either that or head for the lonely comfort of his shower stall. Tonight he'd probably go for a run.

Dustin—you asked if I believed that some people are naturally night owls while others are larks who crave getting up early in the morning. Sure. I'm definitely a night owl. I can't remember the last time I saw a sunrise....

Good, Dustin thought. Another area of agreement. So they'd make love all night and sleep in, then make love again before they finally climbed out of bed.

However, everything I read suggests that most men are naturally aroused early in the morning. If they awake at that time, they have a substantial erection. That interests me. If I insist on staying up late and sleeping in, I may miss my partner's best sexual cycle. So I'd have to say that if it comes down to sleep patterns or finding the best time for amazing sex, I'd chose the sex over sleep any day.
Erica

That's my girl, Dustin thought. She had her priorities straight, and they happened to coincide with his. He hit the reply button.

Erica—any man lucky enough to be in bed with you would probably be erect any time you happened to wake up and take a look. I don't think you'd have to worry about disturbing your sleep pattern to take advantage of his peak sexual cycle.

But there's something to be said for early morning sex. If a man wakes up before his lover, he can sometimes use his tongue to make her come when she's still half-asleep, when she's so relaxed and open that she responds without thinking.

And for the record, I'm a night owl, too. Most of the time.

Dustin

Clicking the send button, Dustin waited for the message to go through before turning off the laptop. Then he climbed from the bed, nursing his erection, and put on his running shoes. Moments later he churned through the twilight, pounding the sidewalks of his suburban neighborhood in an effort to calm his out-of-control libido.

He wanted her to be the one who suggested another visit. He hoped he could last until she'd had enough of this titillation and was ready for a round of the real thing.

Thirty-five minutes later he let himself back into the house, a cleansing sweat dampening his skin. These three weeks had been great for his conditioning. During his stay in Dallas, the only exercise he'd gotten was while he was horizontal, and given a choice, he'd rather have sex than run four miles. If his plans worked out, he'd have to figure out a way to keep in shape.

He automatically checked his answering machine in his combination den and office and discovered he had a message. Messages were common these days now that he was looking for good investment opportunities. He'd had to reject quite a few, but the ones he was considering had great potential. If the economy picked up a little more, he'd be golden and his parents would be secure for the rest of their lives.

Punching Play, he prepared himself for another sales pitch.

"Hi, Dustin, this is Jennifer Madison."

He tensed. Although he'd asked Jennifer to keep tabs on Erica, he'd thought about canceling the request. His constant e-mail exchange with Erica seemed to be enough. Maybe not.

"You asked me to let you know if anything changed in her routine. She's booked a flight to Seattle leaving first thing in the morning, returning day after tomorrow. Looks like she's going for a job interview. If you want the flight times, give me a call."

Dustin stared at the phone, his brain whirling. Damn it! He'd kidded himself that he was getting somewhere with Erica, and she was going off on some blasted job interview! In *Seattle*. She couldn't end up in Seattle. Even Dallas was too far away, but Seattle might as well be Paris. If she ever got established in Seattle, all his hopes would die.

He picked up the phone, grabbed his Rolodex and found Jennifer Madison's number. Her caller I.D. would let her know it was him, so they wouldn't have to waste any time on pleasantries. She answered on the second ring. "Hi, Dustin. I figured you might want those flight times."

"I do." He scribbled the information on a notepad beside the phone. "Thanks."

"You're welcome. Have a safe trip."

"How do you know I'm going anywhere?"

"Just a hunch. After all, I am a P.I., you know."

Dustin laughed. "Give the baby a kiss for me. I'll talk to you when I get back." Then he hung up and ran upstairs to grab a shower and change clothes before he started the drive to Dallas. Good thing he was a night owl.

ERICA HAD BEEN OPERATING on pure adrenaline ever since she'd heard from the *Seattle Times*. The job was exactly what she was looking for—investigative reporting. She was sure she'd end up working on some juicy environmental issues with all the controversy about logging in the Pacific Northwest.

She should be ecstatic that she had a chance to land this dream job. Instead she was lying in the dark not sleeping, thinking about all the reasons she didn't want to go to Seattle. If she didn't get any rest, she'd be too tired to make a good impression during the job interview. Maybe she was sabotaging herself on purpose.

No, damn it, she was going to get some sleep, go up there and nail that interview. She'd never been to Seattle, and she'd heard it was beautiful. A little rainy in the winter, but she could deal with that. She'd rent an apartment with a fireplace.

She concentrated on all the great stories she could write in Seattle—meaty stories about issues that would affect future generations. The timing couldn't be better. The bulk of her newsletter subscribers renewed next month, so she wouldn't have a huge amount to refund. Yes, she might have to go into debt to handle the rest of the refunds, but she'd live frugally and pay it off a little at a time. A person had to sacrifice for her dream.

She'd miss Denise and Josie, but they could come up and visit. She'd also miss putting out the newsletter. Interest had really grown recently, and the e-mails were gratifying. Because of the whole virgin letter thing, she had a bunch of new subscriptions to process. Fortunately she could simply return the checks uncashed with an explanation.

Maybe *Dateline: Dallas* was starting to take off in a big way, but that wasn't her future. It never had been. Denise was getting excited about it, and would probably take it over if Erica asked her. If the Seattle job came through, maybe she should see if Denise was interested in the newsletter. She'd do a good job.

But the truth was, Erica was reluctant to turn it over to anyone, even a friend like Denise. Denise's style was different, which would make the advice column sound totally different. If Erica had decided to franchise, which was a moot point now, she would have delegated the articles and restaurant reviews, but she would have kept the column the same in all the newsletters, and she would have continued to handle it. That column was her.

But the environmental stories she wrote would be her, too. She wouldn't have the same kind of freedom when she wrote them, but she'd be making a bigger impact. All the letters from people struggling with the issue of virginity were very nice, but they weren't on a level with saving old-growth forests.

Except some of those letters had been so poignant. The heartfelt words continued to haunt her, and she'd printed all the letters responding to that column and collected them in a pile on her desk. She was thinking of adding another section to the newsletter in which she could write an essay on topics like this.

But of course, she wouldn't do that, because she intended to land the Seattle job, and the newsletter would either die or be turned over to Denise. Now she really needed to get some sleep. She turned her pillow over to the cool side and vowed to do exactly that.

Instead she thought about Dustin and his last e-mail. She'd decided not to mention the Seattle job offer. If for some reason she didn't get the job, there was no point. He'd wonder why she didn't answer his e-mails, now that they'd become a daily thing, but she could explain when she came back.

If she was hired for the job, she'd break off the e-mail contact with Dustin. She'd known he was trying to seduce her long-distance, and she hadn't been able to resist playing along. It had seemed like a harmless way to ease the pain of losing him. And there was pain, more than she wanted to acknowledge.

Unfortunately, she'd allowed herself to fall a little bit in love with him. Maybe more than a little bit. That was understandable, because the sex had been great and now she was learning that maybe they weren't as ill suited to each other as she'd thought.

Or maybe it was still his ability to get her hot that was influencing her. Sex was such an overriding deal with them that she didn't trust herself to think straight regarding Dustin. Those e-mails always left her aching, and a few times she'd resorted to the vibrator. But a vibrator didn't come close to giving her the satisfaction of a complete Dustin experience, as he'd been so eager to demonstrate. Thinking about having sex with him wouldn't help her sleep, either. Each night she'd tried to ward off thoughts of him by wearing her ugly pajamas with the obscenely huge cabbage rose design.

She had them on tonight, and still she was getting wet and restless. She considered the vibrator in the drawer, rejected the idea, then considered it again. She wanted Dustin, but he wasn't here, and she was getting more agitated the longer she tossed and turned in this bed. Sleep was a top priority. Maybe a session with the vibrator would help.

She opened the bedside drawer and took it out. Battery-operated sex to the rescue. Dustin wouldn't approve, but he never had to know. Besides, she shouldn't care if he knew or not. The vibrator hummed as she turned it on. Reaching down, she pulled aside the material of the boxers. She was so wet.

Trembling, she started to slip the vibrator inside just as the doorbell rang. She gasped, switched off the vibrator and tossed it aside. Heart pounding, she sat up and glanced at the glowing numbers on the bedside clock. Three-twenty in the morning was a strange hour for a visit, even from Denise or Josie. They would have called first, anyway, unless there was an emergency.

She hoped to hell there was no emergency. Maybe she was the victim of a prankster, somebody who got a kick out of ringing doorbells in the middle of the night. Still swollen and moist with arousal, she walked through her dark apartment, stood on tiptoe and peered out the peephole.

Dustin stood there looking tired and unshaven. Unlocking the door with trembling fingers, she flung it open. "Is something wrong?"

"Yes." He stepped inside the door. "You're going to Seattle."

"How did you know?"

Instead of answering, he closed the door and locked it, leaving them in near darkness. A night-light in the kitchen cast a faint glow that outlined the furniture in the living room, but she couldn't see his face.

"Don't go." He reached out and pulled her into his arms. "For God's sake, don't go." Then he kissed her.

She shouldn't have kissed him back. Kissing him back was the one wrong thing to do if she wanted to maintain some distance between them. But she'd been without him for three solid weeks, and she'd switched off her vibrator two minutes ago without getting any use out of it.

He groaned and spread his hands over her bottom. Then, as if by instinct, he reached up under the leg of her boxers and discovered the state she was in. He wrenched his mouth from hers. "How can you leave?" His voice rasped as he stroked her possessively. "All I have to do is touch you and you're ready to come!"

"I—"

"Never mind." He swept her up in his arms and carried her back to her bedroom. "We need to take care of the situation. Then we'll talk."

"Dustin, the reason I'm—"

"You have another man in there?" He stopped dead in his tracks.

"No. My vibra—"

He uttered a pungent curse and headed through the doorway of her dark bedroom. He practically threw her onto the bed before tearing off his clothes. "Take off that stuff you're wearing."

She didn't need to be told. The cabbage-rose outfit sailed into the air to land somewhere at the foot of her bed.

"It's a crying shame." He was down to his boxers before he paused and fumbled in the pocket of his jeans. Then he tossed the condom packet at her. "Open this."

She did. "What's a crying shame?"

"I'm jerking off in the shower and you're playing with plastic, when we should be together. Got it open?"

She handed him the condom.

"We should be together," he said again as he rolled the condom on and climbed into bed with her. Then he cursed again, and she realized he'd put his hand on the vibrator. Grabbing it, he pivoted and hurled it against the wall.

Erica could only imagine how she'd explain that noise

to the neighbors. But then Dustin plunged deep inside her and she realized she'd have many, many noises to explain to the neighbors. She and Dustin loved each other hard and they loved each other loud. She came immediately, and then, while he pumped relentlessly into her, she came again.

Then Dustin exploded with a bellow that probably woke the entire building.

"That will have to do for now," he said, panting. "But don't think I'm finished."

"Okay." She gulped for air and wondered how she'd survived for three weeks without this kind of orgasm, without the feel of Dustin within her, hovering over her, surrounding her with his urgency. He was incredible.

He also seemed different, somehow. She wasn't sure what had happened in three weeks, but he'd lost his hesitancy. He'd ordered her around, and she hadn't even thought to question him. If there had been another man in her bed instead of the ill-fated vibrator, she wondered if he would have thrown the man out, too. He'd been that focused on what he wanted.

"Don't go away. I'll be back." He slipped from the bed and went into her bathroom.

While he was gone she decided the ordering-around routine had to end now. She'd gone along with him before because she'd needed to buy exactly what he was selling. But he wasn't going to bulldoze his way back into her life and tell her she wasn't going to Seattle.

He returned and slipped into bed beside her. "That was part one of my argument." Gathering her close, he nuzzled her ear. "Do I need to continue with my case?"

She responded to him the way she always did, snuggling closer and wrapping her arms around his toned body. But the edge was off her craving now and she was able to put together a coherent thought. "You never told me how you knew I was going to Seattle."

"Jennifer." He nipped at her earlobe.

"You still have someone tailing me?" She was amazed. If she'd thought Dustin would fade into the night, she'd been mistaken. "What if I object to be tailed?"

He ran his tongue around the inside of her ear. "Do you?"

"Yes." She shivered as he continued to make love to her ear. It was difficult to be tough while he was trying to seduce her again.

"Then I'll take Jennifer off the case."

"That's no big concession. You found out what you wanted to know."

"Were you going to tell me?" He cupped her breast and stroked her nipple with his thumb.

"If I got the job."

He slowly released her, turned over and switched on the bedside lamp.

She blinked. "What's that for?"

He leaned on his elbow and gazed down at her. With his beard-stubbled chin and piercing blue eyes, he looked intimidating, definitely not someone to mess around with. "I want you to look me in the eye and tell me that you planned to fly to Seattle, accept a job there, and let me know after the fact."

She stared at him. "You must have been eating your Wheaties every morning for the past three weeks."

"What's that supposed to mean?"

"You're getting an attitude, Ramsey, and I don't appreciate it. Who says I have to report my behavior to you? Do you think having me tailed gives you a right to know everything about me?"

"No." He moved quickly, rolling her to her back and pinning her beneath him. "I think getting the response you gave me ten minutes ago gives me that right. I walked in the door and you were ready to roll.''

"Only because I'd taken out the—''

"So you said. The big question is, why did you remove your battery-powered friend from the drawer?''

She lifted her chin, trying to stare him down. "A girl has her reasons.''

"Anything to do with the e-mail you've been getting from Midland recently?''

"That's my business.'' She wished his body pressing against hers didn't feel so damned good. He made it very difficult to concentrate.

"I'm making it my business. I think this whole charade has gone far enough. It's time for you to admit that we have something special going, something that deserves notice. You can't write me an e-mail about morning erections one day and fly off to Seattle for a job interview the next. That's not being fair to either one of us.''

He had a point, and for once, her debate skills deserted her. She could feel his penis stirring against her thigh, and Lord help her, she wanted him to make love to her again. This time it would be slow and smooth, like that time on the sofa. This time she'd lie back and enjoy the steady thrusting instead of scrambling for her own orgasm.

He searched her gaze. "You want me again, don't you?''

"I want you all the time,'' she confessed. "I've turned into a Dustin junkie, and that scares me to death.''

"Why?''

"Because I need to go to Seattle.''

"No, you don't.'' He lifted his chest and began lazily brushing his torso over hers, teasing her breasts with the tickle of his hair. "You can stay here in Texas with me.''

Because he was weakening her resolve, her words became harsher in tone. "You want me to stay here and play with you instead of doing important work?''

He frowned. "Not just play, although I hope we can do that. Look, I know what you said, that you didn't want to tie yourself down until you were thirty, but—"

"Oh, no, you don't." She pushed at his chest, trying to dislodge him as panic filled her.

"What?"

"Don't you dare start dangling marriage in front of me! You know that's not what either one of us needs right now!" The prospect of marrying Dustin glimmered in front of her like a forbidden dream, one she was afraid she wanted. But it would be her undoing. She'd become part of the establishment, have two-point-five children, probably even a *maid* for God's sake. She'd be selling out.

"Speak for yourself," Dustin said quietly.

"I just did!"

"Yes, you did." His blue eyes clouded over. "And I can tell the concept of marrying me scares the hell out of you." He rolled away from her and stared up at the ceiling.

She hadn't meant to hurt him. She'd felt the need to protect herself from his overwhelming appeal, but she hadn't wanted to inflict pain in the process. Easing to her side, she touched his arm. "This is the job I've been waiting for ever since high school. I told you in the beginning this was what I wanted to do. Now's my chance."

He turned to face her. "So you've been marking time by sending me those e-mails?"

Shame swept through her. She'd been encouraging him because he was the most exciting thing going on in her life. It had been a cruel thing to do if she had no intention of following through. "I shouldn't have kept replying."

"I guess not." He turned away from her and swung his legs over the side of the bed.

She watched, not able to think of anything to say, as he gathered his clothes and started putting them on.

He paused halfway through buttoning his shirt. "What

if you hadn't gotten the job interview? Would you have asked me to come to Dallas for a visit?''

She gazed at him in misery. ''I'd like to think I wouldn't have, but yes, I was thinking about it. We were having so much fun, and I—''

''You thought you might as well take advantage of that until something better came along?''

''Oh, Dustin, it's not like that! I've loved being with you!''

''So I've done a damned good job of keeping you occupied while you waited for your destiny. That's comforting.'' He pulled on his jeans and fastened them. Then he leaned against the wall and put on his boots. ''Guess I'm in the way, though, so I'll just head on out of here.''

Her eyes filled with tears. ''I didn't mean to hurt you. I know that I have, and I don't know how to make it up to you.''

''I'll be fine. I'm tougher than you might think.''

''I'm sure you are.'' Her throat tightened with grief. ''You're the best, Dustin.''

His jaw clenched as he stared at her. ''Goodbye, Erica. Have a safe flight.'' Then he left.

17

ERICA HADN'T TAKEN many plane trips in her life, and never one in which she had traveled alone. The flight to Seattle wasn't crowded, and she ended up sitting by herself in a row of three, staring out the window. Usually she didn't mind having time to think, but this morning was an exception. She didn't much like herself today.

After Dustin had left, she'd given up on sleep and climbed out of bed to shower and finish packing. Several cups of coffee and a box of tissues later, she'd been forced to conclude that she'd been incredibly selfish to continue her e-mail connection with Dustin.

It was no good telling herself he'd only been interested in getting her back into bed. She'd seen the look in his eyes when he'd left three weeks ago. Whether he'd acknowledge it or not, he was getting hooked on her. The marriage topic hadn't really surprised her. Thrown her into a panic, yes, but not surprised her.

She should have seen it coming and ignored his e-mail messages. He'd been so heavily involved, he'd continued the P.I. surveillance so that he'd know if she decided to leave town. Or started dating someone. Oh, yeah, Dustin had it bad.

So here she was, flying off to interview for a job that would help her save the planet, but in her personal life, she had no problem handing out misery galore. What a noble person she was turning out to be. Not.

She'd treated Dustin abominably, when he was the

sweetest, most gentle and caring man she'd ever met. He'd left in a terrible mood, and she'd let him go, knowing he'd driven through the night to get there. There was an excellent chance he'd headed straight back to Midland, which would have been very dangerous on no sleep.

Yet she didn't know how to check on him without making things worse. Any contact from her might be misconstrued. She couldn't toy with him like that, not when she realized how he felt about her.

He'd never told her he loved her, but who could blame him? She'd warned him off so many times he wouldn't dare reveal his feelings. It was a miracle he'd dared to bring up the subject of marriage, and she'd thrown it back in his face, too.

Finally, somewhere over Utah, she admitted to herself the reason that she'd acted so horribly toward Dustin. She was in love with him, too. In love with him and scared to death of that love, afraid it would distract her from her chosen path. How arrogant of her, to think she could stomp all over someone's feelings because they didn't share her vision.

The plane touched down at Sea-Tac International and she took a shuttle into the city. Seattle looked like a postcard—Puget Sound reflecting the blue of a clear sky, seagulls wheeling gracefully over the waterfront, and ferries chugging back and forth between Seattle and Bainbridge Island. Erica surveyed it all glumly. Where was that cold, rainy weather Seattle was famous for? She could have used fog, maybe even a dose of sleet.

The *Seattle Times* staff was friendly and the editor who interviewed her was complimentary about the clips she'd sent with her résumé. Yet when he showed her the bustling area where the reporters worked at linked terminals, she couldn't help but compare the scenario to typing in her cozy little apartment. As she absorbed the urgent pace of a

large daily and remembered the pressure of meeting someone else's deadline, she got a funny feeling in the pit of
her stomach.

A natural reaction to the prospect of change, she told
herself as the editor took her out for a quick lunch. His
conversation centered around the necessity of staying objective, even with a highly charged topic like the environment. The last reporter on the beat had allowed his personal
opinions to creep into his work, which was why he'd been
fired. Erica agreed that was a mistake, but all the while she
thought about the fun she'd had spilling all her opinions
onto the pages of her newsletter.

After lunch the editor took her to her hotel and made
sure she was checked in okay. Then, before he hurried back
to his duties, he offered her the job. Good salary, great
newspaper, excellent opportunity. Her dream job. She
didn't blame him for being confused when she turned it
down.

DUSTIN KNEW he was sometimes reckless, but he wasn't a
total fool. Driving back to Midland without sleep would
have been beyond stupid. Because the Fairmont was familiar to him, even though it had too many memories of
Erica, he drove there and checked in.

Maybe he wanted to be there *because* it had memories
of Erica. Her decision to follow through on her trip to Seattle still seemed unreal to him. He hadn't accepted the
finality of it. He had no luggage, but he was too tired to
care. Once he was inside the room, he flopped facedown
on the bed and fell instantly asleep.

By the time he woke up it was nearly ten and he had
some decisions to make. Driving back to Midland and closing the door on this chapter of his life seemed like the
obvious one. But his business with Erica didn't feel finished.

During his football days, he'd learned that the only way to catch a football was to commit yourself a hundred percent to catching it. You couldn't be tentative, you couldn't go after that ball with a half-assed attempt and expect results. You didn't worry about being creamed by the defensive tackle.

Same thing on the racing circuit. You drove to win, not to be safe. A conservative race might put you in the money, but you wouldn't go home with the shiny trophy.

At first he hadn't realized that building Ramsey Enterprises required the same attitude. He'd felt out of his depth and in need of backup. He'd needed Erica.

His instincts had been right. By reconnecting with her, both mentally and physically, he'd gained enough confidence to take on the family business. For starters, he wanted to tell her that. Hurt and anger had caused him to say some ugly things to her, and he didn't want those to be the last memory she had of him.

But there was more to it. As he lay staring up at the ceiling of his hotel room, he finally admitted to himself he loved her. The seeds of his love had been sown the first night they'd made love ten years ago. They'd lain dormant for years, waiting for the moment when he held her in his arms once more.

He wanted her, wanted her more than he'd allowed himself to realize. But he'd been playing it safe, refusing to say what he wanted and give it everything he had. No wonder she was in Seattle today interviewing for a job. He hadn't put his heart and soul into getting her to change her mind.

Thank God it wasn't too late. Even if she'd agreed to take the job, she could still back out. He realized she could refuse him. He'd dropped passes and lost races even when he'd bet all the marbles. Giving it everything he had wouldn't guarantee success. But if he didn't, he didn't have a prayer.

ON THE PLANE RIDE HOME the next day, Erica came to a few more painful conclusions. Not only had she treated Dustin shabbily, she'd been blind to the other people around her, too. She'd acted as if *Dateline: Dallas* was some kind of joke, a toy she'd used to amuse herself while she waited for a more worthwhile career to materialize.

But her subscribers didn't think it was a joke. They trusted her to tell them about good restaurants and give them ideas on how to spend their free time. People had so little free time anymore. What they had was precious, and they were counting on her to help them use it well.

And that wasn't even considering the advice column. She couldn't ignore the importance of it anymore, not with the letters coming in every day. Yet she'd been willing to cast the column aside as if the people writing to her for guidance weren't really worthy of her continued support.

She knew firsthand that the restaurant owners didn't consider *Dateline: Dallas* a joke. Her reviews had put more money in their pockets, and several had said her newsletter was good for the economy and especially for small businesses. That wasn't something to be taken lightly, either.

Here, in her own little corner of the world, she was doing good things. With the help of her friends, she'd stumbled into a job that she loved doing, if she'd get off her high horse and admit it. Instead of complaining the newsletter wasn't important enough to warrant her valuable time, she should be on her knees in gratitude that she'd discovered such a terrific way to make a living and make a difference.

Franchising to other cities *was* a fantastic idea, and she'd been quite the snob to turn down Dustin's offer. Unfortunately, she'd treated him so poorly that she couldn't expect that offer to still be open. Out of courtesy she'd contact him, awkward though that would be, because she had to be certain he wasn't interested before she went looking for funding elsewhere.

After all, it had been his idea. He'd probably tell her where she could put her newsletter, and she deserved whatever abuse he chose to hand out. If, by some miracle, he still wanted to consider franchising, she'd work very hard to earn back his goodwill. She couldn't think beyond that. She'd be lucky to get that far.

It was dusk by the time she parked her car in the lot beside the apartment building and rolled her suitcase through the entrance. She climbed the stairs, the suitcase bumping along behind her, so glad to be home, so glad not to be contemplating a move to Seattle.

Two days away had put her behind on the newsletter deadline, but she didn't care. Working on *Dateline: Dallas* gave her so much joy she could hardly wait to dig into the next issue. She had another restaurant to review, and she'd planned to cancel her visit for tomorrow if she'd taken the job in Seattle. Now she could go, eat good food and write one of her famous sensuous reviews.

Even before she reached her door she noticed a beige rectangle was taped to it. Probably a note from Denise reminding her to call the minute she came home, wanting a report on the Seattle trip. Erica smiled as she pictured Denise and Josie's reaction to the news that she'd turned down the job and planned to stay in Dallas. A celebration would definitely be in order.

Her two best friends were her lifeline and they'd help her get through the loss of Dustin. She couldn't imagine how she would have made it in Seattle with no Dustin and no Denise or Josie, either. What a fool she would have been—a miserable, arrogant fool.

She wondered how much Dustin's late-night visit had influenced her to refuse the job. Probably more than she realized. She had him to thank for helping save her from making a terrible mistake. Too bad he wouldn't feel like accepting her gratitude.

The beige rectangle had her name on it, printed neatly in handwriting she didn't recognize. So it wasn't Denise. Heart pounding, she untaped it from the door and discovered it was an envelope with a card inside. Dustin. Considering how they'd parted, she wasn't sure she was up to reading it.

But she owed it to him. She pulled the card from the envelope with shaking hands.

It was her kind of card, all right, undoubtedly from recycled material, with pressed leaves embedded into the surface. It didn't seem like the card an angry man would choose. She opened it, knowing she'd see Dustin's name there.

She did, but something plastic fell to the carpeting at her feet. When she picked it up, her blood began to heat. It was a Fairmont Hotel room key.

Quickly she scanned his message. "Sometimes we can't see the forest for the trees. If you'd like to take a walk in the forest with me, please come to my room when you get back from Seattle." Then he'd printed the room number.

He was still in Dallas. Incredible. She'd figured he wouldn't have been able to get away from her fast enough. She'd pictured him putting miles between them as quickly as possible.

But he was still here. He'd waited for her to come back, believing that she'd take the job in Seattle. Maybe he wanted to salvage the friendship. He'd said all along that he valued her input regarding his business. He might be interested in opportunities for investment in the Northwest.

Well, this was her chance to eat crow and ask him if the franchise offer was still open. She'd expected to have to call him or send an e-mail to reopen communication, but he was making it easy for her. As he'd always done.

Placing his room key back inside the card, she tucked the card in the envelope and unlocked her door. She had a shower to take and an outfit to choose. She didn't want to keep him waiting too long.

Less than twenty minutes later she was out the door, dressed quite differently from the last time she'd gone to meet him in his hotel room. She owned one lightweight linen suit, and she was wearing it. She'd treat this as a business meeting, a chance to expand her newsletter career.

Also, she thought an apology was better delivered in a neat little sage-green suit than in casual clothes. Green was a sincere color. She'd read that somewhere. It also matched the card he'd sent her.

As she drove to the Fairmont, her mild jitters gradually became a serious case of nerves. Until now, her interactions with Dustin had been all about sex. Given the way she'd treated him, she figured the sexual games were over, which left her feeling lost. She'd ruined their sexual games, and grief over the loss of their lighthearted fun was beginning to hit her. She had been stupid. So very, very stupid.

In the elegant lobby of the Fairmont, she nearly chickened out. Only a sense of fairness propelled her to the elevators and forced her to punch the number of Dustin's floor. He'd thought of the franchise idea and he deserved to have the first shot at funding it. If she didn't meet him tonight, he'd have even more reason to throw the whole thing back in her face.

She'd brought a little shoulder purse, and she opened it, fishing out the key as she walked down the carpeted hallway. Well, this was it. Swallowing heavily, she stuck the card key in the slot, waited for the little light to turn green and opened the door.

Then she blinked. The room smelled like pine, which

made sense, because at least four potted evergreens were arranged around the room. The only light came from tiny white lights twinkling in the branches of the trees. Somewhere in the room, she heard the sounds of a nature CD, complete with babbling brook and singing birds.

Obviously he'd tried to bring a little of the Pacific Northwest to her, which was touching in itself. Here she'd planned to grovel and he was making grand gestures. Fortunately there didn't seem to be any cart of food, though, so he didn't have a swanky meal in mind. That was fine with her. She was too nervous to eat anything, anyway.

Slowly her eyes adjusted to the dim light as she searched the room for him. "Dustin?"

"I'm here." He walked out of the shadows clad in a tuxedo.

She was totally dazzled. Not only did he look more yummy than any man had a right to, but he'd gone to a *lot* of trouble and expense. Hope bubbled within her, although she warned herself not to get too carried away. But a *tuxedo*. That had to mean something good.

As he walked toward her, he took his hand from behind his back and held out a slender branch of some kind of tree.

Not a rose. Maybe his tuxedo didn't mean what she'd hoped.

With a soft smile he handed it to her. "It's an olive branch," he said. "I think that's what you're supposed to give someone when you want to stop arguing."

While she stood with the branch and absorbed the amazing statement, one *she* should have been making, he moved past her to close the door. The security lock fell into place with a soft click.

She turned, the branch clutched in her hand. "Dustin, I should have come here with an olive branch. I've been insufferable to you."

"Yeah, kind of." He grinned and came toward her. "But sometimes that's how people act when they're confused."

"How did you know I've been confused?" She stared at him, unable to believe he was that psychic. "Did you have someone follow me to Seattle, too?"

"No." He chuckled and shook his head. "No more tails. I took Jennifer off the case. But you have to be confused, because I haven't been clear about what I want."

The way he looked, she was ready to give him whatever that happened to be. Her throat grew tight as she thought about how vulnerable she was right now. The answer to her next question could have vast implications. "What… what do you want?"

"I—" He paused. "You know what? I'm much better at showing than telling. Are you impressed with the tux?"

She nodded, her pulse beating rapidly as she wondered what was next on his agenda. He obviously had one. "I'm impressed with all this. Maybe you stage this sort of thing all the time, but—"

"I don't. And before we go any further in our discussion, you need to know that I'm not fabulously wealthy. My dad left me with a financial mess. I'll probably be able to turn it around eventually, but the money's not flowing like water, believe me."

She was stunned. "You really did need the newsletter franchise?"

"Yeah." He smiled. "My dad bought a couple of weekly newspapers, one in Houston and one in San Antonio. They were struggling, and I thought expanding your newsletter to those markets would mean I could maximize the use of the printing facilities there and maybe help save them. If not, I knew your newsletter would work out, so the plants wouldn't be a total loss."

"Why didn't you tell me that?" She wondered if helping save a couple of weeklies would have made a difference to her. She'd always had a soft spot in her heart for small independent papers.

"Oh, stupid reasons. For one thing, I thought the week-lies would seem bush-league to you after your experience with big dailies."

"But I—"

"It doesn't matter. I've pumped up the advertising department in both cases and I think they're going to be okay, after all. I also want to thank you for hooking me up with the brewery and the water-filter people. Those were two really great leads. Looks like Ramsey Enterprises will survive."

Without her. Boy, had she ever shot herself in the foot. "Dustin, you shouldn't have spent money to impress me tonight. I don't need the frills."

"Don't worry. I didn't spend much. The trees are on loan—my buddy Curtis works for a nursery. And my other racing friend, Roger, happened to have a tux that fits me."

It fit him beautifully, borrowed or not. Her image of Dustin was changing rapidly. She'd been such a fool to make assumptions about his company. She could have checked into it. She'd planned to, and then hadn't bothered, certain he was still part of the monied set.

"Anyway, I think the tux has served its purpose." He pulled at the black tie and it came undone. Then he took off the coat and flung it over the back of the desk chair before starting to remove his cuff links.

Her mouth grew moist and she began to tremble. He wanted sex, after all. But maybe that was all he wanted. She might have killed whatever chance they'd had to nurture their lust for each other into something more.

Well, if he wanted sex, she'd give it to him, any way, any amount. She owed him that much after what she'd put him through recently. "Should I…take off my suit?" she asked as he shrugged out of his shirt. If all he wanted was another adventure in bondage and oral sex, he might like to watch her do it while she was still fully clothed.

"Yes, I'd love you to take off your suit. But I like it. Thanks for dressing up for me." He kicked off his shoes and reached for the fastening of his slacks.

"My version of an olive branch." She laid it on the desk and unbuttoned her suit jacket.

"Your suit, or your willingness to take it off?"

"Both, I guess. Dustin, I have a lot to apologize for. I should probably start with—"

"Getting naked," he murmured. "I've been waiting for this ever since yesterday morning. I didn't bring work with me this time, so I've had nothing to do but dream about you stretched across that bed, ready for me."

She was certainly ready for him. In no time she'd stripped down to her bra and a pair of very damp panties.

"Hold it right there." He'd pulled off his black dress socks, leaving only gray knit boxers with a telltale bulge in the front. He took a long, shaky, breath. "I just want to say that you're...incredibly gorgeous. I've thought it every time I've looked at you, in clothes or out of them. I haven't said it much, and I should have. If I concentrated on you standing there in those little bits of white material, I could probably make myself come, just from the visual stimulation."

She swallowed. "Ditto."

He grinned. "This from the captain of a championship debate team?"

"Some things don't need to be debated."

"No." Fire smoldered in his blue eyes as his grin slowly faded. "I'd like to watch while you take those off."

Quivering with excitement, she reached behind her back and unhooked her bra. Maybe sex was all Dustin wanted now, but she could build on that. She wouldn't scare him with love talk that he might have a hard time believing, anyway. But she'd give him a great ride, and that would be a beginning.

His gaze settled on her breasts. "I look at you and I can already feel the sensation of rolling your nipple over my tongue."

When he looked at her like that, so could she. She moaned softly.

"Now the rest."

She slid her panties down and stepped out of them.

"Toss them to me."

He caught them in one hand and slowly raised them to his nose. Taking a deep breath, he closed his eyes and clenched the white cotton in his fist. When he opened his eyes again, his gaze looked as if it would melt steel. "Lie on the bed for me, Erica. Lie on the bed and spread your legs. Make my fantasy come true."

Walking over to the mattress on trembling legs, she stretched out, the quilted covering cool against her back.

Dustin shoved down his briefs and his erection sprang free.

Slowly, deliberately, she opened her thighs, silently inviting him to enter her.

He slid one knee onto the bed. He had no condom. She watched him with a racing heart, wondering what he planned to do.

"This is what I want," he said, his voice husky. "You in my bed, every night until we grow old. I want that because I love the sex, but I also want it because I love you. I want to marry you, make you pregnant, build a life together. I don't know what shape that life will take, but we have almost no chance if you go to Seattle. Don't go. I know a weekly isn't what you had in mind, but these are great little papers and we have plans for increasing circulation, so I was thinking, if you'd like to write a column about environmental stuff, then—"

"Oh, Dustin."

"Don't say no yet. Think about it. Think about staying here."

Her chest tightened and tears pricked beneath her eyelids. She drank in his words like a woman dying of thirst. This was what she wanted, what she'd wanted all along but hadn't allowed herself to think she could have it.

"Please," he whispered.

"I've already turned down the job."

"You have?" He climbed onto the bed and hovered over her. "You turned it down? When?"

"Yesterday." She framed his face in both hands. "Thank you for helping me see what a mistake that would be. For me, for us." She forced the words past the lump in her throat. "I love you, Dustin. I want to be your wife and have your babies. I'd love to write a column for the weeklies, or do whatever I can to help keep them going. And I'm going to hang on to the newsletter, but the franchising isn't important, if that would be too expensive now."

"It is important." He began to laugh and tears sparkled in his eyes. "We'll do that, too."

"But—"

"Don't worry about anything. We'll work it all out. Together." He studied her face, his laughter dying as he grew serious. "How about the thing about being a mother? Do you really mean that?"

She looked into the eyes of the man who would be the father of her children. "Yes."

"Good, because I'd like to start that project before we get into the franchising thing."

"Like, when?"

"Like, now."

"Like, hooray." Grasping his bottom, she drew him down and lifted her hips.

He slid in smooth and easy. "How's that?"

"Perfect." She gazed up at him and saw years of loving, raising children, molding lives, growing old together. "This is a big step. I hope you know what you're doing."

He smiled. "I do. My plan is to show you how well I know what I'm doing."

As he settled in deeper, she had no doubt about this part. "I'm not only talking about sex."

"I know." He brushed her lips with his. "When I came to Dallas that first time, I thought I knew it all, but I still had a lot to learn."

She sighed, surrendering all her doubts in the warmth of his embrace. "Me, too."

"I think we've finally got it right."

"I think so, too." As he began to love her, she was sure of it.

Epilogue

JENNIFER MADISON GLANCED around her candlelit dining room with a sense of accomplishment. She and Ryan were actually entertaining guests, and they weren't even family members. Dustin had brought Erica to dinner so that Jennifer could meet the woman she'd helped him track down.

Laughter and conversation flowed around the table, and Jennifer soaked it up. Annie was upstairs asleep, and with any luck she'd stay asleep a little longer. Between caring for the baby and running her P.I. agency, Jennifer had skipped socializing for too long. She and Ryan didn't use the dining room except as a place to stack mail.

Well, that wasn't precisely true. Although she wasn't much of a cook, she'd managed to put together a fancy meal for Ryan one night. She looked over at her husband and wondered if he remembered what they'd ended up doing on the table after the meal. He met her gaze and winked. He remembered. They'd even recklessly skipped using a condom, figuring it wasn't a fertile time.

"So for the time being we're keeping both my apartment in Dallas and Dustin's town house here in Midland," Erica said, responding to Ryan's question about who was moving, Erica or Dustin. "I have a few months left on the lease, anyway. Once my friend Denise feels comfortable handling *Dateline: Dallas* by herself, we'll probably give up the apartment and I'll live here."

"But after the wedding next month, we'll rent something

short-term in Houston so we'll have a place to stay while we're launching *Hello, Houston*,'' Dustin added.

"Right. And after that we'll be spending some time in San Antonio. If those two expansions work out, then we might test the concept in Oklahoma City."

"I'm sure the expansions will work out," Dustin said.

Jennifer could feel the crackle of energy between Erica and Dustin. "That's quite a schedule, but you both sound excited about it."

"We are." Erica squeezed Dustin's hand. "But there's no doubt we'll be busy. Dustin has a million irons in the fire, and I've recently started writing my environmental column for the weeklies." She glanced around the festive dining room. "I love everything that we're involved in, and I wouldn't change a thing, but someday…"

"Someday we'll have a home like this." Dustin gave her a meaningful look. "Guaranteed. There's a new builder—"

A baby's wail coming from the small receiver on the china cabinet interrupted him.

"Oops." Jennifer put her napkin beside her plate and stood. "Maybe she lost her pacifier. Sometimes if I get it for her, she goes right back to sleep."

"You mean you wouldn't bring her down?" Dustin seemed disappointed.

Jennifer glanced at him in surprise. "Do you want me to?"

"Um, well, I wouldn't want you to louse up her schedule or anything."

Erica laughed and glanced fondly at Dustin. "He wants you to, Jennifer. He's crazy about Annie. That's one of the reasons he was excited about coming over here tonight. You probably didn't notice his expression when he discovered you'd already put her to bed."

Ryan chuckled. "Better go get her, Jen. Dustin needs his baby fix."

"Okay. Be right back." She hurried upstairs to fetch the main attraction. How cute that Dustin was smitten with the baby bug. She hoped Erica was ready to have kids, because Dustin obviously was more than eager.

Moments later she returned with Annie. "She's wide-awake, so maybe I have a party girl on my hands. She—" The phone rang in her office, and as she counted rings she remembered she'd forgotten to turn on the answering machine.

She started to hand Annie off to Ryan, but then she changed her mind and offered her to Dustin.

"For me?" With a smile of surprise, Dustin took the baby and settled her on his lap.

"Ryan, would you start organizing dessert?" Jennifer said as she ran out of the room toward her office.

After hanging up the phone five minutes later, she started back to the dining room and heard Annie's crow of delight. Thinking that Ryan was playing with her, she was amazed to discover that her husband was still in the kitchen. Dustin and Erica were alone in the dining room playing patty-cake with Annie.

Jennifer paused in the doorway to enjoy the scene. Thank goodness she'd been able to find Erica for Dustin. Watching the two of them with Annie, she had no doubt they were exactly right for each other.

Moments later Ryan came in from the kitchen carrying a tray of four hot-fudge sundaes. Erica and Dustin both looked up, exclaimed over the elaborate desserts, and then gave each other a secret smile. Jennifer was willing to bet that hot-fudge sundaes meant more to them than just a delicious dessert.

Ryan set down the tray and glanced at Jennifer. "Was the call important?"

"Yes. That was Lily. She's found me a private investigator."

"Really?" Ryan looked pleased. "Good. You definitely need some help with the agency." He parceled out the sundaes.

"No kidding. Listen, Dustin, I can take Annie while you eat your dessert."

"She's fine." Dustin kept one arm tucked possessively around the baby while he picked up his spoon.

"Don't give her any," Jennifer warned. "It's way too rich for her."

"Right, mom." Dustin grinned at Jennifer as he dug a spoon into his sundae.

Jennifer decided to keep an eye on him. It wouldn't be the end of world if he gave Annie a tiny taste of the vanilla ice cream, but as enamored as Dustin seemed to be, he might end up feeding her so much he'd give her a tummy ache. Jennifer could do without that.

"I'll watch him, Jen," Erica said.

Jennifer relaxed. "Thanks."

"So you're getting an employee?" Erica asked.

"Looks like it." Jennifer spent a few minutes explaining that Lily and her twin brother Dylan were the founders of the well-known Texas agency, Finders Keepers, an organization near San Antonio dedicated to locating missing persons and reuniting family members. If Jennifer hadn't been working a case for Finders Keepers, she never would have met Ryan, so she was willing to take on anybody Lily recommended.

"So who is this person Lily's come up with?" Ryan asked.

"Interestingly enough, he's part of the Trueblood family tree. His name's Zack Letterman, and he's from the Indiana branch of the Truebloods. Apparently he wants to relocate to Texas and Lily thinks he could turn out to be exactly the guy I need.''

''Let's hope so.'' Ryan glanced over at Dustin. ''You look excessively happy with that baby in your lap. Better be careful or Erica's going to start getting ideas.''

Dustin's smile widened as he gazed at Erica. ''You know what, Ryan? I sincerely hope she does.''

From the heated look passing between Dustin and Erica, Jennifer calculated that in a few months she'd undoubtedly be attending a baby shower. Maybe, if Zach Letterman worked out, she'd have time to shop for a gift.

In fact, if Zach Letterman worked out, she and Ryan could start thinking about giving Annie a brother or sister. She caught her husband studying her, almost as if he could read her mind.

''I'm glad Lily's found you some help,'' he said.

She basked in the warmth of his gaze. He might not be thinking about making babies at this very moment, but he was definitely letting her know that he missed having the time to indulge in crazy, wonderful stunts like making love on the dining room table.

''Yeah,'' she said softly. ''So am I.''

*   *   *   *   *

Don't miss the second
TRUEBLOOD TEXAS *sequel,*
EVERY MOVE YOU MAKE
by Tori Carrington.

Available next month from Blaze.

The Trueblood, Texas
tradition continues in...

 HARLEQUIN® *Blaze*™

TRULY, MADLY, DEEPLY
by *Vicki Lewis Thompson*
August 2002

Ten years ago, Dustin Ramsey and Erica Mann shared their first
sexual experience. It was a disaster. Now Dustin's determined to
find—and seduce—Erica again, to prove to her, and himself, that
he can do better. Much, *much* better. Only, little does he guess
that Erica's got the same agenda....

Don't miss Blaze's next two sizzling Trueblood tales:

EVERY MOVE YOU MAKE by Tori Carrington
September 2002
&
LOVE ON THE ROCKS by Debbi Rawlins
October 2002

Available wherever Harlequin books are sold.

TRUEBLOOD, TEXAS

HARLEQUIN®
Makes any time special ®

Princes...Princesses...
London Castles...New York Mansions...
To live the life of a royal!

**In 2002, Harlequin Books lets you escape to a
world of royalty with these royally themed titles:**

Temptation:
January 2002—*A Prince of a Guy* (#861)
February 2002—*A Noble Pursuit* (#865)

American Romance:
The Carradignes: American Royalty (Editorially linked series)
March 2002—*The Improperly Pregnant Princess* (#913)
April 2002—*The Unlawfully Wedded Princess* (#917)
May 2002—*The Simply Scandalous Princess* (#921)
November 2002—*The Inconveniently Engaged Prince* (#945)

Intrigue:
The Carradignes: A Royal Mystery (Editorially linked series)
June 2002—*The Duke's Covert Mission* (#666)

Chicago Confidential
September 2002—*Prince Under Cover* (#678)

The Crown Affair
October 2002—*Royal Target* (#682)
November 2002—*Royal Ransom* (#686)
December 2002—*Royal Pursuit* (#690)

Harlequin Romance:
June 2002—*His Majesty's Marriage* (#3703)
July 2002—*The Prince's Proposal* (#3709)

Harlequin Presents:
August 2002—*Society Weddings* (#2268)
September 2002—*The Prince's Pleasure* (#2274)

Duets:
September 2002—*Once Upon a Tiara/Henry Ever After* (#83)
October 2002—*Natalia's Story/Andrea's Story* (#85)

**Celebrate a year of royalty with
Harlequin Books!**

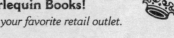

Available at your favorite retail outlet.

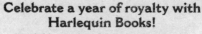

HARLEQUIN®
Makes any time special ®

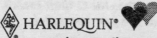

HARLEQUIN® *Blaze*™

**The Masterson brothers—Zane and Grey.
Both gorgeous, both oh-so-sexy.
*Identical?***

Natural-born lady-killers Zane and Grey Masterson are
notorious among the female population of New Orleans
for their "love 'em and leave 'em smiling" attitudes.
But what happens when they decide to switch places—
and each brother finds himself in an intimate struggle
with the one woman he can't resist...?

Find out in...

DOUBLE THE PLEASURE by Julie Elizabeth Leto
&
DOUBLE THE THRILL by Susan Kearney

*Both books available in August 2002,
wherever Harlequin books are sold.*

**When these two guys meet their match,
the results are just two sexy!**

HARLEQUIN®
Makes any time special®